D1403468

Sleeping with the Devil

❧❧

LITERATURE AND LANGUAGE DEPARTMENT
THE CHICAGO PUBLIC LIBRARY
400 SOUTH STATE STREET
CHICAGO, ILLINOIS 60605

LITERATURE AND LANGUAGE DEPARTMENT

Sleeping with the Devil

❦

Vanessa Marlow

St. Martin's Griffin

New York

This is a work of fiction. All of the characters, organizations, and events portrayed in this novel are either products of the author's imagination or are used fictitiously.

SLEEPING WITH THE DEVIL. Copyright © 2008 by Cheryl Holt. All rights reserved. Printed in the United States of America. No part of this book may be used or reproduced in any manner whatsoever without written permission except in the case of brief quotations embodied in critical articles or reviews. For information, address St. Martin's Press, 175 Fifth Avenue, New York, N.Y. 10010.

www.stmartins.com

Design by Kathryn Parise

Library of Congress Cataloging-in-Publication Data

Marlow, Vanessa, 1954–
    Sleeping with the devil / Vanessa Marlow. — 1st ed.
        p.   cm.
    ISBN-13: 978-0-312-36477-9
    ISBN-10: 0-312-36477-6
    I. Title.

PS3558.O3954S58   2008
813'.54—dc22

2007048964

First Edition: April 2008

10 9 8 7 6 5 4 3 2 1

R0413519880

Sleeping with the Devil

Prologue

&&

T ell me again what happened."

I peeked at the sheriff. At first glance, with his stomach bulging over his belt, his thinning hair and sagging jowls, he looked like a typical small-town cop. I could have easily mistaken him for an idiot or a buffoon, but I'd learned my lesson, and I was too smart to be duped by a deceptive appearance. I refused to be drawn in by the false sense of camaraderie he was trying to establish.

He evaluated the cliff face, studying the terrain, the angle, the sheer drop to the ocean hundreds of feet below. His curious concentration didn't miss a single twig or stone on the steep, isolated trail, and though he seemed calm and relaxed, his mind was racing a thousand miles an hour, taking it all in, figuring it out.

The gray water stretched to the horizon, and it merged with the gray clouds, so it was difficult to discern where the sea ended and the sky began. The waves crashed on the shore, shaking the earth with their power. The wind whipped at my clothes, the sound roaring in my ears, the huge, ancient trees creaking at the strain. Seagulls cawed, their plaintive wails bringing a suitable touch of melancholy to the desolate, dangerous spot.

With my anxiety waning and my adrenaline rush dissipating, I felt sick at my stomach and I wondered if—before we were through—I'd vomit all over his polished black boots. I'd always hated heights, and I was suffering surges of vertigo that had me so dizzy I was worried I'd collapse in a bewildered heap, not knowing which direction was up or down.

I yearned to grab the lapels of his coat, to plead with him to permit me to return to the parking lot, but I didn't dare. I couldn't do anything that might be suspicious. If he chose to stay out on the cliff, I had to stay with him.

"I told you," I said. "One minute he was standing there, and the next . . ."

Shrugging, I didn't finish the sentence. After explaining over and over, it was best not to offer new details. In the past few months, I'd become adept at prevarication. I wouldn't provide too much information, for then it would be tricky to keep my story straight. It was better to stick to the basic facts, to let him fill in the blanks.

"It's a long way down," he casually mentioned.

"It certainly is." The men in the rescue crew on the rocky beach were so far away that they could have been ants. "Is he . . . he . . . dead?"

"Oh, yes." He scrutinized me, his astute gaze digging deep. "A fellow couldn't survive such traumatic injuries."

I wailed with dismay, and I shuddered, imbuing the action with what I hoped was the correct amount of shock and horror.

"It's so dreadful." I covered my mouth, not having to pretend I was ill. My nausea was very real.

"Let's go over this again." He stared me down, his arms folded over his chest. His skepticism was blatant and impossible to hide.

At another period in my life, I might have been candid with him. I might have confessed and begged for mercy, but the woman who could have spoken the truth no longer existed.

I gave an anguished sigh.

"It was an accident," I lied. "A terrible, terrible accident."

Chapter One

I met Jordan Blair on a rainy day in January.

At the time, I assumed it was a quirk of fate, that we'd crossed paths at the right cosmic moment and everything had clicked into place. Our immediate and potent connection seemed so natural and effortless that it must have been preordained.

Of course, now I realize it was a tad more complicated than that. I was fairly sure he'd seen me somewhere prior, and I often wondered if he hadn't been following me and become obsessed, but I never stumbled on any evidence to prove how it had happened.

He was the most organized, meticulous person I'd ever known. Nothing with him was random or haphazard, so it was difficult to decipher his motives. Very likely, he'd schemed for months to arrange bumping into me, but the notion of it having been so calculated was too sinister, so I forced myself to believe it had all been chance.

I was vacationing on the Oregon coast with my boyfriend, Steve. We were celebrating the one-year anniversary of the first occasion we'd had sex—an event I scarcely remembered, but which he recalled fondly.

We lived together in a dumpy but cozy apartment in Portland. Steve worked as a salesman in his dad's restaurant supply company, while I was employed at the upscale Mozart's restaurant, where I was a dessert chef.

I was twenty-three years old, and I had been in the city long enough for my acquaintances to decide I was a true Oregonian. With my passion for expensive coffee and exotic food, my brown hair with its spiky blond highlights, my clunky jewelry and trendy black wardrobe, I was too typical to be an outsider.

I rode the train and pedaled my bike rather than driving a car, although this was a financial choice and not an environmental one. I didn't wear leather and rarely ate meat. I marched in demonstrations at Pioneer Square and was a regular shopper at organic grocery stores. I knew all the dance clubs and where the hottest bands were performing, and even though it rained incessantly, I didn't own a raincoat or umbrella.

My salary was pitiful, so I was usually broke, but I loved my job, my life, and Steve. Or at least I thought I did.

We'd rented a tiny cottage at a beach hotel, and soon after our arrival, a huge winter gale had blown in. The rain came down in torrents, wind gusts shaking everything so violently that part of the cottage's roof blew off during the night.

Though our apartment was only two hours from the beach, I had never visited before that disturbing day, so I wasn't prepared for how awful the weather would be. In Portland, it drizzled politely. On the coast, it was an unrelenting, tempestuous deluge.

Steve and I had been trapped inside for nearly twenty-four hours, and we'd started to go stir crazy.

We spent the morning in bed, having sex and coffee, but we could only copulate so many times, and we were anxious to do something else. The hotel furnished slickers and boots, so after lunch we donned them and ventured down the stairs that led to the sand. The scenery was fantastic, what we could see of it anyway, with towering cliffs and slamming surf.

We lasted about ten minutes, then we were soaked, and we headed back to our room. We read books, we played checkers, and we watched television until the electricity flickered out. Initially it was romantic to sit by the fire, but by evening the thrill was gone, and Steve was pacing like a tiger in a cage.

The front desk gave us directions to a restaurant and bar just through the trees, so we bundled up and trudged over, hoping to dine, then quench our boredom with cocktails. Luckily the restaurant was open but serving a limited menu due to the power outage. We were the only souls hearty or desperate enough to stop by, and we had the place to ourselves.

After eating, we went into the lounge, which was very small, with a couple of stools and four tables. As we were chatting, another couple entered, and I couldn't help but notice them — because they were the only other customers, but also because their appearance screamed *money*. They were so attractive, and so stylishly attired, that I speculated as to whether they might be movie stars.

We were close to the exclusive resort village of Cannon Beach, where lots of Hollywood moguls were rumored to keep summer homes, so it was entirely possible that they were famous, and I wanted them to be. It would add an aura of mystery and excitement to an otherwise dreary adventure.

The woman was glamorous, like a fashion model, with long, curling blond hair that probably wasn't her natural color. She was thin as a rail, but her breasts were plump and round and too large for how slim she was, so they probably weren't natural, either.

She had on a slinky red gown with red heels and red lipstick to match, and the dress clearly showed that she didn't have an ounce a fat on her. I gained some satisfaction by imagining her exhausting herself in the gym, a slave to the stair machine, which I would never do.

Of course, Steve—being a typical male—honed in on her right away. He leaned over and whispered, "Did you see that woman?"

"Yes."

"If I bought you a dress like that, would you wear it?"

"If you bought me a dress like that, I'd have to kill you."

He chuckled as we resumed drinking and tried to ignore them, which was hard. They were too magnificent to be in the same establishment with us, and I kept sneaking peeks at them, curious as to what had spurred them to brave the storm and follow us in.

The woman seemed to be our age, mid-twenties, but the man was older—maybe mid-thirties or forty—and I couldn't take my eyes off him. He was tall and thin, too, with black hair, high cheekbones, and a full mouth. He was enigmatic, smoldering with a charisma and maturity that fascinated me.

He was obviously rich, his wrist sporting one of those watches that told time in twelve countries and cost thousands of dollars. His clothes were tailored to hang correctly so that you couldn't miss the terrific torso beneath the fabric. He was in jeans and a leather jacket, slip-on loafers and a denim shirt, as was Steve, but where Steve looked okay and even a little frumpy, this guy looked dynamic and sexy.

They sat at the table farthest from ours, and the woman was propped forward on her elbows, giving the man — and Steve — a great view of her fabulous cleavage. She was sipping her wine, her tongue occasionally flitting out to lick her bottom lip.

Every so often she'd giggle, and it was a sultry sound, her voice suiting her gorgeous anatomy. The man never laughed in return, but would cock a brow or murmur a quiet reply, and I was intrigued by him and what he might be thinking.

Was he wishing she'd shut up? Was he annoyed by her? Or was he simply the sort who didn't exhibit much emotion?

I studied their body language, trying to figure out if they were married, but there wasn't a wedding band in sight, so I didn't suppose they were. There was definitely something sexual going on with them, though.

Were they lovers? Were they about to be?

Since I couldn't hide my piqued interest, I got up and went to the bathroom. I dawdled, evaluating myself in the mirror, checking how I stacked up with the beauty in the bar and cataloging all the ways I came up short. Literally, I was several inches shorter, my black outfit and the thick soles on my black boots making me appear taller than I was.

I was slender, but pleasantly so. I was a cook, and had sampled my share of the broth, so I had a butt and thighs, and my boobs were the appropriate size for my torso.

With my big brown eyes and pale skin, I looked very

young, like a waif, like I should be standing on a corner with a cup in my hand, begging for change.

I started back to the bar when, to my amazement, I ran into the man. He was heading toward the lobby—I wouldn't flatter myself into presuming he'd sought me out on purpose—and we were stuck, alone in the hallway.

Up close, he was more handsome. He was tan, as if he spent a lot of time outdoors, and he was whipcord lean, his stomach the kind of rippled washboard found on male models. His eyes were an icy blue, and they were assessing me so thoroughly that I was completely undone by the scrutiny.

I'd pegged his age as between thirty-five and forty, and I decided forty was the better guess. His face had a few crows' feet and wrinkles, but they gave him a weathered air that was very seductive.

I couldn't quit gawking or move on as I ought, and he seemed swept up, too, perfectly content to tarry as he analyzed me. His intent gaze blatantly wandered to my breasts, his attention so potent that it felt as if he'd reached out and caressed my nipples. They throbbed and poked against the cotton of my T-shirt, and I was so glad I'd kept my jacket on.

I stumbled away, mumbling, "Pardon me."

"Certainly," he politely responded, and we danced about, maneuvering around each other in the cramped space, which only brought us nearer. His thigh brushed mine, and my arm was pressed to his. We both paused, locked in place, a tangible energy flowing between us.

He focused in, as if probing for all my petty secrets, and in a deep, mellow baritone he asked, "Have we met?"

The line was such a cliché come-on that I laughed. Because

he was attractive and wealthy, I'd envisioned him as being overly sophisticated, but apparently I'd imbued him with traits he didn't possess.

"I'm sure we haven't."

"You're so familiar. Would I have seen your picture somewhere?"

I almost stupidly blurted out, *There was a photo of me in* The Oregonian!

I'd recently been featured in a "Best of Portland" charity calendar, where twelve female chefs posed provocatively, arranged behind wedding cakes and ovens, to seem as if we were cooking without any clothes on. *The Oregonian* had carried an article and matching photo about the calendar, with my name, Meg White, in the notation.

I was proud, but embarrassed by my fifteen minutes of fame. Fleetingly, I hoped that he'd noticed it, that he'd recognized me, which was absurd.

As if he would have recollected me from the paper! And if I *was* to be remembered by someone like him, I didn't want it to be because I'd posed naked, against my better judgment, in a charity calendar.

"No," I said, "you wouldn't have seen me anywhere."

It was the moment to leave, and I ordered myself to go, but before I could, he stepped in so that I was wedged to the wall. I was overwhelmed by his height, by the yummy smell of his leather coat. There was a manner about him that was all male, a tough, dangerous masculinity that men always yearn to have but are never quite able to muster. It was indefinable but thrilling, and it appealed to my feminine side, making me wish I was a damsel in distress so he could rescue me.

He bent in and slipped his fingers inside my jacket, resting them on my waist, and I just stood there and let him. I didn't shift away. I didn't frown. I didn't do anything at all. My nipples were so inflamed that if he'd slithered up and stroked one of them, I'd have let him do that, too.

Why was I loitering in a public corridor, allowing him to grope me? I had no idea.

"What's your name?" he inquired.

"Meg."

"Meg. Hmm." He pondered it, then nodded as if that's what he would have picked for me, as if he deemed it to be absolutely right. "How old are you?"

"Twenty-three."

"You're very pretty."

The compliment broke whatever weird magnet held us together. I'd been called many things in my life: interesting, exotic, different, but never pretty. Not even by Steve, and to my ears it sounded contrived, another come-on.

"Thanks." I chuckled, spun, and walked away.

I didn't glance around to see if he was following me, but I was positive he was. I could feel his hot gaze on me like a brand, as if he had X-ray vision. The sensation was eerie, but cool, too, and I reveled in it, a small, vain part of me tickled that he was intrigued enough to stare.

In the bar, I wasn't surprised to discover that while I was off flirting—or whatever it had been—with a stranger, Steve had struck up a conversation with the blond goddess. He was a salesman, so he had a gift for gab, which was the reason he was so good at his job. He genuinely liked people, had tons of friends, and in a situation where I would be too shy to speak, he'd already have learned everybody's address, phone number, where they'd gone to school, and their employment history.

I was relieved that he hadn't moved to her table, that they were still sitting where I'd left them. They talked as if they were old chums, and they were discussing French painters of all things, about which Steve knew nothing, but he was a bullshit artist so he easily carried his share of the exchange.

I ignored them and sipped my drink, thinking about my encounter in the hall and how it had rattled me. Eventually, the dark-haired man returned and slid in next to the blond. He sipped his drink, too. We gaped at each other as Steve and the woman continued to chat, but they were totally absorbed and unaware that the man and I were having our own little drama.

I tried my best to avoid eye contact with him. I studied the ceiling, my reflection in the window, the bartender washing glasses. Whenever I peered straight ahead, the man was observing me with such a determined gleam of appreciation that I wanted to leap up and shout, *What? What are you looking at?*

But I didn't. I didn't care to have Steve realize that the guy was watching me, or that I was watching him back.

He whispered to his companion, and whatever the remark, it brought a sly grin to her ruby lips. She said, "I'm Kimberly, by the way."

"I'm Steve," Steve replied. "And this is Meg."

"Hi, Meg," Kimberly cooed.

I flashed a wan smile and murmured hello. All through the introductions, I felt as if the man was judging me or waiting for me to make a mistake, but what could I possibly do or say that would be wrong?

"We're off to Jordan's beach house," Kimberly mentioned, providing the information that the man's name was Jordan and that he had a beach house. "Would you like to join us? I thought we could soak in the hot tub. Wouldn't that be fun?"

Knowing that it was precisely the sort of invitation Steve would accept, I immediately declined. "Oh, we couldn't impose."

"Nonsense, Meg," Kimberly responded. "The weather is so awful. What else is there to do? You have to come with us."

She was bent forward, the bodice of her dress drooping so that Steve had an unimpeded view of her breasts. I had to admit that they were terrific, and we could see most of them, so it was an easy call to make. The posture wasn't an accident; she was intentionally tantalizing Steve, when I couldn't imagine why. Steve was nice enough, but I mean, really!

She was with Adonis. Why torment poor Steve with what he couldn't have?

Yet, he was hooked like a fish on a line.

"Yeah, we'll come," he agreed, countering my refusal. "It sounds great."

Jordan and Kimberly stood, and we stood, too, but I was very nervous and not able to understand why. We'd gone off before, partying with people we scarcely knew, so why was I hesitating?

They were just so different from us, and the differences mattered in a way I couldn't identify.

"I'm parked out front," Jordan said. "You can follow us."

"We walked over from the hotel," I resisted. "We should be getting back."

"No problem." Jordan seemed to be upping the ante. "You can ride with me, and I'll bring you down when we're finished."

Steve was eager and excited, like a kid with a new toy. "Cool! Let's do it."

Jordan and Kimberly exited into the rainy, blustery gale, and we trailed after them. I slowed my pace, so that Steve would have to debate the situation with me before we climbed in Jordan's car.

"I don't want to go with them," I hissed once they were far enough away not to overhear.

"Why not?"

"I don't know. I just don't!"

"Don't be a stick in the mud. It'll be fun."

"We don't know anything about them."

"So?"

"Jordan might be an ax murderer. Maybe he's scouting us as his next victims."

"Right!" Steve laughed. "Why are you so worried? Lighten up."

We were outside and huddled under the awning at the entrance to the restaurant. Jordan was across the parking lot, helping Kimberly into an expensive SUV. Through the shadows, I could see his eyes glimmering, focused directly on me. Although he hadn't uttered a word, I perceived how keen he was for me to go with him. I was certain he'd intervene to guarantee I didn't escape. Why? Why would my presence or absence be so important to him?

I grabbed Steve's arm and pulled him to a halt.

"This is too weird. Why would they ask us over?"

"Because it's storming, and boring as hell out here, and they're dying for some company."

Even though I'd never previously met them, I couldn't shake the impression that they'd picked us, or had been searching for us. "But why would they want *us?*"

"We're the only human beings available in a twenty-mile radius." He gestured around the deserted lot. Jordan's car was the sole one in it. "Don't make me hang out at the hotel, Meg. Please. If I have to sit there all night, with no electricity and nothing to do, I'll go crazy."

"We could play cards," I petulantly reminded him. "That wouldn't be so bad."

"I played cards with you for three hours today." I scowled, and he hastily added, "Not that it wasn't entertaining, but Meg, they have a *hot tub.*"

He pronounced *hot tub* as if it was the Holy Grail, and I knew I was whipped. It was a luxury he relished and hardly ever had a chance to indulge.

"Okay," I finally grumbled, "but promise we can leave whenever I tell you I'm ready, and that we won't have a big argument about it."

Now that he'd gotten his way, he was all benevolence. "Sure."

"And I want him to take us over to our car. I don't want to be without it."

"Fine. Whatever." He marched across the lot, and I trotted along behind.

"Hey, Jordan," he called, "could you swing by the hotel so

we can get our car? Then you won't have to drive us back later."

Jordan nodded and smiled—not at Steve, but at me. It was settled. He'd won whatever battle we'd been waging. I was going, and I couldn't evade him or the disaster I sensed approaching like an inevitable train wreck.

Chapter Two

⯍

The road to Jordan's beach house wound up a mountain and through some thick woods that were so ominous I wouldn't have been surprised if Sasquatch had leapt out in front of us. The wind lashed at the car and rain beat on the wipers, slamming down so hard that we could scarcely keep his taillights in sight.

My dread increased. If I'd had to return later and find the spot on my own, I never could have, and I couldn't imagine how we'd get back to the hotel without assistance. I felt as if we were the last four people on earth, that we were about to drive off the edge, and I considered ranting at Steve for pushing me into the situation, but I didn't.

I was a grown-up. If I truly hadn't wanted to come along, I could have refused. I'd made my choice and wouldn't complain.

Up ahead, Jordan had stopped at a fancy, two-story log home. It wasn't big, but it wasn't small, either, and it appeared to be new. By the time we pulled in behind him, he'd vanished, so Kimberly ushered us in.

Playing the gracious hostess, she escorted us through the kitchen and living room, which were separated by an elaborate stone fireplace. The décor was tan and black, with comfy couches and plush rugs. One end was lined with windows, and Kimberly advised that it faced the ocean, that in the morning we'd be dazzled by the view of the coastline. I didn't intend to stay till morning, but I kept that thought to myself.

She took us upstairs and showed us into a bedroom with a private bath. It was stocked better than the best motels, with robes, toothbrushes, combs, bathing suits, and any clothes that an overnight visitor might need. I couldn't help wondering how often Jordan entertained and who his acquaintances were that he provided so many accessories.

We still hadn't seen him, and Kimberly babbled on as if his absence was customary, so I could only hope that he wasn't off loading a gun with which he planned to murder us.

I was so jumpy; I couldn't relax. Something bad was about to transpire, and whatever it was, I didn't care to be part of it.

Kimberly gave us directions to the hot tub, which was out on the rear deck, then she went to change, saying that she'd meet us there and to make ourselves comfortable.

As soon as she shut the door, Steve did just that. He strutted over to the four-poster bed and flopped onto it, the mattress bouncing with his weight. He lay on his back, his hands tucked behind his head.

"This is the life, huh?"

"Yeah," I agreed halfheartedly.

"Quit being such a bitch! You're embarrassing me. Knock it off."

He never talked to me that way, so I was astounded by the

out-of-character remark. "I'm not being a bitch. I just didn't want to come."

"Well, that's obvious as hell. What would you rather have done? Jerk off in the dark, in our crappy little hotel? Give me a break."

"This is creepy."

"Why? We've simply been invited to party, not to convert to a new religion. You're being a pain in the ass."

Was I? I'd never had his open and ready acceptance of other people, so I was nervous. It was disconcerting for me to waltz into a stranger's home, to use the underwear he'd purchased and sleep in his guest bed.

"What if Jordan's a serial killer?" Voiced aloud, the prospect sounded silly, but I was like a dog at a bone. I couldn't let it go. "What if he's in the basement right now, checking the manacles to be sure they're working properly before he ties us up and tortures us?"

"You're acting crazy."

"We don't know anything about him!"

"He's Jordan Blair." Steve spoke the name as if it explained the mysteries of the universe. "Kimberly told me at the bar, when you were in the rest room."

"Who's Jordan Blair?"

"He's like this reclusive bazillionaire. He started some sporting goods company when he was about ten years old, then sold it for megabucks when he was thirty."

"Why would somebody like that ask us over?"

"Who the fuck knows?" he crudely snapped. "But he did, so I'm going to put on one of his bathing suits, pop a cold beer, and soak in his hot tub."

"I don't want to do that."

"Suit yourself."

He marched over to the dresser, grabbed some trunks out of the drawer, and went into the bathroom. In a funk, I plopped onto a chair, desperate to join in but too uneasy. When he exited, he had a towel wrapped around his waist, the trunks on underneath. He'd removed his shirt, and he was fatter than I recollected. He was developing a genuine beer gut, and I hadn't noticed.

What did that mean?

"You coming?" he barked.

"No."

"Fine. Sit up here all alone then. I don't give a shit."

He stomped out, and as the quiet settled, I tried to figure out why we were fighting, but I hadn't a clue. Usually he was so considerate of me, and the fact that he'd been rude and abrupt had me worried. We hadn't been in the house a half hour and he was being such a prick. What would happen if we wound up staying all night?

The walls were closing in on me. There was a patio door that led out to a balcony, and I walked over and stepped out into the fresh air. Down below, Kimberly and Steve were chatting, though I couldn't hear what they were saying.

I had no desire to linger upstairs like some kind of freak. Plus, I wasn't particularly keen on Steve being by himself with Kimberly, which was weird. In the entire year we'd been together, even when he was on the road, making sales calls, I'd never questioned his fidelity, and I felt petty to be questioning it now.

Still, Kimberly could have been a lingerie model. What normal male wouldn't be tempted?

I had to go down. There was no other choice. In the dresser, I found several skimpy bikinis that I never would have selected for myself. They were all the same style and hardly covered anything that ought to be covered. They were in a myriad of colors, but red being my favorite, I picked that one.

I had begun to tug off my shirt when I was overcome by an intense sensation that someone was watching me. The curtains were drawn, and the space was small enough for me to be certain that no one was in it with me, but I was rattled again. I changed in the bathroom.

The suit was so tiny, just two patches of cloth over my nipples and a thong that slid into my butt crack. My privates were mostly visible, and I couldn't imagine strutting around with my pubic hair sticking out.

I rifled through the medicine cabinet, located a razor, took a few quick swipes, then posed in front of the mirror. After twirling back and forth, I decided I looked okay. I was thin and healthy, but with real boobs, a waist, and hips. Satisfied, I pulled my T-shirt and jeans over the suit, then ordered myself to the deck.

Steve and Kimberly were in the tub, side by side and much too cozy for my peace of mind. As I neared, there was no guilty flinching or hasty separation, yet I was shocked to see that Kimberly wasn't wearing a bathing suit—at least not on the top. Her perfect, sculpted breasts were bare, the rosy tips jutting out. If she had on the bottom piece, I couldn't tell through the swirling water, but I assumed it was off, too.

Steve's trunks were casually tossed on the patio. So Steve was naked, and Kimberly was naked, and I was . . . what? Embarrassed? Uncomfortable? Angry?

Try all of the above. How was I to force myself to join them? It was bad enough to be next to Kimberly in a bikini, but doing it in the nude wasn't in the cards.

Her fabulous blond hair was pinned up in a haphazard way, the curly strands framing her face. She was cute and sexy in a fashion I never could have managed.

"Hey, babe," Steve called to me, "would you fetch me a beer before you climb in?"

Throughout our relationship, he'd never referred to me as *babe,* so I was astonished. He pointed to a refrigerator over by the wall, and I went to it and retrieved a beer as Kimberly added, "Would you be a darling and refill my wine, too?"

"Sure," I muttered, feeling like the maid.

"While you're at it, help yourself to whatever you'd like."

"I will," I said, thinking I'd need something stronger than wine.

Determined not to snarl at Steve, not to ogle Kimberly's tits, I took them their requested beverages, then I returned to the minibar. There was a shelf of liquor, and I poured myself a straight whiskey. I gulped it down, then poured another, and gulped it, too. It had an instantaneous, soothing effect, giving me the necessary courage to proceed.

I sauntered over to the tub, drinking and pretending I was fine. I didn't want to act like a prude, or to appear squeamish, but I was on the verge of shouting at Steve, something along the lines of, *What the hell are you doing?*

But I refused to behave like a shrew. If he could be so nonchalant about being naked with Kimberly, then I could blithely stand there and observe as he made a fool of himself. I could stand there all friggin' night.

"Where's Jordan?" I asked.

"Oh, he's around," Kimberly vaguely replied. "He hates the hot tub."

"Really?"

"Oh yes. He never gets in."

Why have us over for an activity he detested? My anxiety spiraled.

"He'll probably be here soon, though," Kimberly continued. "He likes to watch, rather than participate."

"To watch what?" I stupidly inquired.

"Well . . . *us*." She giggled, her laughter tinkling like a bell. "What would you suppose?"

A queasy wave coursed through my stomach. It had to be a sexual comment, and it underscored my trepidation about the place and the two occupants. I glanced over at Steve, but he was as relaxed as ever, lounging as if he hung out in the nude with women like Kimberly every day.

"Come on in, Meg," he urged. "The water's great."

"Yes, Meg," Kimberly badgered. "Come on in."

We were like children. They were daring me to do what I didn't want to do, what I knew I shouldn't do, but damned if I was a coward. I yanked my T-shirt over my head, revealing the scant halter of my bikini.

At seeing my upper torso, Steve grinned. "Now *that* I like."

"You do?"

"Oh yeah!"

The remark broke the tension, and I chuckled. It had been ages since he'd gazed at me so passionately, so perhaps there'd be a benefit from the encounter after all. Perhaps it would rev up our sex life, which had grown very routine.

"You should wear red more often," he said.

"Maybe I should."

I unzipped my jeans as both of them stared at me, and the attention made me feel like a stripper. As calmly as I was able, I strolled to the patio table and folded my clothes over a chair, then I climbed in the tub and sat on the rim. My calves and feet dangled in the water.

"It's very hot," I mentioned.

"You'll get used to it," Steve coaxed. "Slide down in."

"Give me a minute."

"It *is* hot, isn't it?" Kimberly agreed.

She sluiced up and sat on the rim, too. As she was directly across from me, I couldn't help but look at her. She'd shaved herself all over, so she didn't have any hair between her legs. I had never viewed myself as overly prim or proper, but the sight startled me. Her knees were spread as if she was eager for me to notice.

Arching her back, she ran her hand down her bosom, her stomach, her thighs. I didn't miss a single inch of the gesture, and neither did Steve. He was completely enthralled, which really pissed me off.

Her exhibition finished, she glided down. In a challenging tone, she taunted, "Why don't you take off your suit, too?"

"I don't think so," I responded. "I'm not much for skinny-dipping."

Steve was annoyed by my reluctance. "Just do it, Meg! It'll be fun."

Kimberly shifted toward him, her breast nestled to his chest, her leg draped over his lap. I was speechless and trying to figure out her game.

Did she want to have sex with Steve? Did she want to have sex with *me* and Steve? Is that what Steve was hoping would occur?

It certainly seemed like it to me, which was bizarre in the extreme. I didn't know Steve had a kinky bone in his body. Could he actually envision the three of us together?

I scowled, but my fury was lost on him. He was too intent on Kimberly and that breast. He was in a virtual fog of desire and so distracted that his eyes were nearly crossed.

"Steve . . ." I said.

"What?"

"Could we go?"

"Go? But we just got here."

"This is kind of weird."

"What is?"

"I want to go!"

"Fuck no. Why are you whining about everything? If you don't want to party, then go watch TV. Stop complaining."

I should have screamed at him, but I was too stunned. His temper and discourtesy were facets of his personality I'd never previously witnessed, so I hadn't developed a method for dealing with them.

I flashed a glare that could kill, but it was wasted on him. He was ecstatic over what was about to transpire, so I couldn't shame or cow him into better behavior.

"I guess I'll find a TV," I grumbled.

"There are hundreds of videos in the den," Kimberly offered, "although they're probably a tad more racy than you'd enjoy."

At the catty comment, I yearned to slap her, but I restrained myself.

I scrambled to the deck, grabbed my clothes, and stormed into the house. Kimberly murmured something to Steve, and he snickered. I was dying to know what they were doing, but I was too much of a chicken to turn and see.

If he screwed Kimberly, what would I do? Was I prepared to break up with him? To move out? To give up all my friends and the life he and I had built? I understood that sex was just sex for a man, but I couldn't handle this. It was beyond me.

Livid and confused, I stumbled into the hall, and I gaped around, trying to get my bearings. Where were the stairs? Where was our room?

I decided I'd snag the car keys, drive off, and leave his sorry ass behind. In the morning, when he arrived at the hotel, I wouldn't be there. He'd have to hitchhike to Portland in the rain, which would serve him right! The bastard!

In a daze, I wandered to the stairs and trudged up them. As I reached the top and rounded the corner, Jordan was at our door. He leaned against the frame as if he'd been waiting for me.

The leather jacket and jeans were gone, and he was wearing only a silky pair of lounge pants and nothing else. He was all honed muscle and sleek lines, his torso mature and seasoned. I'd had my share of lovers before Steve, but I'd never slept with an older man, and I was fascinated. Once again, I felt a surge of the peculiar energy that had sparked between us at the bar. I was drawn to him, my anatomy in sync with his and ready for a more intimate association.

I couldn't have him assuming I was afraid of him, because I wasn't, so I approached till I was so near that our feet were tangled, our legs entwined. He yanked my clothes from my arms and tossed them on the floor, then he stared down at me, curious to see if I'd retreat or flee, but I wasn't about to do either one. It was blatantly apparent that he wanted something from me, and I had to learn what it was.

"Didn't you like the hot tub?" he queried.

"No."

"Don't be angry with Steve."

"What do you mean?"

"Men can't resist Kimberly." He shrugged. "Let him play with her, and forget about it or you'll go crazy."

"You make it sound like they're merely drinking tea."

"I know Kimberly, so I'm sure it's more involved than that."

"Aren't you the least bit"—I almost said *jealous* but settled for—"concerned?"

"I don't care what she does."

"What is she to you?"

"Nothing."

"Then why is she here?"

"She amuses me."

He traced a finger down my cleavage, wedging it under the little triangle that passed for a bathing suit top.

"I knew you'd look good in red," he said.

His statement puzzled me. There had been several bikinis in the dresser. Had he been positive I'd put on the red one? How could he be aware that red was my favorite color? He seemed to be implying that he'd placed it for me specifically, that he'd been confident I'd select it, which was too strange to consider.

I was disturbed and perplexed, and I should have shoved him away, but I didn't. When had I become such a mouse?

Ever since I'd crossed paths with him, I had lost my ability to act or react.

With a simple flick of the wrist, he bared my nipple, and he bent down and nipped at my neck, forcefully enough for it to hurt. I felt as if I was drowning, as if he was plunging to the bottom of the ocean and taking me with him. I had to pull away, to come up for air, and I wailed, "What do you want from me?"

He pushed me to the wall and stepped in. "I want to fuck you," he said. "I want to fuck you all night."

He lifted me, my thighs wrapped around his waist, his loins connected with mine, and he was hard as a rock. He flexed against me, eager for me to feel him, to desire him in return, and oh, I did. I did! He was insistent and firm in a way I'd never experienced with any of my other, much younger lovers.

"I can't," I breathed. "Please . . ."

With that *please*, what was I asking? I thought I'd skitter into my room, to retrieve the car keys and go. Wasn't that what I'd planned? Yet without a whimper of protest, I was allowing him to proceed. He was untying my suit, and in a second the top was off.

He dipped down and sucked on my nipple. He was rough and demanding, but I didn't mind. The excess of stimulation had me dizzy with excitement.

"I have to leave," I said.

"Why?"

"Steve is . . . is . . ."

"Don't worry about Steve," he scolded. "Kimberly will entertain him."

His hand was between us; his fingers slithered into the

bikini panty, about to glide that final inch where they would be inside me.

I panicked. I wasn't loose; I wasn't a slut. I most definitely wasn't the sort to freeze like a statute while he mauled me. I wiggled away and he released me, directing my descent so that I slid down his torso. My heart was pounding, and I was so wet and slippery between my legs that I felt as if we'd had full-on sex.

He studied me, his blue eyes intent but enigmatic.

"I scared you." He seemed surprised that he had.

"I'm not like Kimberly. It's not easy for me to . . . to . . ."

"It's okay." He soothed me as one might a skittish horse, massaging my arms, my shoulders, urging my pulse to a slower rhythm. "You don't have to do anything you don't want to do."

"I want to go to my hotel."

"I won't let you."

"You can't stop me."

"The power's out everywhere."

"It's not out here."

"I have a generator," he claimed, "but at your hotel, you'll be in the dark. I won't permit you to do something so silly."

"So . . . I'll pack my suitcase and head to Portland."

"And abandon Steve to Kimberly?" He was sarcastic, as if he'd suspected I wouldn't fight for Steve.

"She can have him—with my blessing. I just want out of here."

"You can't go."

"I can!"

"I mean it literally. The road to Portland is closed. There was a landslide because of all the rain. It'll be a day or two before it's cleared."

I scrutinized his cool expression, but I didn't know him at all. He appeared to be telling the truth, but how could I be certain?

"I don't believe you," I ultimately said.

"Check for yourself." He motioned to the television in my room and, as if my dilemma had ceased to matter, he walked away.

"I will," I called after him, but he kept on.

I scooped up my clothes and went in, shutting the door behind me, and I channel-surfed until I found a Portland station. The news was all about the bad weather, the power outages, and the blocked highway, so he'd been honest about the situation.

Still, electricity or not, I would have rather been at the hotel, though I had no idea how I'd find my way down the mountain in the storm. Steve's jeans were strewn across the end of the bed, and I rummaged through every pocket, searching for the keys to the car, but they weren't there. I searched the blankets, floor, dressers, closet, and bathroom, with no luck.

When I'd come upstairs, Jordan had been loitering in the threshold, but I refused to accept that he might have taken or hidden them. Why would he?

I sank down on a chair, wondering what to do next.

Chapter Three

❦

I was trapped.

I wanted to march down and demand that Steve help me find the keys, but I was too much of a wimp. I was terrified of what I might catch him doing. Another woman, a braver woman, might have had the temerity to walk into the middle of it, but not me.

I prowled the bedroom till I ran out of steam, then I stopped and sifted through a stack of videos in the cabinet. They were erotic in nature—drenched, hesitant females in showers, handsome, aggressive men urging them into degrading acts—soft porn that was as disconcerting as it was arousing. I put one in the machine, and I relaxed against the pillows to watch it.

At some point I must have dozed off, because I woke with a start. I was disoriented, and it took me a moment to remember where I was. The clock on the nightstand showed that it was after two, which meant I'd been out for nearly four hours. Steve wasn't in the bed with me.

I lay in the quiet, deciding what my next move should be. I hadn't been raped or murdered in my sleep, so the need to escape wasn't as dire as it had been.

Muted voices drifted by, indicating that the party was still in progress. Steve had had plenty of time to soak in the hot tub, so maybe I'd be able to convince him to leave.

Wearing the red bikini, a white robe covering it, I proceeded into the hall and tiptoed down the stairs.

At the bottom, I could peer into the living room without actually entering, and the view was more appalling than anything I could have conjured in my imagination.

Kimberly was naked, on her knees on one of the tan couches, and gripping the rear of the sofa. Steve was behind her, clutching her hips and fucking her for all he was worth. The scene was so awful that it couldn't be real, and I lingered in the shadows, my jaw dropping in shock.

Kimberly looked incredible. With her perfect body, and her curly blond hair swinging free, she was every man's fantasy, but Steve didn't match as her partner. He was chubby and soft, and he'd pulled his swimming trunks down to his ankles. He resembled a goofy character in a raunchy cartoon, so out of place with the glamorous Kimberly that I almost felt sorry for him, and it underscored how strange the night was.

When Kimberly was such a fox, why would she stoop to having sex with *my* friendly, sweet, normal Steve?

He was very drunk, and probably high, too. I could tell from the blush on his cheeks, from how he swayed and staggered, but his condition was scant comfort. Even if he was intoxicated, how could it be an excuse?

This was the last straw for me, and I dawdled, trying to figure out how to make my presence known. Should I storm in, shouting and accusing? Should I stroll over and tap Steve on the shoulder? Should I sneak in and wait until they noticed me? Then what would I say? What was the appropriate comment: *Steve, when did you get to be such an asshole?*

It was then that I spotted Jordan in the room, too. He was sprawled in a chair and studying them, but extremely bored, as if he'd seen it all before and wasn't impressed.

I'd just opened my mouth to speak—what words, I wasn't sure—when he saw me. His icy blue eyes locked on mine, and I was transfixed, staring at him, staring at Steve, staring at Jordan again, and I couldn't say anything at all.

Jordan touched a finger to his lips, motioning me to silence, and like a puppet on a string, I obeyed. He rose and went around the couch so that he was facing Kimberly.

She reached out to him and drew him into a kiss, and briefly, he participated.

"Are you having fun, darling?" she asked.

"Oh, yes," he replied, though with no enthusiasm to suggest that he was enjoying himself. "Turn around and go down on him. I want you to suck him off."

"A fabulous idea."

"You know what I like."

"Yes, I do."

Happy to try whatever Jordan requested, she wiggled away from Steve and slid off the couch and onto the floor. She fondled his balls and cock, lapped at the tip, then took him deep in her throat.

I wasn't a great fan of oral sex. I couldn't get used to all that thrusting. Nor did I like the taste of semen, so the occasions when I'd given a guy a full-on blow job were very rare. Steve liked the act as much as the next man, but I was always so opposed that he'd quit pestering me about it.

In a sort of horrified fascination, I observed them. It seemed as if Jordan was testing me, though I didn't know why he would. I was going to fail; I could already tell. After what I was witnessing, how could Steve and I ever stay together?

Steve grinned at Jordan, and a searing glance passed between them, some idiotically male bond of complicity that I couldn't begin to understand.

"You can be next," Steve advised him. "I don't mean to be a hog."

"You can have her all to yourself," Jordan responded. "I don't mind."

"Thanks!"

Steve flexed with a renewed vigor, and Jordan walked away from them and straight to me. He clasped my wrist and dragged me down the hall and into a bedroom.

As he shut and locked the door, I yanked away. Pacing and cursing, I released the explosion I should have hurled at Steve, but hadn't.

"Bastard!" I keened over and over. "Bastard, bastard, bastard . . ."

I grabbed a lamp and smashed it, receiving a significant amount of satisfaction from how it shattered. I was barefoot, but I continued on, blindly stomping over the shards of glass. I had to have cut the soles of my feet, but I was too upset to notice.

How could Steve do this to me? *Why* would Steve do this to me? Was he thinking I wouldn't find out? Or that if I did, I wouldn't care?

I picked up a vase, prepared to fling it, too, but Jordan was on me, his arms encircling me so I couldn't do more damage. He jerked the vase away, and I fought with him, trying to get at it.

I was in a frenzy, and he wrestled to control me, finally turning me and shoving me against the wall. He crushed his body to mine, his front to my back, so I was pinned in place. I kept swearing, kicking at his shins with my heel, but no matter what I did, he only flattened himself to me that much more.

I could feel every inch of his torso, his chest, his stomach, his crotch. His cock was wedged to my bottom, throbbing with desire.

"Why did you bring us here?" I demanded to know. "What do you want from us?"

"I didn't *bring* you."

"You did!" I insisted. "You wanted us to come. You wanted *me* to come. Why? Why me?"

"Why not?"

My fevered brain couldn't make sense of his answer. I couldn't shake the perception that he'd chosen me for some cruel, sick game.

"I was happy! I was happy with my life, with how things were."

"Were you?"

"Yes! And you've ruined it! Why would you? What did I ever do to you?"

"He fucks around on you constantly."

"You're lying!"

"He said he's out of town a lot, on business. He bragged about it."

"That's not true."

"It is."

The anger swooshed out of me, vanishing so quickly that I was dizzy. My knees were weak, my bones rubbery. If he hadn't been supporting me, I'd have collapsed on the floor in a stunned heap.

Could Steve have been unfaithful? Could it possibly have occurred regularly without my suspecting?

He was gone frequently, staying overnight in cheap hotels, and I had no idea who he encountered while he was away. Disturbing visions flashed in my head, of smoky bars and busty, wasted women, hanging around till closing, following him to his room.

I pushed the images away, refusing to look, refusing to see. I knew Steve. He wouldn't behave like that toward me.

Jordan tugged at the belt on my robe, and he drew it off so that I was wearing only the skimpy bikini. He massaged my breasts, pinching and squeezing the nipples as he bit my neck. He was too rough, hurting me, but I was too numb to care. If he'd been gentle and restrained, I wouldn't have felt anything.

He removed the top of the suit, but I didn't protest. There wasn't any point. I was furious with Steve, and at that moment I might have committed any outrageous act.

We were about to have sex, but it didn't seem wrong. It was like being in a car wreck. You could watch the other vehicle coming, but you couldn't halt its determined approach. All you could do was hold on and pray you weren't injured too badly.

He ripped away the thong, and he clutched my thighs and entered me from behind. I moaned, not in agony but with a resigned despair. I didn't want to do this with him, but I didn't want to stop, either.

"He doesn't deserve you," Jordan declared, his words matching the rhythm of his penetrations.

I agreed. Steve didn't deserve me.

I braced my palms on the wall as Jordan fucked me over and over. It was basic and crude, but I was so bewildered that I wasn't bothered in the least. I felt as if I was being punished, and in some bizarre way, it was just what I needed.

I struggled against him, not because I hoped he'd quit, but because I was desperate to lash out and he was the only one who was near.

"Yes," he hissed, "fight me. I like it when you do."

I increased my skirmishing, twisting away from him, or perhaps he let me go. He shoved me onto the bed and I pulled him down with me. In a tangle of arms and legs, we tumbled onto the mattress. He rolled us till he was on top, and he slid into me.

He gazed at me, his expression frightening in its intensity. I'd never had a lover who focused on me as he did, as if I was the most exotic, most wonderful woman in the world.

I reveled in the attention, delighted to have it flow over and through me, as I met him thrust for thrust. Expertly, he drove me to the edge and hurtled me over. I arched up and cried out, the wail wrenched from my very soul, and he clamped a hand over my mouth, stifling the sound so that we wouldn't be overheard.

Through the entire orgasm, he continued to flex, and as I reached the peak and floated down, he was still very hard, very relentless, and he didn't slow. I had expended so much energy—with the sex, but with being angry and distressed, too—that I simply wanted to curl into a ball, but he wouldn't let me.

"Again," he said. "Again."

"I can't."

"You have to. For me."

He kept on, his tantalizing lips on my breast, his skilled fingers toying with me. Swiftly, he goaded me to the cliff and pushed me over. This time he joined me, but he was very reserved, as if he'd come so often that he was beyond a wild outburst.

With the passion ended, he nodded in contemplation. It was an arrogant gesture, as if I'd participated precisely as he'd planned, and I had provided no surprises.

He retreated from me, though his erection hadn't waned. I'm sure if I'd given the smallest hint that I was in any condition for it, he'd have spurred me to a third orgasm, which I was convinced would have killed me. I was a mess, my body bruised from his ferocity, my emotions careening from depression to dread, and I couldn't have done it again if he'd offered me a million dollars.

He turned me onto my side, and he spooned himself to me, stroking his hand across my hair, down my shoulder, my back.

"I'm so sad," I murmured, unable to swallow the hurt that had replaced the fury.

"I know you are."

"What will happen when—" I needed to talk, but he cut me off.

"Hush for now. Just rest. It's very late."

"But what am I going to do?"

"You don't have to figure it out this very second."

No, I didn't. I could doze for a bit, then wake up and face the situation with a clearer head. It was as if I'd died, as if the next morning I'd be reincarnated as a different person whose new life bore no resemblance to the old.

How could a few short hours have altered everything so completely?

I closed my eyes. I slept.

Chapter Four

❦

I awoke to daylight and silence. I was neatly tucked under the blankets, but I had no idea what time it was. I could see gray sky through the window. Raindrops splattered the glass, but I couldn't hear the wind, so the worst of the storm must have moved on.

As I straightened and stretched my legs, every muscle protested. I ached from top to bottom, and my head pounded as if I was hung over, but I'd hardly drunk anything the prior night.

I glanced over, but Jordan wasn't with me, and I was relieved. I hadn't exchanged a dozen words with him before we'd had sex, and I wasn't positive how I felt about that. I wasn't embarrassed, when I probably should have been, but I was definitely curious as to what we'd say to one another at our next meeting.

I wondered where Steve was and if he had any inkling of what I'd done with Jordan. I hoped not. I couldn't defend my actions, and I did *not* want to explain myself.

I located a clock that showed it was after two, and I groaned and stood, ignoring how my body protested as I tugged on my robe. The pieces of the bikini were strewn across the floor, a blatant and humiliating reminder of my stupidity. I stuffed them into a pocket, not eager to touch them, but not too keen on having anyone else stumble on them, either.

I staggered to the bathroom and took a long, hot shower. When I finished, I couldn't bear to put on the same robe, so I found another in the closet, then forced myself out to face the aftermath. I couldn't hide forever.

I tiptoed into the hall, inching down it as if negotiating a mine field, but I was wise to be cautious. Who knew what I'd discover?

In the living room, there was plenty of evidence of a party. Empty beer bottles and overflowing ashtrays were scattered around, but no one was passed out. Through the large windows, the ocean was visible off in the distance, as well as a significant section of the coast. Steep cliffs extended out into the water, and waves crashed against the rocks.

Any other day, I might have been enthralled and would have paused to marvel at the view, but I was too distressed to pay much attention. I proceeded toward the kitchen, when I literally ran into a maid who was carrying a garbage can and washcloth.

I jumped.

"Sorry," she said, smiling. "I noticed the car out front, but it's so quiet I wasn't sure if anyone was still here or not."

"I was just about to make some coffee."

"I already did. Help yourself."

"Thanks."

I lurched to the kitchen, scrounged for a cup, and sat at the table, sipping away as I pondered my next step. I didn't want to see Jordan, nor was I too crazy about my pending altercation with Steve. If Kimberly walked in, I'd gag.

I was desperate to escape, and it seemed as if everyone was asleep, so it was a good time to sneak out. I hurried toward the stairs but the maid stopped me.

"I was supposed to lock up," she explained, "but if you're staying over, I can come back tomorrow."

"What did Mr. Blair say you should do?"

"Well, he told me to close the place up, but he's gone and you're here, so I'm not certain what he'd want."

"He's gone?"

"He was scheduled to leave this morning."

"I thought the highway was blocked."

"I heard on the radio that it's open. It's only one lane, though, but traffic is getting through."

So he'd split, content to have us—two perfect strangers, and perhaps Kimberly—roaming around on our own. Blair was a lunatic. The urge to flee was growing stronger.

"I need to be going," I advised her. "There are a couple of other people here. At least I think there are. I don't know what you should do about locking up the house."

"It's no problem." She was nonchalant, as if dusting around unconscious guests was a common occurrence. She studied the mess. "I'll be busy for a while yet, and I'll figure it out."

I left her and climbed the stairs. I peeked in every door, positive Kimberly and Steve would be snuggled together. Every bed was mussed, the blankets tossed, as if they'd fucked everywhere, but Kimberly wasn't there, and I guessed that she'd departed with Jordan.

Steve was naked and snoring in one of the rooms—not the one we'd been given—and I darted past it and into ours. Someone had folded my jeans and T-shirt in a neat pile on a chair. As I donned them and pulled on my jacket, I was unnerved to locate the keys to the car, as if they'd been there all along. I was creeped out all over again, and I grabbed them and rushed out.

For a nanosecond, I considered yelling at Steve and nagging at him to drag his ass out of bed and come with me, but I simply couldn't do it. It was two hours to Portland, and at the moment I couldn't have tolerated being trapped in a small space with him. I'd have committed murder.

What would we say to each other? Would we spend the whole ride with him denying he'd had sex with Kimberly? Would we discuss the business-trip infidelities he'd confessed to Jordan? Would he admit what he'd done with Kimberly and regale me with the details? More likely, we'd travel in hostile, resentful silence, a fate that was too dreadful to contemplate.

In the living room, the maid was tidying up. As she saw me dressed, she said, "That was fast."

"I'm heading out," I apprised her, "but there's a guy here. His name is Steve. If he wakes up, would you tell him that Meg—that's me—took the car and went back to Portland?"

"Sure."

It was shitty of me to leave him behind, but I was pissed and dazed, and I didn't care how—or *if*—he got home.

I walked out into the rain, relieved that Steve's car was actually in the driveway. I'd had this inexplicable fear that it would have vanished, that maybe the outside world had evaporated. The night had been so odd. How could everything still be the same?

I stared up at the house, getting my first genuine look at it, and I was surprised by how normal it appeared. It was just a building, with rock chimneys, big windows, and expensive landscaping. It didn't emanate evil vibes, which didn't seem possible. From the instant I'd entered it, I'd felt surrounded by wickedness, as if there'd been something in the air or walls that had pushed me to act as I had.

I *had* to blame it on the house, for I refused to acknowledge that I'd participated of my own free will. Steve had behaved very badly, but so had I. What could be the justification for either of us?

I snagged the keys from my pocket, and as I did, a scrap of paper fell out. I glanced down, stunned to see a note from Jordan. It contained several phone numbers, with the initial *J* written underneath.

I shuddered, envisioning him jotting the message, searching for my coat and slipping it in. Could he really imagine I'd contact him? Why would I? Was he assuming we'd have sex again?

He was a man, so probably yes. He'd be pleased with what we'd done. I, on the other hand, was very uneasy.

The encounter had been too aggressive, too severe, but I'd liked it anyway. His conduct appealed to some mysterious facet of my feminine side that had enjoyed his forcing me to obey. What did that mean?

I was afraid to learn the answer.

I crumpled the note and tossed it into the bushes, then I slid into the car, started it, and sped away. The road curved down the mountain to the highway. Within minutes, I was at our hotel.

I crammed our stuff in a suitcase—Steve's, too, when I could have been the ultimate bitch and left it—checked out, and drove off. A few hours later, I was in our apartment, drinking scotch and puffing on a cigarette. I didn't smoke, but one of Steve's friends had forgotten a pack, and it seemed an appropriate way to pass the time as I waited for him to call or to slither in like the despicable snake he was.

I glared across the room, where a drooping banner that read *Happy Anniversary* was hanging by some tape. Steve had bought it before we'd gone to the coast to celebrate. There was a wilted bouquet, snuffed-out candles, the dirty dishes from an intimate supper. All of it mocked me with what had been lost.

I wanted to take off, but where would I go? I didn't have any family to assist me. I'd been an abandoned child, raised by an elderly aunt who'd been deceased for years. I had no siblings or cousins. I had some friends, but they were people I knew through Steve and more his friends than mine. I had numerous coworkers at the restaurant, but I'd never impose on any of them. The prospect was ludicrous.

Payday wasn't till the following Friday, so I was low on cash, which made it hard to consider finding a new place.

Technically, the apartment and furniture were Steve's. When we'd gotten together, I'd moved in with him, bringing only personal items such as clothes, books, and CDs. If we were to split up, *I* would be expected to go, and at the notion of giving it all up, I was depressed and tired. I couldn't make any plans or take action. I was too conflicted, unable to reflect or proceed.

There was a rapping on my door. I opened it, recognizing that it would be our neighbor, Marie. We shared the top floor of an old, remodeled, run-down mansion. She was grinning and happy to see me. At her last visit, Steve and I had been laughing and joking, preparing for our weekend getaway.

"I thought there was a light on." She waltzed in as she usually did, without a clue that anything was wrong. "How was the trip? Was it all flowers and romance?"

"It wasn't exactly romance," I muttered.

"What happened? Is Steve okay?"

"He's fine—I suppose." To my horror, tears filled my eyes, and I pressed against them with the heels of my hands. "God, everything is so fucked!"

"What is it?"

She led me to the couch, where I related what I could of the sordid story. Of course, I conveniently omitted my own transgressions. I wasn't about to mention Jordan and me.

"Steve did that?" She was as shocked as I could have predicted. "I can't believe it."

"Neither can I. It was so weird, like his body was invaded by aliens."

"Where is he now?"

"I left him there."

"You didn't!"

"I did. He was passed out, and I figured *fuck him*."

"But . . . but . . . how will he get home?"

"I have no idea."

"Jesus, Meg. That's harsh."

"I know, but I was so pissed off."

She poured herself a scotch, and lit up a cigarette, too. We smoked and drank in the quiet. Finally she asked, "What will you do? Will you break up with him?" She peered around the room, trying to picture it without my meager possessions tucked away in the drawers and shelves.

"Wouldn't you?"

"I don't know. He's such a great guy. I don't understand this at all."

"You think I do? The man, that Jordan Blair, he claimed Steve was bragging that he screws around on me constantly when he's out of town."

She frowned. "That can't be true."

Just then, Steve's footsteps sounded on the stairs, and she rose. "See what he has to say," she counseled. "Don't make any decisions while you're angry."

"I won't."

She scooted out and into her own apartment as he tottered in. I was on the couch, staring at him, my fury palpable, but on observing his disheveled condition, some of it faded. His coat was soaked, his hair and shoes, too, an indication that hitch-hiking had been a tad difficult. His eyes were bloodshot, his skin pasty, his hands shaking. He looked like shit and was obviously in the middle of the worst hangover in history.

"Don't say a fucking word to me," he hissed, and he stormed into the bathroom, raced to the toilet, and puked over and over. The disgusting commotion continued for so long that I wondered how he could still be alive, but I could tell he was. He was rampaging like an enraged elephant.

I sat for an eternity, but I didn't check on him. Eventually, I snuggled down on the cushions, pulled an afghan over me, and went to sleep. At one point, I vaguely noted him stumbling into the bedroom and falling into bed.

When I woke in the morning, it was time to get ready for work. I showered, dressed, and crept out. I should have talked to him, but I couldn't stomach the shouting that was certain to ensue. Plus, my own behavior was extremely suspect, so the moral high ground had collapsed beneath me.

By taking the coward's route of sneaking away, I was merely postponing our confrontation, but the delay was fine by me.

As I arrived at the restaurant and strolled into the kitchen, my partner in desserts, Jeffrey, was toiling away. At thirty, he was short and pudgy, with curly brown hair and glasses. He loved clothes, wine, cooking, and other men. He was openly gay and never hid it.

I must have appeared as if *I* was the one with the hangover, because he glanced up and scowled.

"What happened to you?"

"What do you mean?"

"Darling, were you pecked by a gaggle of geese?"

I chuckled miserably. That was an accurate description of how I felt. I ached everywhere. Even my veins hurt. I couldn't conceive of staying all day, of concentrating sufficiently to bake anything remotely edible. As I donned an apron and hat, I tried to remember the simplest recipes, but my synapses weren't functioning and I resigned myself to being a hazard.

I dragged myself through the motions of stirring and mixing. Jeffrey frequently sniped at me because I'd forgotten to decorate a plate or set a beeper. The rear door banged occasionally, and I kept jumping, sure it would be Steve slinking in to apologize, but it never was.

As the afternoon wound down, my boss and the restaurant's owner, Pam Owen, barreled in, all smiles.

A typical Portland native, she was civic-minded, involved, and respected for her energy and ideas. She did everything by consensus. We couldn't even decide on the order we'd take our lunch breaks without having a staff discussion to vote on what was fair.

She was the one who'd thought up the infamous chefs' calendar in which I'd been featured to raise money for her favorite charity, Children's Hospital. The photo had resulted in the article in the *Oregonian* and other dubious spots.

I was in the June slot, for the month of brides, and I'd actually been dubbed "Miss June" in the caption. I was mostly concealed by a giant wedding cake. The only parts of me that were visible were my head, which was covered with a flirty chef's hat, and a bare arm and foot, so it seemed that I was naked, when I wasn't. The photographer had taken pictures of me at his studio—in a tank top and shorts—then he'd spliced me into the scene as if I'd been lurking behind the cake all along.

I had a dollop of white frosting on my finger, and my head was tipped back as I pretended to eat it. The pink end of my tongue was showing, and I appeared to be licking at the concoction in sexual ecstasy.

The carnal tenor was disturbing. My face was like a caricature, my brown eyes bigger and more luminous than they really were. I looked like a nude little girl, so perverts all over the city were no doubt enthralled.

"I have marvelous news," Pam gushed. "You'll never guess!"

"Guess what?" I asked.

"We sold a thousand copies of the charity calendar."

"A thousand? But it just went on sale."

"One of our benefactors bought them."

I couldn't imagine why anyone would. "Who was it?"

She leaned nearer, whispering as though it was a military secret. "I'm not supposed to know, but it was Jordan Blair."

I dropped my spoon on the floor, dough splattering, and I forced myself to calm down as I slowly and casually stooped to retrieve it.

I feigned ignorance. "Jordan Blair? Who's that?"

"Haven't you heard of him?"

"No."

"He's one of Portland's premier citizens. I met him years ago through his wife."

The bastard was married? To Kimberly? "His wife?"

"Yes, she served on the board of directors with me before she drowned in that awful boating accident. She was the sweetest young woman."

"So he's a widower?"

"Oh yes. Poor man. He never got over her death, so he's a bit of a recluse, but who wouldn't be, hmm?"

"Why would he want all those calendars?"

"Who knows?" She laughed and walked on. "He's rich as Croesus. Maybe he'll burn them in his fireplace and heat his penthouse."

"Maybe," I agreed halfheartedly.

I stood, frozen, the temperature by the ovens seeming to have plunged a hundred degrees. I shivered.

On TV programs, homicide cops always insist that there's no such thing as a coincidence. I'd posed for a risqué picture. I'd crossed paths with Jordan Blair in a dangerous, sexual way. Then he purchased a thousand copies of the calendar at twenty dollars a pop.

He couldn't know I was in it, I told myself. *He just couldn't.*

I picked up a clean spoon and began to stir.

Chapter Five

ひ&

I worked late, putting off my appointment with Steve until the last possible moment. As I punched out and left through the back door, he was waiting for me in the parking lot. He was balanced on the trunk of Pam's car, his coat collar turned up, his hands jammed in his pockets.

We glared at each other, fury and regret passing between us. My anger rolled toward him, and he correctly interpreted my mood.

"I'm sorry," he said.

"Are you?"

"I was a total shit."

"We're beyond the *total shit* stage. You've moved into some level of assholeness that I can't describe."

"I made a mistake."

"A mistake?" I marched over to him. It was dark and misting, but there was a street lamp overhead and I wanted to be near enough to peer into his eyes so I'd know if he was lying.

"I was in the living room! I saw her giving you a blow job!"

"I didn't know that," he murmured, appearing ashamed.

"Blair was tickled to death to inform me that you fuck around every chance you get. He claimed you bragged about it."

He flinched as if I'd punched him, but despite my keen evaluation, I couldn't decide if he was upset because Jordan had tattled or because Steve hadn't said any such thing. When the comment would hurt me so much, why would Jordan Blair invent such a terrible falsehood?

"I don't screw around on you, Meg. It's not true."

"After what I witnessed, how could you expect me to believe you?"

I stormed off, wondering where I was going, but recognizing that there was only one place: our apartment. Or I could stay at Marie's across the hall. My life was so intertwined with his that we were like two strands of a rope.

"Meg," he called, sounding desperate, "don't leave me over this."

Against my better judgment, I halted and whipped around. "Why shouldn't I?"

"Because I love you, and I couldn't bear it."

He looked like a whipped dog, so sad and miserable that it was difficult to maintain my rage. He'd always been so nice to me, and he was so fucking *sorry*. How could I be mad when he was oozing remorse?

I wished I was smarter or wiser. This sort of catastrophe landed on women all the time, and I'd previously told myself that if it ever happened to *me*, I'd be so gone. But I couldn't ascertain the best resolution. In light of my own antics with Jordan, wasn't I just as culpable? Who should be casting the first stone? Not me.

"I was drunk," he said.

"You think that makes it okay?"

"No."

"You were sober right at the beginning."

"Yes, I was."

"So . . . why?"

He shrugged, finding it hard to put the sordid episode into words. "My common sense flew out the window. There didn't seem to be any reason not to do whatever I wanted."

I spun away to stomp off, but he reached out and clasped my arm.

"Just come home," he pleaded. "Just come home and talk to me for a while."

It was nine o'clock at night. I stared down the black street, the rain falling, the cars whizzing by. I could go with him or I could go alone, but I'd still end up at the same spot.

I had to be the biggest fool alive. For a lengthy, charged interval, I studied him, then demanded, "Promise me that you won't ever do anything like that again."

"I promise."

I didn't believe him.

Was this to be our future? Him telling me stories and me doubting him?

I felt that we'd been poisoned, that our relationship would suffer the devastating toxin of deceit and betrayal forever.

I sighed and started toward our apartment, my feet making

the choice my mind and heart couldn't make for me. I plodded into our building, climbed the stairs, and proceeded directly into the bathroom to shower and change.

I spent the evening listening to music and watching TV, while he was overly solicitous and avoided me. I was like a ticking bomb, and he realized he could do the wrong thing and I'd explode. We survived the tedious hours without a flare-up, then I slinked off to bed without a good night. A long time later, he followed. Eventually he drifted off, but I never did.

I gazed at the ceiling, pondering Steve and Kimberly, how he and I would never be the same as we had been. I thought about Jordan Blair being a benefactor of Pam's charity, about his buying the calendars.

Steve was up early, and he tiptoed around and left. Once I heard his car motor revving, I crept to the window and spied on him as he sped away.

As I stepped into the kitchen, I saw a note he'd placed on the table for me: *Please don't leave without calling me first.*

He'd gone to work, imagining that I'd pack my bags and flee before he got back. He was hoping I wouldn't, but was unable to have the conversation that would persuade me otherwise.

What did I want? What should I do?

I brewed some coffee, and I sipped it as I peered out at my neighborhood. Down on the sidewalk, Marie hurried to the bus stop. Farther down the street, the restaurant's discreet sign, Mozart's, was visible through the trees.

I could keep it all or I could toss it away.

Like a robot, I went to the bedroom and pulled on my chef's pants and smock. I forced myself to the kitchen and grabbed a pen. On the bottom of Steve's message, I wrote: *Will be home about 8:00.*

I guessed I was staying.

For a few weeks, it was awkward, but gradually we adjusted. We didn't mention Kimberly or Jordan Blair. I didn't ruminate about Blair or how he'd ignited a dangerous spark inside me. We didn't discuss the encounter, or how much Steve had enjoyed what he'd done with Kimberly.

Steve was more considerate than ever, and I was kind, too, trying to assuage my guilty conscience and ignore the qualms I was having over my decision to remain. I'd become what I loathed in other women: I'd taken the easy route so that I could hold on to the familiar. I'd been too much of a coward to stand my ground, to leap into the unknown, to part with what mattered to me.

The world seemed grayer than it had been previously, but I carried on. Yet I relentlessly questioned my actions, and nothing satisfied me anymore, so it was a relief when Pam invited me to go with her to the resort town of Sun River.

It was a couple of hours southeast of Portland in the Cascades. I'd never been, but she often visited, to ski in the winter and golf in the summer. She was contemplating a second restaurant and planned to tour rental properties. She wanted advice about the kitchen, and since I was her only cook, besides Jeffrey, who wasn't busy with a wife or kids, I was picked to accompany her.

We traveled on a Tuesday, with intentions of inspecting potential sites on Wednesday, and returning to Portland on Thursday. As I stood on the curb in front of our building and she drove up, I waved at Steve who was watching from an upstairs window. He waved back, and I faked a smile. The tension between us had never really abated, and I was glad to be going. I wished it could be for more than three days.

Pam was funny and interesting, and we had a cordial trip into the mountains. She'd booked us into the main lodge of a convention hotel that was much more elite than I'd anticipated. The guests were rich and bored, but fortunately the dress code was casual, so I wasn't too conspicuous in the clothes I'd brought.

We settled in rooms that were across the hall from one another. Pam encouraged me to explore, have a massage, or swim, but I was a tad overwhelmed. My sole moment of excitement was a drink in the bar prior to joining her for supper.

We had a great meal, with Pam and I dissecting every recipe, and at the end, as we were finishing our coffee, Pam glanced up and grinned.

"Oh, look who's here! Meg, you're in for a treat!"

She knew people everywhere, so I shifted in my chair to discover who was approaching. When I saw Jordan Blair trailing after the hostess, my heart almost quit beating.

It was clear he hadn't noticed us yet, and I didn't want him to. Pam was trying to get his attention, while I was struggling to keep from sliding under the table. My cheeks were red with embarrassment, my hands shaking as my brain raced, grappling with what I should say to him.

"Hello, Jordan," Pam greeted him as he neared.

"Hello, Pam." He replied amiably, as if they were old friends which, from her description, they probably were. "What are you doing in Sun River?"

"I'm scouting restaurant locations."

"I'd heard that you were. Let me know when you start searching for investors."

"I will." She was ecstatic over his offer. "How about you? What brings you up in the dead of winter?"

"Here for the skiing."

"Lucky dog. *Some* of us have to work for a living."

"And some of us don't."

They both chuckled as if her working, and his not, was a private joke between them.

In a very calculated manner, he gazed over at me and asked, "Who is your lovely companion?"

"Jordan, this is my premier dessert chef, Meg White."

"Hello, Meg."

"Hello."

Could he tell how terrified I was? If he alluded to his beach house or the party, or gave any hint about our having met before, I'd kill him.

"I think I've eaten your desserts," he claimed.

"Of course, you have," Pam said. "When you were in last month, we specially ordered the soufflé for you, remember?"

"I do." There was a polite pause, and he added, "You're very talented, Meg."

What did he mean? Was it a sexual innuendo? Was he teasing me? Was he flirting? Did it mean nothing at all except that he'd been at Mozart's and had tried my soufflé?

"Thanks," I mumbled like an idiot.

"Don't let us keep you." Pam waved him on.

"Nice to see you again." He continued on down the aisle.

I don't recollect the rest of the meal. Jordan was across the way, dining with two other men, and I was completely distracted by him. His back was to me, but I couldn't help feeling that he was focused on me all the same.

Pam and I stopped in the bar and had a brandy while he was still in the restaurant. We were seated so that when he was in just the right spot, we were staring at each other. I kept lurching to the side, out of range, but Pam didn't appear to notice how disconcerted I was.

Pam wanted to have another drink, but I pleaded fatigue and returned to my room. While I'd been out, a note had been shoved under the door. It was on a sheet of hotel stationary, and it contained a room number and the word *Midnight*. He'd signed it with the initial *J*.

From the instant he'd first bumped into us in the restaurant, he hadn't left it, so how and when had his message been delivered? He had to have been aware—before he came down to supper—that I was in the hotel. But how? How had he known?

Had he, simply by chance, seen me in the lobby as we were checking in? Or had it been more premeditated than that? Had he somehow learned that I would be in Sun River with Pam? If so, he had to be there explicitly to cross paths with me, and he had. But with what intent?

When he'd provided his phone numbers to me at his beach house, he must have been expecting me to call. Had he been waiting all these weeks?

The notion was absurd, but strangely exciting. I was flattered that a man like him—rich, sophisticated, older—would be so interested in me, and I wasn't certain what to make of it. I paced, trying to decide what to do.

I was much more intrigued than I should have been. Did I

dare go to him? The only reason would be to have sex. He wasn't the type to bother with chatting or watching TV, so there was no other purpose for him to have invited me.

A vision of Steve and my life in Portland flashed in my head, but it all seemed so far away. Recently, I'd been so unhappy, irked and disappointed in my relationship with Steve. My job was tedious, my friends boring.

Staying at the resort, I felt as if I'd become someone else, or that I was acting out a part in a stage play. My world at home had ceased to exist, or had been put on hold. I could do anything, without repercussion or consequence, but could I? Should I?

It was after nine, midnight three hours away. I was in turmoil, my conscience shouting at me to behave myself, but my resolve was weakening. The more I thought of why I shouldn't join him, the more I wanted to.

The minutes ticked by in slow motion, and as the time approached, I determined that I couldn't go to him. I'd scrounged through a drawer and found a map of the large property. He was in another wing, on the top floor, which looked out toward the mountains. The distance made me feel better.

Sitting on the mattress, I observed as the red numerals on the clock flipped to 12:00, then 12:05, then 12:15. At 12:20, I clicked off the lamp and lay down. My pulse was pounding, and I was terribly sad, as if I'd dodged a bullet or relinquished something important, but I refused to rue or regret.

I'd dozed off when there was a quiet knock on my door, one that was so soft I wasn't sure I'd heard it. I didn't move till I heard it again.

I rose and went to let him in.

Chapter Six

As he entered, I gestured for silence. I didn't know if Pam was still awake, but I didn't want her to hear me welcoming a man into my room. Nor did I want her to peek out and see that it was Jordan Blair. I couldn't predict what her attitude would be, and I would have hated to have to explain my connection to him.

We stood in the narrow foyer, assessing one another. I was wary, and I didn't trust myself. With him, my common sense flew out the window, and considering how he'd tempted me previously, I was terrified of what I might do.

He was in jeans and a button-down cotton shirt. The sleeves were rolled up to reveal his strong arms, his skilled hands. I tried not to notice how sexy he was, or to recollect how fabulous his fingers had felt on my body.

"How did you learn that I was in Sun River?" I asked. Before we went any farther, I had to have an answer.

"Does it matter?"

Did it? Well, yes, if he came specifically to find me. Why would he?

"Why did you buy all those calendars?"

He evaluated me as if I was nuts. "What calendars?"

"The calendars! The calendars! You bought a thousand copies."

"I don't know what you're talking about."

"You're lying." I had no idea if he was or not, but I enjoyed accusing him.

He switched subjects, hurling an accusation of his own. "You never called me."

He was upset that I hadn't, which surprised me. With him being so attractive, women probably never rejected his advances. Maybe I was the only one who ever had. Could it have made me irresistible to him? Had I become a challenge?

"No, I didn't."

"Why not?"

I scoffed. "I didn't think you were serious. I couldn't imagine why you'd want to see me again."

"Don't you know why?"

"No."

Cradling my face, he leaned down and kissed me. It was very sweet, very gentle, and it tickled my insides.

"Let me show you."

He clicked on all the lamps, so the space was brightly lit, then he led me to the bed. I was attired in what passed for pajamas with me, an old pair of sweats and one of Steve's T-shirts. He grabbed the shirt and yanked it off, then he untied the drawstring on my pants and tugged them away.

In a few seconds, I was naked.

He eased me down so that my back was on the mattress, my calves dangling over the edge. He wedged himself between my thighs, lifting them so that my privates were displayed. I'd never pictured myself as a particularly modest person, but this was too much too soon.

I tried to press my legs together, but I couldn't budge him.

"You're very beautiful, Meg," he murmured.

"I am not," I felt compelled to protest, even as I was secretly thrilled by his opinion.

"You are!" His tone cut off any argument.

He cupped me, then bent down and began licking me. He was so adept at it that I forgot how timid I'd been about being exposed. Without a whimper of complaint, I allowed him to proceed, but before it really got interesting, he halted and nibbled up my stomach to my nipples. He rooted and sucked, teased and pinched, and the anticipation was agony.

"Please . . ." I managed, wanting him to hurry the hell up, but he was content to dawdle.

"We have to do it at my pace," he told me. "You can come when I decide it's time."

"Let me!" I demanded as I arched up, desperate to finish.

"No."

"Jordan!"

"You've always had boys as your lovers. You need some lessons on how to fuck an adult man."

He commenced again, dipping down to torment me with his tongue till I was at my limit, then he'd return to my breasts. He had the patience of a saint, while I was in such a state that I worried my heart would burst. I didn't know how he could keep from ripping his jeans open and having at it, but he was happy with the slow tempo.

I ached, I wept, I begged, but I couldn't convince him to go faster.

Eventually he unzipped, but even then he didn't enter me, and I couldn't figure out how he stood the suspense. He inserted the tip of his cock, then a bit more, as he toyed with my nipples, with my clit.

We were scarcely acquainted, yet he was so attuned to me, giving me such pleasure, but seeking none of his own. I was fascinated.

When he ultimately pushed in all the way, with that one thrust I was so aroused that I came and came until I wondered if I would ever stop. I'd never experienced anything like it, and as I spiraled down, I was limp, my bones and joints drained, but he was barely fazed by what had occurred.

He retreated, and he had me sit up so that I could watch as he undressed. His body was a sight, hard and buff and fit. I was eye level with his erect penis, and he clutched it and brushed it across my lips, but I refused to take him. He frowned, intent, determined that I comply with his request, but I shook my head.

"I can't do it," I said. "Not yet."

Not ever, I thought to myself. I simply wasn't a blow job kind of girl, and if that was what he was hoping for, he would be disappointed.

"It's all right," he soothed, the tense moment passing.

He shoved me onto the pillows and arranged me. Then, with no finesse or coaxing, he was inside me. He fucked me and fucked me—there was no other word to describe it. This wasn't sex; it wasn't lovemaking. It was something inexplicable and exhilarating that was beyond my frame of reference.

The night sped by in a frenzied haze. He kissed me and touched me, moved me and posed me. His caresses made me come over and over, each of my orgasms more potent and more sizzling than the last, while he never joined me, not till the very end.

I was pleading with him for a rest, telling him I absolutely couldn't do it once more. Yet he spurred me to the precipice, and he finally spilled himself, letting go without a condom, and me being too stupid and inundated to insist he use one.

Through the entire encounter, he peered down at me as if I was magnificent. And I have to admit that I felt pretty damn great. He was handsome and rich, and for some reason he liked me. The notion was terrific, and I was more than a little smug.

Despicable as it sounded, Steve did not cross my mind. Nor did I waste any energy pondering what this second betrayal meant.

As Jordan slid out of me, I glanced at the clock and was stunned to note that we'd been at it for hours, that it was after six. Pam expected me for breakfast in the dining room at seven. Then we would snoop out restaurant properties. The prospect had been exciting, but suddenly it had ceased to be quite so significant.

I couldn't bear to leave, couldn't bear to be away from Jordan. The relationship developing between us was very different, and I was eager to pursue it. I couldn't imagine it extending past our short jaunt in Sun River, or if it did, that I could find any chances to sneak off with him in Portland.

Did he even live in Portland?

I suffered no remorse or guilt over my zeal to engage in infidelity. What a cheating slut I was turning out to be!

He broke the silence. "When are you meeting Pam?"

"At seven."

"I wish you didn't have to go. I'd like to stay here all day."

My feelings exactly. "Me, too."

"Let's get you up."

I wasn't ready to crawl out of bed. I was cozy and exhausted, my muscles sore, my innards protesting. I had bite marks all over, my thighs tender and bruised from his powerful thrusting. I wanted to doze for awhile, then start in again. What I *didn't* want was to drive around looking at real estate.

With me as an unwilling participant, he dragged me to my feet and led me to the shower. He switched on the heat lamps and adjusted the water so that it was extra hot, then he helped me in and climbed in with me, scrubbing me as if I was a young child who couldn't manage alone. He lathered me with soap and shampooed me, then rinsed me thoroughly.

With the steam and the water sluicing over us, the moment was incredibly erotic. He trailed down my front and knelt before me, washing my crotch, examining my pubic hair.

"You have to shave your pussy for me."

"Jordan . . ."

"You have to shave it!" he commanded, as if the topic was settled. "Promise you will."

I'd never considered such a thing. It was demeaning, and it pandered to male fantasies I didn't like, but he was adamant, and it mattered to him so much. All I could do was nod.

We finished, and he dried and dressed me, though he

remained naked himself. He picked through my satchel of clothes, selecting what I should wear, even though it wasn't what I'd have preferred. My stuff was pretty much all black, so it wasn't a big deal, and he was so pleased when I agreed to his choice that it was worth submitting rather than arguing.

When he wouldn't let me put on panties, we tussled briefly, but I relented on that issue, too. He claimed that while we were apart he wanted to envision me in just my jeans and nothing underneath.

I gave in, liking that he would be tantalized by raucous thoughts of me while I was away.

He observed as I dried my hair, as I applied a dash of makeup. As I was about to swipe on some lip gloss, he said, "Hold on a minute."

He went over and retrieved something from his shirt. When he came back, he had a tube of lipstick that was a bright shade of red I never would have owned.

"You walk around with lipstick in your pocket?"

He shrugged, but didn't respond.

"Why red?"

"Try it."

He gestured toward the mirror, and after I complied, I was amazed to see how it accented my black clothes, my creamy skin. In his other hand he had a pair of earrings. They were dangly and sparkly and not the sort of simple posts I typically wore. Once again, I donned them without objection, and it was immediately clear that I appeared more exotic, more mysterious and bewitching.

I twirled from side to side, liking the small changes, how they'd emphasized me in a whole new way.

"What do you think?" I asked.

"I knew they'd be perfect."

He stepped nearer and turned me, trapping me against the sink, with him positioned so he could peer over my shoulder into the mirror. He cupped my breasts.

"I like it when you do what I say," he murmured.

"I can tell."

"It's exciting when you obey me."

The word *obey* was a little much for me, but he was assessing me in the rapt fashion that I was quickly liking too much, so I didn't fuss.

He was hard. I could feel his erection as he fiddled with my zipper, as he jerked my pants down around my flanks. I was astounded that he had any stamina, but I couldn't possibly join in. My female membranes were stretched and rubbed raw.

"God, I can't do it again," I told him as he thumbed my clit and pinched my nipples.

"You have to."

"I can't. I'm too sore."

"You can't refuse, Meg. I won't allow you to."

There was a bottle of lotion in my bag, and he unscrewed the cap and swabbed it over his penis, then he centered himself and pushed. The lotion was cold, and it made him so slippery that he glided right in, but I couldn't stifle a painful gasp. I'd never had so much sex in such a short amount of time. I was in agony, but he couldn't be deterred. He gripped my hips and began to flex.

"Watch us," he said. "Study our reflection. See how beautiful we are."

He had at it, with me bent over the bathroom counter. I

looked so unusual and striking, while he was nude and brooding behind me. We moved like dancers, straining to a silent rhythm.

He toyed with me till I came—I couldn't believe I had it in me!—and when it was over, my knees buckled. He propped me up so I didn't fall to the rug. He didn't come, but pulled out without concluding, and he was extremely arrogant, satisfied that he'd gotten his way.

I was leaned over, balanced on my elbows, as I laughed at him and myself.

"What do you call this? Death by orgasm?" I was struggling to catch my breath, to steady my pulse.

"There are worse ways to go out."

"I should shower again."

"No. I want my scent all over you. I want you to remember."

"As if I could forget!"

I glanced at the clock. It was a few minutes past seven. Pam was very prompt; she'd be wondering where I was, so I couldn't have bathed again anyway.

"I have to go."

"I know."

I was desperate to ask if he'd stop by later, if he was staying on at the hotel, but I wasn't sure how to question him without sounding overly possessive.

He saved me. "I want to be with you tonight. I want to fuck you all night long."

"Okay."

"When will you be finished with Pam?"

"Probably not till after supper."

"Sneak away as early as you can."

"I will."

"You know my suite number."

"Yes."

"Shave your pussy, then come to me. I'll be waiting."

He helped me into my coat and urged me to the door. I reached for the knob, then paused and drew him to me. I kissed him on the mouth, lazy and slow, with lots of tongue.

"I'm glad you're in Sun River," I boldly said.

"So am I. Now get going."

" 'Bye."

"Phone me as soon as you're back."

"I will."

I stepped into the hall, and to my dismay Pam was running a bit behind and was just leaving, too.

"Good morning, Meg."

"Good morning."

"How nice to see you first thing. We can walk down to the dining room together."

I smiled and headed for the elevator as my door swung shut with a muted thud. If she'd noticed Jordan lurking in the shadows, naked and gazing at me with a great deal of lust and affection, she gave no hint.

Chapter Seven

⌾⌾

On Thursday morning when I met Pam for breakfast, I was a mess but working to hide it. Since leaving Portland, I'd hardly slept, but I was buzzed with adrenaline, running on fumes, and I was too worn out to understand just how tired I was.

Jordan and I had spent every extra moment together. We'd had sex over and over until I didn't recognize my body anymore. My lips were swollen, my thighs raw from the rasping of his whiskers. There were bruises on my back and buttocks. I felt as if I'd been pressed through a meat grinder, as if every bone and pore had been wrenched into a new position, but it was a superb sensation.

I was happy, more alive than I'd ever been.

Nothing remotely similar had ever happened to me. He was so different from every other man I'd ever known, so passionate and experienced, so absorbed with giving me pleasure. I couldn't remember how I'd gotten along without him in my life, and I couldn't imagine being away from him, or returning to the city and resuming my regular routine.

I had to advise Pam that I wouldn't be riding to Portland with her, but I couldn't figure out how to start the conversation. She'd want to know why, but my relationship with Jordan was too special to mention. For some absurd reason, I couldn't bear to share my secret.

We ordered, but our discussion was stilted. Not on my end, but on hers. She was studying me as if I had my clothes on inside out, or had food stuck in my teeth, and I kept glancing down to see what was wrong, but nothing appeared to be.

Pam made small talk, about the properties we'd visited, the drive home. I could barely listen to her, and I yearned to leap up and shout, *I don't care about any of it!*

I had been completely altered, had metamorphosed into someone else. It seemed as if Meg White had died and another woman, a more spontaneous and greedy woman, had taken her place.

When the bill came and we were finished, I still hadn't piped up, and the situation grew even more awkward as she muttered, "I have to ask you a question. Feel free to tell me if it's none of my business."

"Sure. What is it?"

"Jordan Blair phoned me last night."

"He did?"

"He claims you'll be staying over for a few days—with him."

I couldn't decide what was worse: her having discovered my intentions or Jordan having intervened. I was an adult and perfectly capable of notifying her myself. I hated to have him butting in, though part of me was thankful that he had.

How should I confess to my boss that I required a vacation so that I could lounge at a fancy resort and screw my new boyfriend? I had no idea.

Suddenly embarrassed, I stared down at my plate. Guilt swept over me. "Jordan called you?"

"Yes." She hesitated. "You know, if you needed some time off, you could have approached me yourself. You didn't have to be afraid to speak up."

"I wasn't."

Worry creased her brow. "Are you positive you should do this?"

"No." I chuckled miserably. "But I'm doing it anyway."

"It's just that he's"—she paused, searching for the appropriate word—"so much older and, well . . . more *sophisticated* than you are, Meg. I don't mean that in a bad way. I'm merely stating the obvious."

"When we're together, it doesn't seem to matter."

She leaned over and patted my hand. It was a motherly gesture, bestowed on a girl who'd never had a mother. I felt even lower, a dunce who was making one awful choice after the next.

"Where do you see this going?" she inquired. "What do you expect from it?"

"I'm certain it's a brief fling. I'm Meg White, and he's . . . he's . . . Jordan Blair."

"Yes, he is." She scrutinized me, then sighed. "I'm sorry. I shouldn't have said anything."

"No, it's all right. I don't mind."

"I shouldn't have pried." She was so concerned about me! "Promise you'll be cautious, hmm?"

"Of course I will be."

Shortly after, she left, but she'd jotted her private cell number on a piece of paper and slipped me a hundred dollars. I tried to refuse the money, but she wouldn't let me. She declared that it was in case something happened, in case I had to find my own way home—a fear that I thought was groundless and bizarre.

Then she was gone, and I was so relieved. I dawdled at the table, drinking too much coffee, till she'd had plenty of time to check out. I didn't want to bump into her in the lobby and suffer through another clumsy encounter.

I was annoyingly aware that this was a terrible decision, that I shouldn't do it, but I couldn't stop. I *had* to proceed, and I couldn't explain myself or change directions.

As I stood to head out, the hostess brought me a note. It was from Jordan, apprising me that he'd had the maids pack my bag and empty my room, that I should come straight to him. I grinned, glad that I wouldn't have to waste a single second with mundane chores, and I could be with him immediately.

I crammed his note in my pocket and hurried for the elevators. I had plans for the day, risqué, rough, outrageous plans, and I couldn't delay.

He was waiting for me—before I could knock, he opened the door to his suite. I rushed through and into his arms, hugging and kissing him as if I hadn't seen him in years, as if we were catastrophe survivors about to be rescued.

We tore at each other's clothes, stripping ourselves, then tumbling onto the bed.

"You shouldn't have called Pam," I scolded as he kneed my thighs apart and entered me. He thrust in the steady rhythm I loved, and I bit down on a gasp.

I was so sore!

"I couldn't have her say no. I couldn't let you go away with her."

"I wouldn't have. I couldn't."

"You're mine, Meg."

"Yes, Jordan, I'm yours."

"Swear to me that you'll never leave me."

"No, I never will. I swear."

He was smiling at me, his face so beautiful, his expression so tender and filled with desire. I was amazed that someone so wonderful could have grown so attracted to me. I never wanted to be separated from him, and my vow swiftly took on a deeper significance.

I was determined to always be by his side.

We ate, we sipped champagne, and we had sex for four days and nights. He never tired of me, never needed to rest. He was so attuned, so eager to please, goading me to riveting heights of lust and relaxation. I was trapped in a bubble of hedonism, where the outside world had ceased to exist, where there was only excitement and increasing levels of titillation, and I wished the sojourn would never end.

By Monday morning, when Jordan had to be back in Portland, I was bouncing between exhilaration and exhaustion. The lack of sleep had energized me, or perhaps I was so out of it that I didn't realize my fatigue.

Colors were brighter, sounds louder, smells more potent. I was cruising at a frenetic pace, as if I was on amphetamines.

I stepped out of the shower, and as he dried me with the towel he said, "I want you to move in with me."

"I will."

"You have to break up with Steve."

"I know."

Poor Steve. In the period I'd been away, I'd left him precisely one phone message, lying to him with a story that I'd met an old friend from high school and had remained behind to visit with her.

"It has to be over with him today," he insisted. "When we return to Portland, you can't go home."

"I won't."

"We'll swing by your apartment and pick up your things."

"Okay. Where do you live?"

Considering how I'd been carrying on with him for an entire week, it was a ridiculous question. How could I have fucked him so rabidly without pausing to learn the answer?

"I own several houses, but mostly I stay at my penthouse in downtown Portland. If you don't like it, we can live wherever you want."

"What should I bring with me?"

"Everything or nothing. You can grab just the necessities for now, then we can send for the rest later on."

I was embarrassed to admit the meager status of my belongings, but still, I wanted my stuff.

"I can get it all this afternoon. It'll fit in the trunk."

"You won't ever have to go back?"

"No."

"Good."

There was no need to discuss it further. I was giving it all up: the cozy apartment, the friends and the lifestyle, the man I'd assumed I loved. Steve's parents had always been so kind. They'd welcomed me as a member of the family, and since I'd

never had one of my own, their acceptance had meant everything to me. After this betrayal, they'd never speak to me
again.

I didn't care. I was ready to move on.

Jordan had ordered new clothes for me from a shop in the
hotel, and he helped me put them on. They were expensive
items I'd ever have purchased for myself. The dress was a silky
red sheath, with red heels to match, and there was lingerie and
stockings, as well as sparkly earrings and a necklace that I
suspected was real diamonds, but I was too naive to know for
certain.

The ensemble made me look different, sexier and more mature than I'd ever envisioned myself being. I was a fox, and
though it was vain and silly, I delighted in the modifications. It
was like playing dress-up, and I was proud to see my reflection
in the windows in the lobby, strolling on the arm of such a rich,
handsome man.

We flew to the city, the trip transpiring in a blur, with people fawning over me simply because I was with him. I scarcely
had time to take it all in before I was huddled next to him in
the rear of a dark sedan and heading toward my apartment.

Out in front of our building, there was no place to park, so
the driver stopped in the middle of the street and walked around
to open my door.

"Are you sure you don't want me to come up with you?"
Jordan asked as he had repeatedly.

"No. I'll just be a minute."

He kissed me, hard. "Hurry."

"I will."

Quickly, I pulled away, nervous that I might be seen embracing him. If a neighbor noticed and mentioned it to Steve, he'd be hurt by the information. He would still be at work, and my cowardly plan was to snag my things without talking to him about it.

I realized that I was being a total shit and I owed him better, but I couldn't hang around to hash it out. My prior life was dragging me under, drowning me in the mundane. I had to be with Jordan, and nothing else mattered.

I rushed up the stairs in my heels. I hadn't owned a pair in years and my feet were killing me. Jordan had been so complimentary about how they set off my legs that I hadn't complained, but as soon as I was inside our apartment, I kicked them off and raced around in my stockings. I retrieved Steve's suitcase from the closet, laid it on the bed, and as if the room was on fire, I started throwing my possessions into it.

There was a knock on the door, and I winced as I heard Marie say, "Meg, is that you?"

I cursed and went to greet her. I didn't have the patience to chat, couldn't stand to have her barging in and delaying my escape. On observing my outfit and jewelry, her eyes widened with shock—and maybe a touch of dismay.

I had tossed CDs and books on the couch, and the suitcase was visible in the bedroom. She frowned.

"What on earth? Are you moving out?"

I tugged an anxious hand through my hair. The trendy spikes had vanished. Jordan had combed it down and over, claiming the altered style was necessary with the dress, that it accentuated the angles of my face, and as usual he was correct.

"I guess I am."

"Why?"

I blushed, my cheeks growing hot. "Ah . . . I met somebody."

"You never told me."

"It was recent."

"How *recent?*"

"When I was in Sun River."

"You're going to live with him? Now?"

"Yes."

"Oh, Meg, are you sure you should?"

"I have to."

"What about Steve?"

Yes, I mused, feeling terrible. *What about Steve?*

"I have to do this. I'm sorry."

"You don't have to be sorry. I'm just surprised."

"Me, too. It was pretty sudden."

To my horror, Steve's happy strides sounded, vaulting up the stairs, and I froze. He wasn't supposed to be home! I wished the floor would open and swallow me whole. I did *not* want to speak with him!

What could I say? There was absolutely nothing that would make it easier for him to bear or that would justify my conduct.

He rounded the corner, smiling and hastening to me. "Meg! You're finally—"

At seeing my attire and Marie's concerned expression, he stumbled to a halt.

"What's going on?"

"I gotta go," I said, more to Marie than to him.

"You're leaving?" he asked, stunned.

"Yes."

"For good?"

I nodded.

"But . . . I thought everything was okay between us."

"It was," I insisted. "I just . . . just . . . need something else right now."

"What?" He was confused and angry. "What else could you possibly need?"

"I couldn't begin to describe it."

"You look like a fucking hooker. What'd you do to yourself?"

Longingly, I glanced at the suitcase, at my CDs and other stuff. I felt as if I was choking. "I was here for my things, but I'll send someone for them."

I skirted around him, but I avoided his gaze and fled down the hall.

"Meg! Don't do this!" Marie scolded as Steve hollered, "What if I have to contact you? Where will you be?"

"I'll call you."

I bounded down, taking the steps two at a time, my nylons snagging on the wood. I sprinted outside and ran, the wet sidewalk soaking my feet, the rocks cutting into my soles.

The driver was standing in the rain waiting for me as I staggered over and fell into Jordan's arms.

"I saw Steve," he said. "I was about to come after you."

"I'm fine," I lied. I was on the verge of hysteria, and I laughed wildly. "I lost my shoes."

"I'll buy you twenty more."

He kissed my forehead, and I snuggled against his chest, my ear over his heart, its steady beat reassuring me.

I'm doing the right thing . . . I'm doing the right thing . . . I'm doing the right thing . . .

The refrain rang through my mind as the driver slammed

the door, sealing me in. There was such an air of finality that I shuddered.

In a matter of seconds we'd pulled away, and my street and apartment building disappeared. Across the river, I could see the city's skyscrapers, where Jordan's penthouse was located, where I would soon reside with him in glorious splendor, where I would wallow in love and in passion.

I shut my eyes and listened to the rain pelting the windows.

I never looked back.

Chapter Eight

W hat happened to you?"
      "I decided to change my look."
   "It's fabulous, darling," Jeffrey gushed, "absolutely fabulous."

   He was coming in to start the evening shift, while I was concluding my afternoon of baking and getting ready to leave.

   He evaluated my new hair style and color, which was
longer, and a rusty auburn parted on the side. My makeup
had been selected for me by a special cosmetologist Jordan
had hired. She'd proclaimed that I needed brown lashes and
natural-hued shades, and my perfectly plucked brows gave me
a constant expression of surprise.

   I wasn't positive how I felt about any of it. When standing
in front of the mirror, it was exciting to see such a beautiful,
sculpted face, but it wasn't *my* face. A stranger stared back
at me.

"Do you really like it?" I asked. "You're not just being nice, are you?"

"I couldn't have picked better for you myself. What does Steve think?"

So far, I'd managed to keep my personal drama a secret, though my coworkers had to be growing curious as to what was wrong with me. Previously, I had been a model employee and team player, but now I was habitually late, sneaking in and hoping my tardiness wasn't conspicuous. I was always tired, and I continually made mistakes that I rushed around, trying to hide.

It was a small kitchen, with an efficient staff, and there were only so many people to cover for me, only so many ways I could screw up before they complained to Pam.

Luckily, she hadn't said anything—yet—but it was just a matter of time.

"Actually"—I gazed down at my rolling pin—"I broke up with Steve."

"Get out of town!" He stepped closer and whispered, "When?"

"A couple weeks ago."

"You didn't tell me!"

"It occurred kind of fast. My head's still spinning."

"Where are you living?"

"Downtown. I moved in with somebody else."

"Anyone I know?" He chuckled and wiggled his brows.

"No." I shrugged. "Weird, huh?"

"I wouldn't necessarily describe it as *weird*. It's certainly sudden." He studied me, the lenses of his glasses making his eyes glimmer. "Are you okay?"

"Why wouldn't I be?"

"I don't know. You seem . . . different."

It took him so long to settle on the word *different* that I couldn't help but wonder what other terms he'd considered prior to choosing that one.

"I'm great," I insisted.

"Well . . . good."

We assessed each other, dozens of remarks floating between us, but we couldn't latch on to any of them. An awkward silence ensued as I thought about Jordan and his chauffeur, who would be outside, impatiently waiting for me. Their presence was thrilling and bizarre; it underscored how far I'd traveled beyond the Meg I'd been.

"I should be going," I finally murmured.

"Sure . . . sure . . ." He waved me toward the door.

I grabbed my coat, and as I scooted out, he called, "I miss your spiky hair."

"I do, too," I mumbled and walked on.

Jordan's car was down the block in the shadows, which seriously annoyed him, but I demanded he park where no one would notice. I was embarrassed by the prosperous turn my life had taken, and I didn't want my coworkers to see. Nor was I too keen on having Pam realize that I'd cast my lot with Jordan.

I didn't comprehend why I was so worried about her opinion, but I sensed that she wouldn't be pleased. When I'd always liked her so much, I couldn't bear to disappoint her.

I slid into the backseat, marveling at how quickly I had adapted to the changes. Jordan's penthouse was in the tallest skyscraper in the city's center, and it loomed over the other buildings. I didn't have to cook, or shop, or do laundry, or scrub the toilet, which was fine by me. I hadn't wasted a single second lamenting the loss of such dull tasks.

"How was your day?" he asked.

"I'm exhausted."

"You should quit."

"I love my job."

"I understand that, but I hate to see you so tired. It's silly to work so hard when you don't have to."

"I know."

"I could phone Pam right now. I'll tell her you're done. It's too draining."

"Not tonight. Okay?"

"Okay."

He'd given me everything a woman could want, even my own charge card and plenty of cash to spend, so he was correct that I didn't need to be employed.

I wasn't stupid, though. For some reason, he was intrigued by me, but it seemed like a fairy tale that could end as abruptly as it had started. My salary from the restaurant was pitiful compared to the gifts he lavished on me, but the money was mine, and I earned it. The independence it provided was vital.

When I yielded to him in so many ways, he couldn't accept my continuing at Mozart's. He was angry at what he viewed as my defiance, and we constantly quarreled over the issue. Offering a truce, I slipped my hand into his, and I kissed him on the cheek.

"I'm sorry," I said, though I wasn't. "I didn't mean to raise a fuss."

"You didn't. When we get home, how about if I draw you a hot bath?"

"I'd like that."

"You can soak your sore muscles."

"It sounds like heaven."

I smiled, but tamped down a sigh. I had no doubt what a bath would entail. His tub was like a swimming pool with water jets and bubbling soaps. He'd undress and get in with me, and we'd have sex for hours, probably all night. When dawn arrived, I would stumble to bed, doze for a few precious minutes, then rise and stagger to work in a trance.

The driver dropped us at our building, and we took the executive elevator to the top. A special key was required to operate it, which I didn't have. When I came and went on my own, I used the main lobby and navigated the security desk.

As we stepped inside, my breath caught—as it always did—when I entered the living room. The entire wall was floor-to-ceiling windows that looked out across the Willamette Valley, the lights from thousands of houses twinkling like stars. By day it was even more spectacular, with Mount Hood off in the distance and filling the eastern horizon.

I paused, taking it all in, feeling like Cinderella at the ball.

He pressed some buttons on a control panel. Romantic candles glowed; music began to play.

"Let's clean you up."

"An excellent idea. I smell like chocolate cake."

"Really?" He nibbled my neck and licked my skin. "Chocolate is my favorite flavor. I may have to eat you all up."

He led me to the bedroom, where lingerie was laid out on the bed, and food arranged on the table in the corner. I never saw his chef or ran into the maid. They were invisible, but they knew the precise instant I'd be away and when I'd return. They rushed in, did their chores, then left, so that Jordan had me all to himself.

I proceeded to the shower, stripped, and climbed in. For once, he didn't join me, and though it was a traitorous thought, I was glad for the solitude. I was never alone anymore. At the restaurant I was surrounded by noise and people, then at home I was with him every second. There was never a moment to sit quietly, to listen to CDs, or veg in front of the TV.

I sagged against the shower tiles, letting the water pummel me. I was so fatigued, I wondered when I'd crash and burn and how painful the landing would be. I couldn't careen down such a destructive path, but I couldn't slow the pace.

I finished and dried myself, then I wrapped the towel around me and tucked the corner between my breasts. I couldn't get over how exquisite everything was. The cotton of the towel was so soft, the soap so fragrant, the shampoo so gentle. It wouldn't be so bad to be rich, to live like this forever.

Would it happen? How long would his infatuation last? How long would he let me stay?

Before meeting him, I'd never worried much about money or the lifestyle it could buy, but experience had altered my perception. Anything seemed possible. I could conceive of myself being married to him, a wealthy, fashionable socialite, and the image surprised me.

I hadn't realized I harbored such materialistic tendencies. When had I become so grasping?

I walked into the bedroom. While I'd been washing, he'd

removed his clothes. He was relaxed on the bed, sipping a glass of wine. When he saw me, his attention definitely perked up.

"Take off your towel."

I wasn't yet at ease with the nudity he enjoyed, and besides, the lamp was on and the drapes were open. We occasionally had sex when they were, and I'd be so nervous, terrified that some voyeur with a telescope might be spying on us.

"Let me close the drapes."

"No. Come here."

He held out his hand, expecting me to blithely obey, which I usually did.

"I'm closing the drapes!"

I drew them shut, then I went over to him. He dragged me down, rolling us so that he was pinning me down.

"You spoil all my fun," he scolded.

"How?"

"I like to think that others are watching while I fuck you."

"That's sick."

"It is not. It's very erotic."

"No, it's sick. Trust me on this."

He chuckled. "Spoken like a prim virgin. Haven't you ever seen two people fucking? It can be very arousing."

"Well, your friend Kimberly was giving Steve a blow job that time. I have to tell you that it didn't do a thing for me."

He chuckled again. "Do you miss him?"

I didn't have to hesitate or lie. "No."

I'd never mustered the courage to call Steve, had never sent anybody for my stuff. I'd simply told Jordan that I didn't need any of it.

I hadn't talked to Marie, either. I don't know what she and Steve thought about what I'd done. I often envisioned them, huddled together, having the suppers I used to have with them. They'd dissect every detail of that final, horrid afternoon, but no matter how they tried, they'd never make sense of it.

"How about you?" I teased. "Do you miss Kimberly?"

My question brought outright laughter. "No."

I'd inquired about her before, and he claimed she was merely a cheap date, when I didn't suppose there was anything about her that was *cheap*. He insisted he hadn't seen her again, and I couldn't decide if I believed him or not.

We had constant sex, so he couldn't have the energy to screw around on me. Or could he? He was insatiable.

If I found out he was still sneaking around with her, how would I react? He wouldn't tolerate any jealous hysterics, so I couldn't get a picture in my mind of how it might play out. As with so much of my life lately, I ignored the disturbing prospect.

He reached over to the nightstand, and he pulled a rope from the drawer.

I scowled. "What's that for?"

"I want to tie you up."

He'd raised the issue previously, but I was wary and kept refusing. "We've been through this a hundred times."

"I want to, Meg."

"So? I'm not comfortable with it."

"Do you trust me?"

"Of course."

"Then why are you afraid?"

"I'm not afraid. I'm just—" I paused, trying to unravel the basis of my reservations. "Okay, maybe I am afraid."

"Of what?"

"Of not knowing what will happen." I'd never had a lover who was into such rough sex, so many of his suggestions bothered me. I was never eager to participate, but his requests seemed so important to him, and my acquiescence thrilled him so much, that I wound up agreeing.

"It'll be very exciting for you. I promise."

"Yeah, right."

"The bindings heighten the tension, which will increase your enjoyment. And mine." I flashed such a skeptical look that he added, "I'll prove it to you."

I was already weakening. "Swear to me that you'll release me if I ask you."

"You know I will."

He gazed at me so intently, making me feel as if my consent could change the world.

"We can try it. Just this once."

I was such a wimp! How did he persuade me to do these things? Why did I let him?

He wrapped the cord around my wrists, then lifted my arms and secured the other end to the headboard. The knot wasn't very tight until I tugged on it, and it became obvious that I wouldn't be able to free myself.

The realization panicked me. My pulse raced.

"Can you loosen it?" I begged.

"No, it's fine. Don't worry."

"Jordan!"

"Hush."

He removed the towel so that I was naked, and he touched me everywhere. He wasn't hurting me, but with my being bound, each caress seemed like a violation. I kept flinching, expecting something awful to transpire.

He took a jar from the drawer and daubed the contents on his fingertip.

"What's that?"

"It's a scented cream. A mint. It will be warm on your skin."

I rose up, struggling to see what else was hidden in his stash. I'd rummaged around earlier in the morning and hadn't stumbled on any sex toys. He must have shopped for them while I was at work, which emphasized the fact that I had no idea what he did in the day while I was out.

I knew he stayed busy. The penthouse had an office, complete with desk, phone, computer, and fax machine, but he was never in there while I was home. It was the same with his fitness. His body was rock hard, and one of the bedrooms had been turned into a gym, but I never saw him use it, when he had to exercise relentlessly to be in such great shape.

He massaged the cream into my nipples, my belly button, between my legs. On my nipples it was very soothing, but down below, my feminine tissues were raw and inflamed, and it burned.

"I don't like it," I complained. "It's too hot."

"Close your eyes, Meg. Go with it."

"I don't want to *go* with it! It doesn't feel right."

"Stick out your tongue."

"No."

"Do it, Meg."

I yanked on the ropes. "Let me loose!"

He ignored me. "Your tongue, Meg. Stick it out."

We engaged in a staring contest I couldn't win, and ultimately I complied. He smeared it on my tongue, then on his own, and he kissed me, the flavor so strong it was a bit nauseating.

He shifted up my torso till his cock was level with my face. I watched as he swabbed the cream on it, as he placed it on my lips.

"Open for me, Meg."

I shook my head. "I can't."

"It's time to show me that you'll do it for me. I've been very patient."

"No."

"I bought the cream just for you, Meg. To make it easier. Now open."

I was mutinous, ready to fight him, though with me being trussed like a goose, I could never succeed. This was the exact situation I'd feared by allowing him to tie me up. He could order me to do anything, and I didn't have much choice in whether to obey.

"I don't want you to come in my mouth," I said. "I don't like it."

"I won't."

"If you're lying, I'll kill you in your sleep."

He leaned down and kissed me so tenderly. "Do it for me. I want this from you."

When he coaxed me so sweetly—I was still such a sucker for him!—I couldn't resist, and I did as he'd commanded. He was very restrained, which was a relief. He inserted the tip and barely flexed, as if having me practice, then he pulled away and trailed down to my breasts.

He nibbled and played, pushing me up and up the ladder of desire, and he was correct: the bindings increased the titillation. I felt as if I was in the middle of an erotic fantasy, that he was a pirate raping me, that I was the spoils of war.

As usual, he'd keep on till I was at the edge, then he'd draw away, not letting me come. He'd return to my mouth, giving me more of his cock, staying at it longer and longer.

He poured me some wine and helped me drink it. He poured me some more. I was so tired from work and lack of sleep that it instantly relaxed me. He scrounged in the drawer again, and he produced a small bottle filled with clear liquid.

"What's that?" I asked.

"It's an aphrodisiac. Have you ever tried one?"

"No."

He added a few drops to my wine, stirred it with his finger, then held it out. "It will augment the pleasure."

"It's a drug?"

"Not really. It merely heightens your senses."

I wasn't adverse to taking recreational drugs, but I wasn't keen on them when I didn't know what—or how potent—the effect would be. I swallowed a tiny sip, not nearly as much as he would have liked, and he forced more and more down my throat until the glass was empty.

Shortly, my privates started to ache, my veins to throb. I grew very warm. My peripheral vision was fuzzy. My limbs were leaden, my torso dead weight. I couldn't lift off the pillow, but I didn't care that I couldn't. I was awake but lethargic, happy to float on a tide of contentment.

He nuzzled up my body, and this time when he wedged his cock in my mouth, I didn't mind. He thrust vigorously, but I let him proceed without a murmur of protest. He reached down and fondled my pulsing nipples as he whispered soft words of encouragement that fit my stupor.

When he finally came, I decided that it hadn't been so difficult to do it for him after all.

Chapter Nine

❦

I rolled over and peeked at the clock. It was ten fifteen on a Wednesday morning when I should have been at work at ten. I groaned. I couldn't imagine how many more occasions I could oversleep without being fired.

My head was pounding, my eyes gritty, and I felt like shit. I'd been off for the prior forty-eight hours, and Jordan and I had spent the entire interval in bed. There were bruises all over my body, our incessant fucking leaving me ragged and torn, and the intensity had completely drained me.

I yearned to have a day to myself, where I could rest and catch my breath, but we were in a cycle of eroticism that I didn't know how to break. His attention made me feel cherished and special, but I wished we could slow down, that we could behave like a normal couple.

We never went out to dinner, never took in a movie or went to the mall to shop and hang around.

Every minute with him was high drama, extreme exchanges, and passionate interactions. I'd started taking odd drugs whenever he suggested it, was drinking more than I ever had, and finding fewer opportunities to eat. I'd lost weight, so my clothes were loose and baggy.

He insisted that he loved the newer, skinnier me, but I thought I looked gaunt and haunted.

When I'd first met him, our attraction had seemed glamorous and electrifying, but now it was just grueling. Considering how excessively he pampered me, I was such an ingrate, but I was desperate for a peaceful interlude where I could collect myself and figure out what I was doing.

As I dragged myself out of bed, I was woozy from fatigue and a poor diet. He woke and frowned at me.

"Where are you going?"

"I need to get up. I'm late for work."

"I don't understand why you don't quit. If you did, we could be together every second."

It was an argument with no resolution, so I didn't respond. I stumbled to the shower, praying the pulsating jets would rattle me to consciousness.

I was washing my hair, the shampoo sluicing off me, when he climbed in behind me. He gripped my hips and shoved me to the wall, his erection pressed to my ass.

"Jordan, come on!" I elbowed him in the ribs. "I don't have time for this."

"Make time."

"I'm late!"

"I want you."

When he was hot with desire, there was no dissuading him. Usually I was eager to oblige, thrilled with how he lusted after me, but at the moment I was simply irritated.

I tried to wiggle away, and I grappled for purchase, my palms slipping on the wet tiles, but I couldn't escape. He clutched my thighs and entered me, fucking in the slow, determined rhythm he could sustain for hours. He had more stamina and self-control than I'd known a man could possess.

I was sore, and I was weary, and I began to cry. I stood there, hands braced, legs spread wide, tears dripping down my cheeks. Though the streaming water hid them, he had to realize I was weeping, but he didn't stop. He kept on and on, and when he came, he collapsed against me, his cock still wedged deep inside.

His mouth at my ear, he whispered, "Don't ever say no to me."

"I won't."

"I love you," he declared. "I can't bear it when you refuse me."

He'd never previously told me that he loved me, and I rippled with gladness and relief. I'd been hoping that I was more to him than a wild fling, and I hated the notion that he'd brought me home for a few months of sex and would toss me over when he grew bored. I couldn't stand to think that I'd given up everything for him unless he had genuine feelings for me.

"I love you, too," I vehemently answered, meaning it.

Satisfied with my submission, with my words, he withdrew from me.

"Let's get you dressed."

"I have to hurry."

I felt as if I'd dodged a blow, that we'd been at an impasse but had skirted around it. He took charge, which he was so proficient at doing, drying me and helping me with my hair and clothes. Within minutes, we were descending to his waiting car, when I hadn't seen him phone anybody to have it ready. How did he do that?

He dropped me at the rear of the restaurant, having the driver pull directly into the parking lot where my coworkers could observe us. I was too frantic to protest.

I raced to the door, but tiptoed in. It was twelve forty, with the lunch rush in full swing. Everyone was running in circles, my absence causing exactly the sort of problems I'd envisioned. No one commented, although I noted a waitress glancing at the clock. Luckily, Pam had gone to a meeting, so I didn't have to deal with her, but I was positive someone would complain. I had to have pushed the envelope on what they would tolerate.

I hadn't eaten again, and I was so busy that I was reduced to sneaking tiny bites as I sliced and prepped. I was queasy, dizzy, and so sluggish that I might have been trudging through a dream.

The afternoon was a blur, and I remained into the evening, striving to make up for lost time, to get a jump on some desserts that Pam needed for a private party at the end of the week.

As I finished and was grabbing my coat, anxious to creep out unseen, Pam appeared from her office. I'd been so distracted that I wasn't aware she'd arrived.

"Meg, there you are."

"Hi, Pam." I couldn't look her in the eye.

"Can I talk to you? It will just take a second."

"Sure."

There wasn't any way I could decline. I'd scarcely spoken to her after that awkward day in Sun River when I'd stayed behind to be with Jordan. Since then, she'd been her typical courteous self and hadn't mentioned it—or him—again.

We went into the small room, and she sat at her desk while I moved papers and junk onto the floor so that I could sit on the chair across from her. It was very quiet. A faucet dripped. Dishes clinked in the kitchen.

Was I about to be fired? I was so exhausted that it would almost be welcome.

She stared and stared, then said, "We haven't chatted in ages. How have you been?"

"Good."

It was the truth and a lie. I was better than I'd ever been; I was worse than I'd ever been.

"I noticed recently that you've been coming in late. A lot."

"I'm sorry. It won't happen again."

As if my tardiness didn't matter, she shrugged away the remark.

"How's Jordan?" At the question, my surprise must have been apparent, because she added, "I heard you're living with him."

I wondered who had told her. "Yes, I am."

"That's going well? You're happy?"

"Yes." I smiled, but struggled to keep it in place. What was she actually asking? "We've had loads of social events and stuff like that—that he has to attend—every night. I'm tired in the mornings and I can't get up when I should. I'll knock it off."

She nodded, scrutinizing me, then she frowned. "You know, Meg, one of the waitresses claims that she spotted bruises on your wrists."

My heart pounded, my cheeks flushed with shame. "Really? That's weird."

There was a lengthy, severe silence.

"If you were ever in trouble," she ultimately said, "or if you were *afraid* about something, you could come to me. You realize that, don't you?"

"Of course, but why would I need to?"

No way in hell would I admit that Jordan regularly tied me up, that he reveled in it and I allowed him to proceed without objection. My wrists were always bruised. So were my ankles.

I tucked my hands under my thighs, out of sight.

"She was wrong," I insisted.

"Was she?"

"Yes."

"Show me."

"Show you what?"

"Your wrists. Let me see."

I was mute with shock and mortification. I couldn't answer the allegation; I couldn't do what she'd demanded.

"I'm fine."

She sighed, then picked up one of her business cards and jotted on the back. "This is my private cell number. I gave it to you before, but I wasn't certain if you still had it or not."

"No, I didn't keep it."

"If you ever need me, you can call me any time. Even if it's the middle of the night. I wouldn't mind."

"Thanks, but I can't imagine why I would."

"You just never know," she replied, looking shrewd and wise.

I crammed the card in my pocket and left, walking slowly as if everything was great, when in fact the discussion had been the most humiliating I'd ever endured.

I was in agony. My boss—whom I liked and respected so much—had practically accused me of being a battered woman!

Jordan and I were extremely passionate individuals, and our relationship was different from the kind that was acceptable to others. I wasn't interested in an apathetic partner or bland sex. I'd moved beyond it into another realm that a normal person couldn't grasp or appreciate. Not that I could explain such a thing to someone like Pam. She'd never understand.

As I stepped outside, I was overcome by a wave of nausea. I was starving, had worked like a dog, hadn't truly slept in an eternity. I dashed behind the dumpster and puked and puked, but there was nothing in my stomach.

I stood and swiped a sleeve across my mouth, my face tilted toward the mist that was falling.

Since I hadn't phoned Jordan yet, he wasn't there, so I had a few minutes to calm down. Someone said my name, and I turned and jumped as Jeffrey emerged from the shadows.

"Meg, is that you?"

"God, you scared the shit out of me." I took a deep breath, fending off another surge of vomiting. I didn't know if he'd observed me, but I didn't want to have to rationalize my condition.

"What are you doing here? I thought you went home hours ago."

"I came to check my schedule." Appearing embarrassed, he kicked at a rock. "Are you okay?"

I forced a chuckle. "What is it with everybody all of a sudden?"

"What do you mean?"

"I just got the third degree from Pam. I'm *fine!*"

"Wanna have a drink?" he suggested. "I never see you away from the restaurant anymore. We never hang out together."

I couldn't remember when I'd last trotted off to have a beer. The days when I'd been free to party with acquaintances seemed so distant that I couldn't recollect what that period of my life had been like.

It was already far past the time when Jordan would be expecting me to call for a ride, and he'd be starting to worry.

I could have invited Jordan to join us, but I simply couldn't conceive of him and Jeffrey socializing. Plus, I was convinced that Jordan wouldn't approve of me having Jeffrey for a friend, which was absurd, but I was too worn down to have a huge fight about it.

"I'm whipped"—it was definitely the truth—"and I need to head out. How about a rain check?"

He shrugged, his disappointment clear. Nervously, he tugged at his coat. He seemed very young, very shy, and he was diligently ducking my gaze.

"I have to tell you something," he muttered.

His tone indicated that it would be bad and would make me angry.

What was up with these strange confessions? Was it a full

moon? Was it chemicals in the water or air? I couldn't bear another frank discussion, not after the one I'd just had with Pam.

"What?" I snapped, more harsh than I should have been.

"I'm only informing you because I love you. You know that,
right?"

"What is it?" I repeated, too tired to be civil.

"I know some people who know some people who . . .
well . . . know Jordan Blair."

Jeffrey had learned about me and Jordan? Had the whole
fucking world heard about us? Why couldn't it be my own private business?

"And . . . ?"

"You use a condom with him, don't you?"

"A condom?" I scowled, confused, then his intent dawned
on me and I laughed hysterically. "You think Jordan is gay?
Trust me on this: Jordan is not gay."

"I'm not saying he's gay." His expression was stony and
serious. "I'm not saying that, at all."

"Then what are you saying?"

"Rumor has it that he'll do anything with anyone. I want
you to be cautious, to be safe."

I understood that he cared about me and he was trying to
help, but he was so wrong. "Jeffrey, I swear. Jordan is the
most hot-blooded, regular, heterosexual male I've ever met."

"You're sure?"

"Positive."

"But you should make him use a condom anyway."

"I do! I'm not stupid." It was probably the biggest lie I'd ever
uttered. On one fruitless occasion I'd insisted on protection, but

Jordan had refused so stridently that I hadn't raised the issue again.

"You have to quit being late," he warned, abruptly switching topics. "You're going to get fired."

"No, no. Pam and I talked. We're cool. Everything's okay."

Jordan's car pulled into the lot without my having contacted him. I was irked by his arrival, by his hovering, but at the moment I couldn't do anything about it. The headlights swept over us, the engine idling as the driver stopped and exited to open the door for me.

"I have to go," I said.

Jeffrey studied the car, then me, then the car again.

"I miss you," he countered. "It's not the same anymore."

"It's *exactly* the same," I fibbed. "Nothing's changed, and nothing will."

He assessed me, both of us recognizing my promise for the falsehood it was, then I walked away without a good-bye. I slipped into the backseat, where Jordan was waiting for me. As he put his arm around me, I felt as if I couldn't breathe, as if I was suffocating on the trappings of the life I'd built for myself.

We sped away, the dark interior concealing the tears that flooded my eyes. I couldn't figure out why I was sad.

"Who was that?" Jordan asked.

"One of the other chefs."

"What did he want?"

"He needed a day off. He was hoping I could trade shifts with him."

I had no idea why I didn't dare speak Jeffrey's name aloud,

or why I would have to concoct a story. I just knew Jordan wouldn't like me to associate with Jeffrey, and I was too on edge to defend the innocent conversation.

"You told him no?"

"Of course."

"Good. I can't have you working more than you already do. It's too much."

"I'm exhausted," I agreed. "Let's hurry home. I could sleep for a week."

Chapter Ten

❧❧

I stood in front of the mirror, studying my reflection. I was still dying my hair auburn, but it was much longer now, having grown out from the distinctive, spiky cut I'd treasured.

I applied my makeup, using natural shades of peach and brown, while going heavy on the mascara and liner because Jordan liked it that way. He'd purchased a slinky, silvery dress for me, and I shimmied into it. I never would have selected the bright garment for myself, but as usual he was correct in recognizing that it matched the new me.

The tiny straps hugged my bare shoulders, the flowing fabric falling below my knees. The plunging bodice displayed plenty of skin, highlighting how much weight I'd lost.

My breasts were nearly nonexistent. I resembled those fashion models who starved themselves. I was gaunt, my cheekbones severe, my hipbones jutting out.

I appeared exotic and foreign, like someone I didn't know, and I was confused about the changes. On the one hand, I looked very chic, very rich and sophisticated. On the other, I grieved for the person I'd been. I felt as if I'd hacked off a limb, that a vital part of me had vanished, and I wanted it back but couldn't find it.

I sat on the bed and strapped on the heels that went with the dress.

Jordan had wanted a certain bottle of wine, and he'd gone out to get it, so for once I was alone in the apartment, and it was very quiet. There was a phone on the nightstand and I gazed at it, thinking I should call someone. But who? And why was I so reticent about picking it up and dialing?

Since I'd run off with Jordan, I hadn't talked to any of the people who used to fill my day. My life had always been busy, as it was now, but with a different sort of chaos. There had been parties, and Sunday afternoon football games where Steve's buddies stopped by with beer and pizza. We'd often danced the night away at our favorite bars or enjoyed big family suppers at his parents' house.

Did anybody speculate over where I was or what I was doing? Did anybody miss me?

I don't know why I'd never contacted any of them, not even Marie, with whom I'd once been so close. In my drive to meld myself to Jordan, I'd been in a rush to shed my previous connections, but there had also been the implicit awareness that Jordan wouldn't have liked me to continue the relation-ships.

It was silly to be afraid merely because he might disap-prove, and I couldn't figure out how I'd tumbled into such a peculiar trap. If I opted to have friends outside my bond with him, it wasn't any of his business. Why let him dictate to me? Before I'd met him, I never would have tolerated it. Why was I now?

I grabbed the receiver, and I was stunned to discover that my fingers were shaking, as if I was doing something very wrong. I punched in Marie's number, and I waited and waited. When her machine clicked on, I couldn't decide if I was sad or relieved. What would I have said anyway? When months had passed, what could possibly be appropriate?

I hung up, and the worst wave of melancholy swept over me. I yearned for my old life, my old acquaintances, the old me. I picked up and dialed again, choosing Steve's number, refusing to wonder why I would.

On the third ring, he answered. "Hello?"

His voice was so familiar and it conjured such pleasant memories. I couldn't speak a word and I sat there like a statue. What precisely had I been hoping to tell him? I hadn't a clue.

"Hello," he repeated.

In the background, Marie asked, "Who is it?"

Marie had always liked him so much. Were they together? It hadn't occurred to me that he'd have moved on, that he might be getting on just fine without me. In fact, from the moment I'd left, I had hardly ever thought of him.

Surprisingly, he said, "Meg, is that you?"

I heard Jordan returning with the wine, and very carefully I placed the receiver in the cradle. I was frantic, as if I'd committed an unpardonable sin, which was absurd, and I took several deep breaths, trying to slow my pulse and smooth my ragged emotions. I seized a Kleenex and dabbed at my face and eyes, terrified that he'd note I was upset and would want to know why.

What would I say? *While you were out, I buzzed Steve so we could catch up?*

The notion didn't bear contemplating.

"Meg, where are you?" He sounded worried, as if I might have scooted out while he was down in the lobby.

"I'm just finishing with my clothes," I replied.

"Let me see."

I wobbled into the living room, doing my best to be graceful in the wretched shoes. In my pre-Jordan world, I'd rarely owned a pair, and it was difficult growing accustomed. They didn't seem worth the bother, but then again, when he saw me in them, his appreciative assessment eased some of the agony.

"Very nice." He made a circular gesture, indicating I should vamp for him, and I did. The hem of my skirt twirled in a goofy, feminine way that didn't fit my image of myself, but that had a spectacular effect all the same.

"Not bad, huh?" I mumbled, embarrassed.

"Not bad, at all."

He was wearing a dark blue suit, and it was the sole occasion I'd ever observed him so formally attired. He could have emerged from the pages of *GQ* magazine or maybe *Forbes*. He definitely resembled the successful entrepreneur and millionaire he was purported to be.

I sauntered over and fiddled with the lapels of his coat. "You're looking very sexy, yourself."

"Am I?"

"Oh yes."

We were about to embark on our first real date. We were

actually having dinner at a restaurant. When he'd suggested it, I couldn't believe he wanted to do something besides climb into bed. I was desperate for it to transpire, and I kept expecting some drama to arise that would prevent us from going. I felt like a prisoner breaking out of jail, a slave racing to freedom.

"I got you a gift," he mentioned.

"What?"

He pulled a pearl necklace and earrings from his pocket. The necklace had a delicate ivory cameo dangling in the center that would accent the neck of my dress and draw attention to my cleavage—or lack of it.

I smiled. "Wow. They're pretty."

"Turn around."

He hooked the necklace and helped me with the earrings, then he took a step back to admire his handiwork.

"Perfect," he said.

"Do you think so?"

"Absolutely. Let's go."

"Don't you want to have some of the wine?"

"It's late, and we're about to miss our reservation. We'll have some when we get home."

We slipped into the elevator and it whisked us down to the sidewalk. In minutes, the driver had deposited us at a restaurant on the banks of the Willamette River. I didn't recognize the name, but from the décor it was obviously expensive and exclusive. The employees fawned over Jordan as if he was a regular customer, and their overt respect was disconcerting. It underscored how little I knew about him.

In the period we'd been together, I hadn't uncovered any

relevant tidbits; he hadn't met a single associate or had guests to the apartment. He hadn't shared anecdotes about his childhood or stories about his family.

He seemed to have sprung from nowhere, to have no connections to anyone, which wasn't true. The reality was that I spent lengthy hours slogging away at my job, and I had no idea what he did while I was away. He might have had lunch in this very spot twice a week, but I didn't know. How weird was that?

Whenever I inquired as to how he kept himself busy, I'd get vague answers about conferences or appointments, but I couldn't delve to the heart of how he earned his fortune. It didn't appear that he did much of anything. He was so wealthy but had so much leisure time, while I worked like a dog and was always broke. Our situations were skewed and unfair.

We were seated at a table facing the water. With the longer spring evenings, it was dusk, so we had a fabulous view of the mansions on the other shore. Sailboats drifted by, and the snowy peak of Mt. Hood glimmered off in the distance.

Our meal had already been ordered—a testament to his elevated status—and as soon as we were comfortable, the wine and appetizers were served, but still the moment was awkward. Our relationship was so private, our behavior a constant lesson in decadence, so it was bizarre to be sitting across from him in a public place like a normal person.

We were a handsome couple, and I could see people—particularly women—taking furtive glances at us. Or perhaps they all knew Jordan and were checking him out, trying to identify the unknown female eating with him. I hoped I lived up to their fantasies but doubted I could.

"What's the name of your company?" I asked, needing to

fill the silence and figuring I ought to learn something about him that wasn't sexual.

"I don't have a company anymore."

"Then what kinds of meetings are you always attending?"

"I'm in discussions with my bankers and accountants."

"Is it a full-time job, managing all your money?"

I meant it as a joke, but he responded in all seriousness. "Yes."

"You seem to have a lot of it."

"I do."

"What sort of business did you own?"

"Sports equipment. I designed snowboards, surfboards, things like that."

"Were they good ones?"

"Top of the line. Only the best."

"Why surfboards?"

"I grew up in southern California."

This was news. "Really?"

"Yes." He studied me. "You're so beautiful these days."

"Thank you."

"I like how your hair is getting longer."

"It's different," I said.

"It's better," he said.

It was typical of him to shift the conversation to me. As opposed to most men, he never talked about himself. Whenever I probed for details, he would switch the subject to me. He was so fascinated, and in the beginning I'd been flattered and amazed, but we were beyond the initial stages of our affair and progressing into something more enduring. I was determined to pry out some facts.

"Tell me about your family," I pressed.

"Tell me about yours."

"You first."

"A mother and father. No siblings," he curtly explained. "And you?"

"No mother or father. No siblings."

"No mother or father? What? Were you birthed by wolves?"

I chuckled. "No. I was an orphan, raised by my aunt. How about you? Are your parents alive?"

"My mother is."

"Do you ever see her?"

He scoffed. "Rarely."

"Is she in California?"

"She's in a mental hospital there."

I dropped my spoon on the floor. "A mental hospital?"

"She was committed years ago."

"And she's still there?"

"She can't ever leave. She was judged insane."

"Insane . . . ?"

"Yes. She murdered my father."

"Why?"

"Why was she found to be insane? Or why did she kill my father?"

"Why did she kill him?"

"Why does anyone?"

"Were you close to your father?"

"No. He was a sadistic asshole."

No wonder he declined to discuss his past! His expression was inscrutable, as if he was daring me to inquire further, and

I wished I hadn't snooped. His family history was a mine field I didn't care to navigate. Yet I mustered my courage and forged on.

"I heard you were married once."

"Who told you that?"

"Pam Owen, I think. Were you?"

"Yes."

"What was her name?"

"Brittney."

"Pam said she died."

"In a boating accident."

"How did it happen?"

"We were sailing at the mouth of the Columbia. Just the two of us. The currents are very treacherous where the river flows into the ocean. Our boat was swamped by a huge wave."

"Do you miss her?"

"Every day."

He sipped his wine, our forks clinked on the china. The comment was the appropriate one to make, but it was delivered with no hint of emotion, and I thought of his lavish penthouse. There wasn't a picture of her anywhere.

An odd frisson of disquiet slithered down my spine.

We proceeded on to other topics—mostly me—with him whispering the things he wanted to do to me when we got home. Usually, I was ecstatic over how I aroused him, but in the middle of an elite restaurant and surrounded by wealthy diners, the conversation unsettled me. I kept trying to steer it to safer, more innocuous issues, but without success. He was focused on me and what he had planned.

The waiter removed our plates and was offering dessert when the maitre d' escorted a couple by our table. Jordan glanced up at the woman and recognized her, but without any visible reaction. The woman, however, blanched in astonishment, then halted.

"Hello, Jordan," she sneered. Her greeting oozed hatred. "Fancy meeting you here."

She was very pretty, a slender brunette, and probably thirty years old. The man with her, most likely her husband, was urging her forward.

"Come on, Ashley," he entreated, "head to our table. Don't start anything."

She ignored him and hissed at Jordan, "What are you doing here, you sick fuck?"

The remark was uttered just loudly enough that nearby customers scowled their disapproval. Jordan didn't flinch, though his mouth quirked as if he was humored by her temper.

"Who's this?" Ashley demanded, her attention suddenly riveted on me. She thoroughly assessed me, her fury acute and unnerving. "Her hair's still auburn," she pointed out. "I guess she has some time left."

"Ashley!" the husband scolded. "Come on!"

"Meg," Jordan said, "let me introduce you to Brittney's sister, my sister-in-law."

"We're such a nice, *happy* family, aren't we, Jordan?" she taunted. "Will you be joining us for Easter dinner?"

She bent toward me so that she was directly in my face, and I wasn't sure what she intended to do. I leaned back in my chair as she wrapped her fingers around the cameo on my necklace. I worried that she'd yank it off and wreck it, but instead she gave it a light—almost affectionate—tug, then she glared at me with disgust.

"You're wearing a dead woman's jewelry," she claimed. "Doesn't that bother you?"

She tossed the cameo against my skin and stormed away.

I was embarrassed and horror-stricken, while Jordan wasn't fazed in the least and seemed amused by Ashley's outburst.

Once my heart slowed to a more normal rhythm, I said, "She doesn't like you very much."

He shrugged. "She never did."

"Why not?"

"She's convinced I murdered Brittney."

For a second the earth stopped spinning, and I actually asked, "Did you?"

"What do you think?"

I suppose I should have leapt to his defense, but what emerged from my lips was, "I don't know."

"Would you like to examine the Coast Guard reports? I have them at home in a file."

The prospect of him being some kind of homicidal maniac was preposterous, and quickly I came to my senses. "No."

"She's crazy," he advised.

"I can tell." I peered around and couldn't see where they'd been seated, but I didn't want to linger and furnish her with a chance to accost us again.

"Could we go?"

"I have to take care of the check."

While he finished with the waiter, I went to the rest room, which was located in a hallway off the entry foyer. As I rounded the corner, I was dismayed to stumble on Ashley and her husband huddled in the narrow corridor. She was crying and he was consoling her.

"No matter where I am," she was complaining, "he shows up. He has to be following me! Maybe he's tapping our phones so he knows my schedule."

"You're reading too much into this," her husband replied, striving to be rational.

"He does it on purpose!" she insisted. "To throw her death in my face. The fucker! He killed her and nobody gives a shit."

"Ash, it's been six years," her husband soothed. "Let it go."

I hated that I'd eavesdropped, and I moved to tiptoe away when Ashley's husband noted my intrusion. He glanced up and frowned. Ashley whipped around and evaluated me, her angry gaze traveling down my dress, to my shoes. Her pity was obvious.

"God, this is so incredible." She gaped at her husband, her eyes pleading. "Don't you see it?"

"No, what?"

"She looks just like Brittney. He's turned her into Brittney." Shivers coursed down my arms.

"Excuse me," I muttered, "I didn't mean to interrupt."

Suddenly Jordan was behind me, his hand on my shoulder. "Let's get out of here, Meg."

Ashley couldn't resist needling me. "Auburn isn't your natural color, is it?"

"No." I couldn't believe I'd responded to her.

"He made Brittney dye her hair auburn, too, a few weeks before he murdered her."

"Jesus, Ash!" her husband snapped. "Sorry, Jordan."

"It's okay, Bill."

My cheeks on fire, my temper raging, I whirled away and fled, with Jordan hot on my heels.

She called after us, "On the day he forces you to dye it blond, run like hell!"

Chapter Eleven

❧

I was in the bathroom when I thought I heard the elevator ping out in the living room. I thought I heard Jordan talking to somebody, too, but the stereo was on so I wasn't sure.

If we had a visitor, it was the first one in all the time I'd been with him. I should have been more curious, but it was late and I was whipped. After juggling work and Jordan for a week, I was determined to fall into bed. It was Monday night, the beginning of my weekend, since I had Tuesday and Wednesday off. Knowing Jordan's capacity for carnal activity, I'd get very little sleep over the next forty-eight hours.

My job was on the line, and I couldn't keep screwing up or missing shifts. I had to snag whatever rest I could.

I didn't mind the sex; it was still hot and potent, but I was desperate to snooze before he started in. If he decided to tie me up, to feed me weird drugs, or any of the other stuff I always ended up trying, I was so weary that I'd refuse, and I wouldn't be civil about it. He'd be angry when I had no energy left for quarreling.

The instant I hit the pillows, I dozed, and I awakened with Jordan nuzzling my neck, urging me to open my eyes, but I fought his efforts to rouse me.

"Please, God, let me keep sleeping," I mumbled, meaning it, but not meaning it, too. "I'm exhausted."

"I have you all to myself for the next two days. I want you. I can't wait."

He wedged himself between my thighs, and he entered me and thrust away. I was only half-conscious, reveling in the attention but blissfully distracted by fatigue so that it felt as if he was making love to me in a dream.

I expected him to secure my hands over my head, but he didn't, which surprised me. He shackled me so often that we never removed the cords from the headboard. They were my constant companion and part of our carnal ritual. Jordan enjoyed the bondage, and he'd taught me to enjoy it, too. And I usually did, unless he got too rough.

When he wanted something from me, I quickly ceded the battle, until it had become our pattern. There were simply behaviors that he desired, that mattered much more to him than to me, and when I consented, I made him so happy.

He nibbled at my breasts, then down my front, to my mons, and he tongued me, licking my clit and puss. I always shaved now, having resigned myself to the fact that it was what he liked and not worth arguing about. He stuck his fingers inside me, stroking them back and forth. When he poked them into my anus, I frowned and arched up, but I didn't tell him to stop.

I detested anal stimulation, and he knew I was uncomfortable with it, but he'd torment me anyway. The more I complained, the longer he'd continue, so I was silent. He played for a while, titillating himself, while I drifted on the brink of slumber, aware of him and what he was doing, but not fully alert. Ultimately, he maneuvered his way up my torso.

"I've never sodomized you," he whispered.

"No, you haven't."

He mentioned it occasionally but hadn't forced the issue, which was a relief. I'd never attempted it and wasn't eager to. His comment made me wonder again why he'd picked me as his sexual partner. Compared to him, I was an absolute prude, but then he garnered an enormous thrill from wheedling me into trying things that scared or disgusted me.

"I'm going to give it to you in the ass sometime. I'll do it when you've been bad and I need to punish you." He was kissing my cheek, my chest. "You'll let me, won't you?"

"Of course," I said. It was easier to agree.

He moved off me and sat on the edge of the bed. He was rummaging through the drawer in the nightstand, but I was too tired to glance over and see what he'd retrieved.

He filled a glass with liquor and mixed some drops into it. "Here, drink this."

"I don't want to. I didn't eat much today. My stomach's upset." Which was true.

"I think I'll have some," he replied.

I was stunned. But for a rare sip of wine, he never drank or took any of the drugs he gave to me. I'd asked once why he didn't, and he claimed he didn't like to have his senses dulled by alcohol, and that the aphrodisiacs had no effect on him, so it was pointless to ingest them. I suspected the real reason was that he hated losing control.

"I want to try something new," he explained, "something we've never done before."

"Sure," I concurred without hesitating.

"Hold on. I'll be right back."

I dozed off again, and I don't know how long I laid there. I heard him return, and he climbed onto the bed and stretched out, but someone else climbed onto it, too, and snuggled on the opposite side of me. I was confused, lethargic, and not feeling exactly sober, even though I was.

My eyes flew open, and I gaped about, anxious to figure out what was happening.

"Hello, Meg," Kimberly cooed. "Remember me?"

She was on her elbow and hovered over me, her blond hair curled around her perfect face. She was naked, a breast nudging my arm, and she smiled, but it was a smirk that seemed to say, *Look where you are now!*

Dazed and baffled, I shook my head. "Jordan . . . no . . ."

"Do it for me, Meg," he urged, coaxing me to acquiesce. "I want to watch the two of you together."

"No!"

He ignored me and slid away to pull a chair next to the mattress. He'd put on a pair of the lounge pants he wore for sexual games, and he nodded to Kimberly, as if instructing her to commence.

"Jordan!" I protested more loudly as Kimberly bent down and sucked on my nipple.

I was ashamed to admit how exciting it was, and for a bit I actually reclined and let her proceed. What did it matter?

I could shut her out and pretend it wasn't occurring, that it was all an odd, erotic dream. I would entertain Jordan, would conclude as rapidly as possible, then get the sleep I was desperate to have, but as soon as I caught myself considering the notion, I rebelled against it.

It wasn't that I was repulsed by the concept of a threesome, or that I was too uptight to do it with a female in order to arouse Jordan. I loathed Kimberly and had from the moment she'd hit on Steve in that accursed bar out on the coast. I'd later questioned Jordan about her, curious for more details about who she was and how they were acquainted. He'd insisted he'd merely dated her, which I regarded as a dubious claim. I was convinced she was a prostitute. She had to be. No doubt he was paying her, and I wouldn't participate.

How had they hooked up? Why had they? I imagined the two of them discussing me, haggling over various acts she would perform, over how much her involvement would cost, and I was sickened by the prospect.

Didn't he understand anything about me? Why would he presume I would do this with her?

For the first time since meeting him, I wanted to leave, to run away and never come back.

Kimberly shifted so that she was on top of me, our nude bodies melded all the way down. Her abdomen and thighs were pressed to mine, her breasts, too. It felt decadently marvelous, much better than it should have, and I was disgusted all over again.

Her bare pussy flexed into me, and it dawned on me that she'd probably shaved for Jordan because he asked her to.

How well did they know each other? Had Jordan been seeing her without my being aware that he was?

"Let's give him a good show," she murmured, laughing her annoying, sultry laugh. "He'll be so hot for you when we're finished."

She tried to kiss me on the mouth, but I jerked away so that she bussed my cheek instead. I started to cry—I couldn't help it—and rolled away from her. My heart pounding like crazy, my stomach heaving, I worried that I was about to vomit all over the floor.

I was so drained and everything seemed wrong: my choices, my decisions. I didn't want to live like this, didn't want to be so overwhelmed. In the beginning, my affair with Jordan had been exhilarating, and I'd been lured by his fascination for me, but now it was all so exhausting.

There were no peaceful interludes, no simple situations. Our entire relationship was high drama, intense behaviors, obsessed passion and togetherness. I just wanted to be alone, to be away from both of them.

I was usually so complacent and submissive that he'd likely supposed this was one more coercion I'd accept, one more degradation I'd allow. But he'd crossed a line and pushed me beyond my limit.

There were many things I could and would do for him, but this was not one of them.

Stunned, shaken, I sat up, and Kimberly had the gall to scoot over and snuggle herself to me. She stroked my shoulder. "Don't be afraid, Meg. It'll be fun."

"Get your hand off me or I'll break your arm."

"Relax. I'll make it easy for you. Let me do all the work."

She rose up on her knees, draping herself across my back, and she reached around and pinched my nipple. I shrugged her off and stood, glaring at Jordan. I was so angry that if I'd been holding a gun, I'd have shot him.

"Get her out of here."

"I want this, Meg," he said very quietly, very earnestly, his blue, blue eyes pleading with me to relent. "I want you to do this for me."

"Get her the fuck out of here!"

I screamed it so shrilly that I felt I'd stripped my vocal chords, then I ran into the bathroom and slammed the door as hard as I could. I spun the lock and paced like a caged animal.

I was frantic with despair, moaning and pulling at my hair. I didn't know what to do, didn't know where to go or what should happen next. I didn't belong with him, but I had cut every tie, had burned every bridge. I didn't so much as have a friend who'd let me crash on her couch.

I wondered if this was why people committed suicide, if they came to a point where they finally realized how alone they were in the world.

I stopped and braced my palms on the counter, and I evaluated my ghastly reflection. When I'd arrived home, I'd been too tired to shower and I'd fallen into bed without washing my face. Mascara was smudged across my cheeks, my hair was standing on end as if I'd been trying to yank it out by the roots. I was skinny as a rail, my ribs and hip bones sticking out like a starving refugee's.

I looked completely insane.

My legs buckled and I collapsed to the floor. Naked and

freezing, I lay there in a state of shock. Blindly, I groped for a towel, and I tugged it off the rack and dropped it over my torso.

I huddled in a ball, not comprehending how a person could be so disconsolate and still be breathing. I prayed for my heart to quit beating, or that I would vanish into thin air, but I wasn't lucky enough for either one to transpire.

What am I going to do? What am I going to do? What am I going to do?

The refrain echoed through my mind, and eventually my shivering slowed. I slept.

Sometime later—a long time later—the door opened, the lock clicking as Jordan let himself in. He picked me up and carried me to bed. At least, I thought he did. I was so groggy and sluggish that I wasn't certain. He nestled me under the blankets, tucking me in as if I was a young child, then he turned out the lamp and crawled in with me. His warm, nude body was spooned to mine, his strong arms encircling me. He caressed me as he whispered soft words that were hypnotic, that lulled me into an even deeper sleep.

When I woke again, I'd been curled in the same position for so many hours that I could barely force my muscles to respond. I rolled over and stretched my legs. From the sunlight flooding through the curtains, it seemed to be afternoon, but I couldn't see the clock so I wasn't sure.

The events of the prior night came rushing in, and anxiously I glanced around, but neither Jordan nor Kimberly was with me. I sighed with relief, and I was very still, listening, trying to hear if anyone was out in the apartment. It was eerily silent. After my manic performance in front of Kimberly, perhaps Jordan had left in the hopes that I'd sneak out and be gone before he got back.

When he finally peeked in to check on me, I could have pretended I was asleep, but I didn't. Obviously he'd been watching me, waiting for me to awaken, and it was disconcerting, knowing he'd observed me when I was in such a pitiful, helpless condition.

We stared and stared, his gaze as inscrutable as always. I'd never been able to tell what he was thinking, and I couldn't now. As for me, I felt as if my skin had been stripped off with a sharp knife, as if every bone had been crushed in a vice.

I'd given up so much to be with him, had sacrificed and surrendered so many little pieces of my character, that I didn't recognize myself anymore.

"What time is it?" I croaked, my voice sounding broken.

"It's eight o'clock."

I nodded. My outburst had happened around midnight, so I'd been out for hours, yet I didn't feel rested. Maybe genuine rest would never be possible again.

He entered, carrying a tray. He put it on the dresser, then walked over and eased a hip onto the mattress, perching hesitantly, as if I might start screaming again.

"I thought your stomach might be upset. I brought you tea and toast."

"Thank you."

He surprised me by adding, "I'm sorry."

I understood that he was talking about Kimberly. "Are you?"

"I didn't know you'd mind so much. You've been so eager to try everything else. I just assumed . . ." He let the sentence trail off, and he seemed flustered and abashed, which I'd never previously witnessed from him. "I didn't mean to hurt you. I never could."

I looked away. "I hate her."

"I didn't realize that."

"Have you been . . . been screwing her all along?"

"No. I ran into her yesterday and I invited her over. I wasn't thinking."

"I don't want to ever see her again."

"You won't."

I studied the far wall. "Swear it to me."

"I swear."

He climbed in behind me and cuddled himself to my back, an arm draped over my waist, his leg over mine. "Don't leave me over this, Meg."

A few tears dribbled down my cheeks, and I was amazed that I had any left to shed. "I don't know what to do now, Jordan."

"I'm begging you not to go. Tell me that you forgive me, that you'll stay."

"Oh, Jordan . . ." He made it difficult to remain angry. I didn't want to fight. I just wanted . . . what?

I had no idea.

"I love you, Meg. I've loved you from the first moment I met you."

It had been the same for me. "I love you, too."

"Marry me."

I frowned, not certain I'd heard him correctly. "What did you say?"

"Marry me. I'll spend the rest of my life showing you how much you mean to me."

"You're crazy."

"No, I'm very, very sane. Marry me, Meg. Say yes."

I closed my eyes, and I prayed that the right response would magically appear so that we could have a fairy tale ending, but there was only him and me and the mixed, potent feelings I had for him.

What if I declined? What if I stomped out and never saw him again? Could I bear it?

The answer was clear: I didn't have the strength or the will to go.

"Marry me," he repeated. "Let me prove how sorry I am."

When he was so repentant, how could I refuse?

Like a fool, I replied, "Yes. Yes, I will."

Chapter Twelve

*

W ith this ring, I thee wed."
Jordan slipped the gold band onto my finger, and I smiled, thinking he was the handsomest man in the world and I was the luckiest woman.

I ignored the empty room, not pausing to consider how weird it was that no friends or family had joined us. Once Jordan had proposed, there hadn't been any reason to delay, so we'd followed through immediately. There hadn't been time to order invitations, or book a hall, or speak with caterers, but I'd never craved a wedding like that anyway.

I'd convinced myself that the day was too special to share with anybody else. I wanted it to just be me and Jordan, soaking up all the excitement and happiness we could. The only other people in attendance were the judge and his bored clerks, who served as witnesses.

The ceremony sped by in a fog of bewilderment, and I could scarcely believe it was really occurring.

Much before I was ready, the judge closed his book, congratulated us, had us sign some papers, and it was over. We strolled out of his chambers, down the steps of the courthouse, and out into the rainy afternoon. We dawdled on the sidewalk, laughing over what we'd done, over having acted so impulsively.

Jordan halted and kissed me, right out in the open where anyone could see. When he was usually so reticent about public displays of affection, I took it as a positive indication for the future. The previous few weeks—which had been so awkward and stressful—were behind us, and this was a new beginning.

"What shall we do?" he asked. "This all happened so fast, I didn't plan a honeymoon."

"We can go later." I glanced up at the overcast sky. "Maybe somewhere sunny and warm?"

"Why not now? Let's swing by the apartment and make plane reservations. We can be in Mexico or Hawaii in a couple of hours."

It sounded like heaven, and it was on the tip of my tongue to agree, but I couldn't. I'd missed so much work, and I simply couldn't miss more without being fired.

I probably should have shrugged off my job. I was married, with a rich husband to support me, but the restaurant was my last link to the person I'd been before meeting Jordan, and I couldn't relinquish it.

If I didn't bake desserts at Mozart's, I wasn't sure what would become of me. Oddly, it seemed as if I'd be a woman with no past and no history.

But I couldn't explain my feelings to Jordan. He was more and more insistent that I give it up, while I was more and more adamant about staying on. The harder he pushed, the more I resisted. We were at an impasse, and on this day of all days, I wasn't about to quarrel.

"It's fine," I said, "if we just head home and lock ourselves in. You won't hear me complaining about having you all to myself."

"Actually, I'd rather drive out to the coast."

"To your beach house?"

"Yes. We'll have even more privacy."

I wasn't crazy about returning to the beach house. I had awful memories of it, and I still vividly recalled the terrible vibes I'd sensed, as if the property had been enshrouded in an evil cloud. The malevolence seemed to have trailed after me, making me behave in ways I never would have prior to my going there.

Though it was idiotic to imagine it, I felt as if the house had caused me to lose Steve, to lose Marie and Jeffrey, that it would ultimately cost me my chef's position. If I risked a second visit, what peril might befall me?

I shuddered to think.

"Let's do it," he urged. "My car will be here in a minute. We'll take off."

"Without stopping by the apartment?"

"The place is stocked with everything you could possibly require."

I remembered the packed dresser drawers, the red bikini, and the white robe. "I'd like to have some of my own clothes."

"You won't need clothes," he pointed out, chuckling. "I intend to keep you naked."

"Animal."

Just then his driver approached, maneuvering through the heavy traffic and pulling up next to us.

"Come on." Jordan took my hand and helped me in. "We can drink champagne all the way."

"I have to be back Thursday morning," I informed him.

He frowned. "What for?"

"I have to work."

He sighed, looking as if he was about to respond in a fashion I wouldn't like, but it was obvious that he didn't want to quarrel either. "Sure."

"Promise me that I can be back on time."

"I promise. Let's go."

Shortly, we were speeding down the Sunset Highway, the Portland metro area vanishing in our wake. The champagne was very cold, very good, and when we arrived two hours later, we'd finished—or rather, *I* had finished—three bottles. Jordan hadn't had more than a few sips, while I'd imbibed freely and was pretty buzzed. I hadn't meant to drink so much, but I'd needed liquid courage to face the dreaded house again.

Perhaps my first wifely proposal would be that we sell it and buy another somewhere else.

The notion that I could make the suggestion, that I now had the right to request and demand, was a bit overwhelming. In my rush to wed him, I hadn't considered all the ramifications. He was wealthy, and I'd married him, so I was wealthy, too. I could go anywhere, do anything, and it was thrilling to have so many options.

He opened the front door and let me in as the driver motored off, leaving us alone. As I walked through the living room, the silence was eerie, the isolation much more extreme than I liked it to be. I stared out the picture windows, gazing down the mountain toward the ocean.

There were no other signs of occupation, no homes, telephone poles, or electric wires. There were just thick woods, gray sky, and gray water as far as the eye could see.

Someone had been in and left chilled champagne and hors d'oeurves, which had me suspecting that Jordan planned to bring me here all along. Since the wedding had concluded, I'd been with him constantly and he hadn't made any phone calls, so he must have completed the arrangements earlier.

Why not simply tell me? Why keep it a big secret? Or was he worried I wouldn't want to come? That I'd want something different or more grand?

I suppose another female might have expected a glamorous destination, but not me. This wouldn't have been my choice, but merely because of my previous experience. If that occasion had been a tad more pleasant, I'd have been perfectly content.

He locked the door, sealing us in, and he came up behind me and started nibbling my neck. I'd skipped breakfast, missed lunch, and couldn't predict when supper would happen, so I was starving and gobbling canapés as if they were the last food on earth.

I'd moved to pop a bite in my mouth when he reached out and took it.

"Hey!" I protested.

"Do you have any idea how many calories are in those things?"

"No. How many?"

"Too many."

"So?"

"You're my wife now, Mrs. Blair. I can't have you getting fat on me."

I peered down at my torso. I was skinnier than I'd ever been, to the point of emaciation. "I don't think it's possible. Not when you keep me in bed all the time so that I never have a second to eat. And my name's not Blair."

"What?"

"I'm not changing my name to Blair."

"Of course you're changing it."

"No, I'm not."

I don't know what possessed me into the small show of defiance. It must have been the champagne talking, because I hadn't really thought about it. I had no great attachment to my surname of White, but some stubborn part of me was desperate to retain it.

"Your name is Meg Blair. From this moment on, that's what it will be."

"It is not."

"You're being ridiculous"—a muscle ticked in his cheek— "and I won't argue about it."

"Maybe I want to argue about it."

"It's nonnegotiable." He nodded toward the rear deck. "Go take your clothes off and get in the hot tub."

"The hot tub? I don't want to."

He snickered in a manner that sent chills down my spine. "Oh, Meg, haven't you realized it by now?"

"Realized what?"

"What you want or don't want doesn't matter to me at all."

"What a shitty thing to tell me."

"When you're deliberately trying my patience, it's difficult to be civil."

I couldn't conceive of anything more gross than sitting where Kimberly and Steve had to have screwed like rabbits. "It's my wedding celebration, too. I ought to have some say in how we spend it."

"You will have, but first I'm fucking you in the hot tub. When we were here before, I didn't have the chance."

"Did you want to?"

"I was mostly hoping to see you do it with Steve and Kimberly, but you refused, so we'll do it now. Just the two of us. Go!"

He was growing angry, swiftly reminding me how much he hated it when I didn't immediately obey, and I guess I was fairly drunk, because I was on the verge of throwing a full-fledged tantrum.

"Do you always have to have your way?"

"I'm much happier when I do."

"I've figured that out."

In a temper, I stomped to the deck and yanked off my dress. It was a silky, cream-colored sheath with a short jacket, and feminine lace around the neck, sleeves, and hem. I tossed it in a pile on the wood planks, not bothering to fold it or lay it on a chair, then I climbed into the tub and sank down, my back to the door. I wasn't about to sit there, gaping and anxious for the glorious instant he appeared.

An eternity passed before he joined me, and by the time he did the water had relaxed me, the champagne, too. I'd had plenty of opportunity to persuade myself that I was content to be Meg Blair, and that it would be fun to have sex with him in the hot tub.

When dealing with him, I needed to be more spontaneous. He was impetuous in a way that I wasn't. He'd settle on an idea and expect me to try it, whether it appealed to me or not. If I wanted to avoid continual bickering, I had to learn to be more accepting of his quirks and whims.

I was determined not to fight, especially on my wedding day. It boded ill for the future, had me questioning my decision, when I wouldn't reflect on it. The deed was done, and I could only move forward. I wasn't the wildest woman in the world, and I had to be more carefree, less ready to complain.

When he finally stepped outside, I glanced over and smiled. He smiled, too, and came bearing gifts: a freshly opened bottle of champagne and a plate of calorie-laden snacks.

I recognized it for the truce it was, and I was relieved.

"If I didn't know better," I teased, "I'd say you're trying to get me drunk so you can take advantage of me."

"My plan exactly."

He slipped in with me, and we made love for hours. He turned me and twisted me, rode me and fondled me, well into the evening and beyond. We kept on till we'd exhausted ourselves, and as we headed for bed I'd concluded that fucking in the hot tub hadn't been so bad, after all. I couldn't believe I'd been such a bitch about it.

I crawled on top of the blankets, my skin dry and chapped from the heat and chemicals in the water. He warmed some scented oil and massaged me everywhere, and I fell into a deep sleep.

When I woke it was late in the morning, and for once I felt

great. Other than a slight headache from the champagne, I'd had a full night of rest, I'd devoured a ton of munchies, and I'd pampered my poor, abused body. All in all, it was shaping up to be a terrific day.

I grinned and stretched, contemplating how easily I'd adapted to Jordan's affluent lifestyle. It would only get better; we would only fall more in love.

I heard him tiptoeing up the stairs and peeking in. He was wearing a pair of jeans that hugged his fabulous butt, his exquisite thighs, and he was carrying a tray of yummy-smelling food.

"Good morning," he said when he saw that I was conscious. "I'd about given up on you."

"The ocean air agrees with me. And the massage. I might have to insist on having one every day."

"You can. In fact, I can hire you a private masseuse if you'd like."

"You would?"

"Sure—as long as you let me watch when it's happening."

"You and your *watching*." I laughed. "Were you born a voyeur or have you evolved into one?"

He thought for a moment. "I think I came this way."

He sat on the edge of the bed and propped me up against the pillows, then he fed me bites of breakfast till I'd cleaned the plate. There were waffles and sausages, hash browns and fruit.

I pushed the last forkful away. "No more, no more. I'm stuffed."

"A bottomless pit." He rubbed my bloated stomach.

"I haven't eaten that much in an entire year. Did you cook it?" If he had, it was a side of him I hadn't seen. Other than brewing an occasional pot of coffee, he'd never so much as opened a drawer in his kitchen.

"Yes."

"Wow. A man of many talents."

He chuckled. "I'm fibbing. It was delivered earlier. My only involvement was nuking it in the microwave."

He put the tray on the dresser, then he returned to me and removed his jeans, letting me drool as he bared every delicious inch. He stroked his hands across my face, fluffing my hair.

"Who's Marie?" he asked much too casually.

My initial reaction was panic, my mind racing to figure out the safest reply, when it dawned on me that I was being absurd. There was no reason not to answer truthfully.

"She was—*is*—my best friend."

"You called her without notifying me."

My dread surged as I struggled to recollect that lonely evening when I'd been desperate to hear her voice, when I'd picked up the phone and dialed. I'd felt like a criminal. "I didn't know I needed your permission."

"You don't, but you see, I can't understand why you never mentioned the call."

"It was no big deal. She wasn't even home."

"So you weren't hiding it from me?"

"Of course not."

He stared at me, then very quietly he said, "Is there anything else you'd like to confess about that night?"

My heart dropped to the soles of my feet. I'd dialed Steve, too, and Jordan had to be aware that I had, so I don't know why I lied.

"No. There's nothing to tell. I called her, she wasn't there, I hung up. That's it." I glanced away as if I was embarrassed. "Look, if you don't want me to contact her again, just say so and I won't."

"Okay. I don't want you to contact her again."

I'd been positive he'd shrug it off, so I rippled with annoyance. "Why not? She's very nice."

"She's not a suitable acquaintance."

"And I'm so fucking great? Too good for my old friends? Why? Simply because I married you?"

"Yes. You're mine, and you have to conduct yourself in a manner befitting your new situation."

"She's very nice," I repeated.

"She's not an appropriate companion for you."

I was so angry that I nearly punched him, and I'm not certain why I didn't. If I hit him, he'd probably hit me back, and I wasn't in the mood for an out-and-out brawl.

What did it matter anyway? I hadn't made any attempts to maintain a connection with Marie, not even on the most superficial level. Jordan had ordered me never to speak with her again, but so what? After so many months had passed, if I knocked on her door, she'd slam it in my face, and I wouldn't blame her.

I tamped down my fury and slid away from him. "I'm going to take a shower."

"You do that."

I stomped into the bathroom, and I took my time washing so that I wouldn't have to confront him right away. Why couldn't I converse with him like a normal human being? Why couldn't I stick up for myself?

I wasn't a child, but I always let him treat me like one. I

never said what I really thought. I yielded to him in all things, until he was so accustomed to my acquiescence that when I dared to stand my ground it threw our entire relationship out of kilter. I had to establish some boundaries, some rules by which we were to interact.

I dried myself and tugged on a robe. I was eager to discuss the dilemma, which I viewed as a serious glitch in our marriage. We had to resolve it.

I proceeded into the bedroom and he was still there, lounging naked on the bed. He was waiting for me, aroused and stroking his erection.

"Come here," he said.

I went over without hesitating, but from the way he assessed me, I was almost afraid of him. He could be forceful and demanding, but he'd never lost his temper. Yet suddenly he seemed ready to lash out.

"What is it?" I asked.

"You shouldn't ever lie to me, Meg. Or try to conceal things. I'm very disappointed."

"What are you talking about? I haven't lied to you."

"Are you sure?"

"Yes."

"When you called Marie, who else did you call?" He paused, his incensed gaze digging deep. "Before you respond, you should remember that I live in a high-security building. I'm apprised of every piece of information that comes in or goes out."

I licked my lips, wondering why I was so scared, why I felt like I'd done something unforgivable.

"Steve," I finally mumbled.

"What did you say? I can hardly hear you."

"I called Steve."

"Yes, you did." He nodded, pleased. "I'm trying to figure out why you would. Can you explain it to me?"

"No."

"Were you lonely? Do you miss him? Were you hoping to get back together? What?"

"I don't know why." It was the truth. I'd felt so isolated that night, and it had been a stupid impulse.

"You have to be punished, Meg. You realize that, don't you?"

"Are you crazy? Punished how?"

"I'm going to show you."

"But I didn't even speak with him! When he answered, I hung up."

He stood, uncurling as if he was a cobra about to strike. "Lie down on the bed. On your stomach."

"Jordan!"

"Lie down."

I didn't run. I didn't scream. I didn't fight him, and I've never comprehended why not. Like an automaton, I did as he'd commanded. I crawled onto the mattress and stretched out, my face buried in the pillow. He was rummaging around, but I was too terrified to look and see what he was about to do.

He came over and braced himself with a knee on the bed, a foot on the floor, a hand between my shoulder blades.

"I'm doing this because I love you, Meg. You understand that, don't you?" I tried to rise up, but he pushed me down. "Because I love you. That's why."

He smacked a belt across my buttocks, the stinging strap

cracking over and over against my bare flesh. I clasped at the blankets and bit down, refusing to cry out. It didn't really hurt, not as much as I would have suspected. I was more humiliated than anything.

Luckily, it ended quickly. He tossed the belt away and climbed onto the mattress, his weight crushing me. His erection was huge and prodding into my thigh. He was excited by the whipping, by the violence.

"Tell me you're sorry," he whispered behind my ear.

"I'm sorry."

"I hate it that you make me discipline you."

"I'm sorry," I said again. "I didn't mean to upset you."

He entered me and fucked me forever, without a peep of protest from me. I was ashamed to have been beaten, to have been so complacent. Yet I felt so guilty, as if I'd committed an unpardonable sin, as if I deserved to be punished as he'd insisted.

When he finished, he pulled out of me and moved away without a word. I rolled onto my side, hugging my knees to my chest. With the brutality concluded, he was very solicitous. He covered me with a quilt, rubbed my back, and kissed my hair.

"This is all your fault, Meg," he advised. "You caused this to happen. Next time you'll think before you act. I just know you will."

"Yes, I will, Jordan," I replied like a puppet.

"Now, you need to rest and contemplate your behavior. We'll talk about it later."

He left me alone, and I wanted to die.

Chapter Thirteen

⊙⊙

I sneaked in the rear of the restaurant, hoping no one would notice me. I'd missed an entire day without calling and was now several hours past the beginning of my regular shift. I felt as if I was standing under a glaring spotlight, and I was certain everyone would see me slinking in and point a condemning finger.

I hung up my coat and grabbed a hat out of the cupboard, then walked into the kitchen as I tied an apron around my waist.

Jeffrey was stirring batter in a large bowl. He was up to his elbows in tasks, with pans spread everywhere, recipes started but not completed, cakes that had been baked but not frosted. He glanced at me, his expression stony, but he didn't comment. As if I was invisible, he continued with his mixing.

"I'm sorry I'm late," I murmured as I moved to the table, trying to decide the best way to leap in and assist.

"Are you?" His tone was bland, as if my presence or absence had ceased to matter to him.

"We were at Jordan's beach house." When this drew no response, I stupidly babbled, "It's out on the coast. There was some confusion as to when our driver was supposed to pick us up."

I didn't add how kind and remorseful Jordan had been after our quarrel, or how passionate the interlude had turned out to be after the initial fight. He'd treated me like a queen, had pampered me till I was exhausted from his constant attention.

Our driver hadn't made a mistake. I'd overslept, after having stayed up—celebrating—for nearly forty-eight hours. We'd enjoyed full use of every bed, every chair and couch, every patch of carpet and floor. I had rug burns on my back, bites and bruises on my chest and thighs, and one particularly nasty mark around my neck from where Jordan's interest in tying me up had gotten out of hand.

I'd concealed it with a turtleneck sweater, which was bulky and hot, but I couldn't have worn a regular shirt.

Jeffrey shrugged and whirled away, intently and deliberately studying a shelf of pans.

Feeling like a fool, I repeated, "I'm sorry."

"No, you're not." He spun to face me. "You're busy with your fancy apartment and your fancy clothes and your fancy *chauffeur*, and you can't be bothered about anything else."

"That's not true."

"I've known you for a long time, and I never realized you could be so fucking selfish."

"I'm not."

He rolled his eyes. "Whatever."

"I got married on Tuesday." He was the first and only person I'd told, and I'd assumed my announcement would set the discussion on a different course, that he might congratulate me or tease me about my wedding night.

"Why would I care that you married some rich, perverted psychopath?"

"I can't believe you'd say such a thing. You've never even met him."

"God, you are so blind."

My cheeks flushed bright red. "I thought you'd be happy for me."

"The mayor's brunch is tomorrow. We're doing it. Did you forget?"

"No," I fibbed.

"And we have three other private parties to cater over the weekend."

"I know."

"I've been working extra, covering for you, *lying* for you when you're not here."

"I appreciate it."

"No, you don't. All of a sudden you think the whole fucking world owes you a favor. You don't think anybody has a life but you."

"Why are you so pissed at me?"

"Take a look in the mirror, Meg. Take a fucking look in the mirror."

He stormed out of the kitchen, the door slamming with his exit, and his hostility stunned me. I'd never seen him lose his temper before. I wasn't sure how to deal with this side of him, wasn't sure if I should go after him or if I should let him cool down.

Two waitresses walked in, carrying dishes for the dishwasher. As if I was a pariah, as if I had a disease they didn't want to catch, they ignored me and swiftly scurried to the front room.

I was shaking, not certain what to do next, when Pam emerged from her office. We stared and stared, then she said, "Meg, would you come in here, please? I need to speak with you."

"I've got a lot to do." I gestured to the numerous projects Jeffrey had started, indicating all the chores that were more important than her. My eyes pleaded for sympathy, for more time.

"This will only take a minute."

Not giving me a choice, she pulled her door wide, an obvious command. Like a felon to the gallows, I trudged over, and I could barely keep from falling to my knees, from clutching the lapels of her jacket and begging for mercy.

She didn't sit, and she didn't invite me to sit, either. We stood, gaping, the moment too awkward for words.

"What's happened to you, Meg?" she finally inquired, her disappointment evident. I was so ashamed.

"I'm sorry." It seemed that all I ever did these days was stumble around apologizing.

"I feel like I don't know you anymore."

"I'm still the same. I just . . . just . . ."

She held up a hand, cutting off any explanation. "Don't make excuses, okay? We're a little beyond them."

"I meant to be here. I really did!"

"Yesterday was Jeffrey's parents' fortieth wedding anniversary. When you didn't show up, I simply couldn't spare him."

It had been so long since I'd truly talked to Jeffrey that I hadn't been aware of any family gathering. "There was a party?"

"A very big one, but he couldn't attend. Because of you, Meg. Because you weren't here when you were supposed to be."

"Oh God . . ."

She evaluated me as if I was an alien species, then she reached out and tugged at my turtleneck, drawing it down so she could see the mark Jordan had left when he'd squeezed the rope too tight.

"Do you want to tell me about this?" she asked.

I yanked away, the collar snapping into place. I was mortified, unable to look at her, so I gazed at the far wall. "We're in love, Pam. We're so in love."

"I'm positive you've convinced yourself that's what it is."

"It is!"

"Whatever you're doing with him, whatever is occurring between the two of you, it's only going to get worse and more dangerous. You understand that, don't you?"

There was a rational part of my brain that recognized her advice as necessary and valid, that I should heed her warning, but it was drowned out by the independent and stubborn part of me that was too proud to admit I was wrong.

"It's different with him," I insisted. "It's so passionate."

"Really?" Her detached assessment wandered down my body. Was she wondering what other secrets were masked by my clothes?

"We're newlyweds," I proclaimed, as if that justified every wicked thing that was transpiring.

"Are you?" she blandly replied.

I smiled, tremulous, hoping—once again—for congratulations, but none was forthcoming. "We've been celebrating and getting a bit wild. That's all."

She nodded, her shrewd concentration delving through bone and pore. "What should I do with you, Meg? I'm curious as to your opinion."

"Give me another chance."

"I've given you dozens."

"Give me one more."

"This job used to matter to you, but it doesn't anymore."

"I love working here!" I declared. "I'll do better! I was late today, but it's the last time. I swear!"

"I think you're sincere, which makes this all the more sad."

"I am sincere!"

"Actions speak louder than words. You know that." She paused, appearing resolved. "I've never fired anyone before, and I don't want to fire you."

Her message was extremely clear. "But you don't want me to keep on, do you?"

"No."

She was throwing me a rope, letting me hang myself, and it was almost a relief to have it over.

"Actually"—I was completely humiliated—"I just came by to notify you that I'm quitting. That's the reason I stopped in. To inform you of my decision once and for all. I'm so busy now, being married and . . . well . . . you know."

"Yes, I do know."

She walked around her desk and opened the drawer. My final paycheck had been prepared, and she handed it to me.

"I'll miss you," she said, but there was no hint in her expression that she would.

"I'll miss you, too. Thanks for the opportunity you gave me. I appreciated it very much."

"You're welcome. Best of luck in your next endeavor."

It was such a cold separation, I couldn't bear it. My employment with her was my sole tether to all that was real and normal. There were so many other things I wanted to tell her—how proud I'd been to work for her, how distressed I was about leaving—but any confession was pointless.

I had turned to go when she murmured, "Be careful, Meg."

"I will."

I stepped into the kitchen, which was suspiciously empty, and in a daze I lurched away, not even remembering to grab my stuff. No one rushed out to say good-bye. No one waved or wished me well.

I stood in the parking lot, a heavy shower drenching my hair and shoulders, but I didn't notice. I felt invisible, so lacking in substance that I could have floated away.

There was a bar across the street, and I proceeded over to it. My cell phone was in my coat, in the restaurant, but I'd never go back to fetch it, so I asked to use the bar's. I called Jordan, but he was in a meeting and couldn't come for me. He sent his driver. I'd never thought of the man as a chauffeur, and couldn't now, especially after Jeffrey had hurled the term at me as if it was an epithet.

I went out into the deluge and dawdled on the curb. After a lengthy wait, the car sped up. Soaked and freezing, I climbed in and watched the streets fly by as we headed downtown. Once we arrived at our building, I checked in at the security desk, took the main elevator up to the penthouse, and let myself in.

I edged over to the windows and peered out across the valley, eager to be soothed by a view of Mount Hood, but it was shrouded in gray rain clouds. It seemed as if I was trapped in a glass bubble above the city.

It was very, very quiet, and I was all alone.

Chapter Fourteen

'D o you like it?"
I twirled in a circle, showing Jordan the dress he was about to buy me. It was another slinky sheath with a low neckline. I had dozens of similar dresses hanging in my closet. Since we never went anywhere, it was silly to have so many, but he had such fun picking them out that I couldn't complain.

"I don't know if that shade of blue is your color." He glanced at the fashion consultant who'd brought several items up to the penthouse. "What do you think? Maybe if she was blond?"

"Definitely," the woman answered. She understood who was paying and had agreed with his every comment.

"I'm not dying my hair again," I protested. "Not just so I can look better in a blue dress."

The woman hovered, fluffing my auburn hair, which was now down to my shoulders. "You have such big, brown eyes. A touch of blond might be good on you."

"It's not happening."

"You could have a few lighter streaks added," she persisted. "It would really galvanize your appearance."

"Not happening!" I repeated, and I glared at Jordan, giving him a frown that indicated I was finished with modeling clothes.

He made his final choices and ushered the woman out. As the elevator whisked her away, I was almost sad to see her go.

I rarely talked to anyone besides Jordan, rarely went out on my own. He didn't like to shop in stores, relishing the privacy and service his money afforded him. When I needed something, he'd have a salesperson drop by and he would stay around to help with my selections. He had exquisite taste, so I didn't mind, yet he was with me most of the time.

If he had a meeting and I was left to my own devices, I was nervous about going out, which was stupid. I was an adult, and I was certainly capable of climbing in the elevator, but the longer I lounged in the penthouse, the more difficult it became to set out on my own.

Jordan liked to know where I'd be and when I'd return, and he'd question me so relentlessly regarding any plans that it wasn't worth the bother of an excursion. Although he never came right out and said he didn't want me to leave the apartment, I was always wary.

If I engaged in an activity that didn't involve him, I had to endure his silent censure, and I'd learned the hard way not to incur his wrath. He had a temper and he wasn't afraid to unleash it. I was determined not to do anything that would encourage him to lash out at me ever again.

I was docile, I was complacent, I was obedient, and I was

sickened by all my groveling. I spent many hours alone, so I had plenty of opportunity to ponder the rut into which I'd fallen, but I couldn't figure out how it had occurred. The best I could deduce was that everything mattered to him more than it did to me. He wanted me to behave in a specific manner, and it was so exhausting to go against him.

He searched through the pile of new clothes and retrieved some lingerie.

"Put this on," he said. "I want to see you in it."

I knew the outfit would lead to kinky sex, followed by a marathon in bed. At that moment I wasn't feeling particularly amorous—it being three o'clock in the afternoon—but I didn't argue.

"With heels?"

"The black ones I like so much."

"I'll be out in a minute."

I proceeded to the bedroom, thankful for the solitude as I tried on the black bra and garter belt, the black stockings to match. I added some dangly earrings and bright red lipstick, the type Jordan insisted I wear, then I walked out without pausing to study my reflection in the mirror.

I was fully aware of how I looked: like a drug addict wasting away, like a very skinny prostitute.

"Very nice!" he murmured as I entered the living room.

"Do you think so? I'm not too thin?"

"You know how much I like you in black."

I couldn't keep myself from smiling. Even though the constant sex was draining, I remained eager to make him happy. He loved seeing me naked, undressing me, arousing me, spoiling me. He made me feel special, as if I was the most incredible woman in the world. I couldn't comprehend why he had such a knack, or why I was such a sucker for his attention, but my heart still pounded whenever he gazed at me with lust and affection.

"There's something I need you to do for me." He clasped my hand and escorted me to one of the rear bedrooms.

"What?"

I wasn't too keen on his surprises, and I dragged my feet, in no hurry to go along like a lamb to the slaughter, but I couldn't halt our forward progress.

He pushed open the door, urging me in, and I was dismayed to see a video camera on a tripod next to the bed. The blankets had been removed, leaving just the sheets, but they'd been changed to red satin. I visualized myself lying on them in my lingerie, how riveting and decadent it would be.

"I want to tape us," he explained.

"No." I stepped toward the hall.

"You didn't even ask how come."

"That's because you couldn't give me a good enough reason."

He grabbed my arm, preventing my retreat. "I want this, Meg. I won't let you say no."

"Why? Why make me do these things I hate?"

It was our first quarrel since the day at the beach house. He'd apologized so profusely, had been so fucking *sorry*, had sworn never to strike me again, and I'd believed and forgiven him.

"You shouldn't assume I'm *making* you do anything," he maintained. "You should participate because you're my wife, because you love me and it's important to me."

"But . . . why take pictures? I don't understand you."

"I like to watch, you know that. What could be more arousing for me than to have us on film?"

"Why not just get your head in the moment and enjoy it while it lasts?"

"I'd like to observe you from a distance—in a manner that I can't when we're actually doing it. The only other way I could arrange it would be to invite another man up here, to have him fuck you while I sat in a chair." He cocked a brow, as if daring me. "Would you let me?"

"Are you out of your freaking mind? Of course, I wouldn't."

"Then let me tape you."

"No."

I yanked away and marched to our bedroom, amazed that he didn't yell or demand. Perhaps our relationship was evolving. He trailed after me, not contrite but not angry, either. He pulled me onto the bed, and we had a rough and rowdy bout of fucking that concluded with a blow job I now condescended to give him whenever he didn't get his way.

He viewed it as a consolation prize. I viewed it as a small price to pay so that I didn't have to do something even more dangerous or distasteful.

After we finished, he poured me some wine, and we snuggled while I drank it. Very quickly, I drifted off, and when I woke it was the next day, the apartment very quiet.

I was groggy and disoriented, my head throbbing, my stomach queasy. I stood up to go to the bathroom, and I was hit by such a wave of vertigo that I had to hold onto the nightstand for balance.

As my vision cleared, I realized that I was naked. When I'd

fallen asleep, I'd been wearing lingerie, but it was now strewn across the floor. I was confused by the sight, struggling to remember disrobing, when I noticed that the video camera was positioned at the foot of the bed, the cables running to the electrical outlet in the wall.

I froze, my thoughts so muddled that it took several seconds for it to register that he'd taped me. He'd taped me! In light of my excruciating headache, he'd probably drugged me, too, so that I was unconscious through the whole disgusting episode.

Feeling violated, I shivered, wondering what he'd done — what *I* had done.

I assessed my body, checking for marks or scratches, but I didn't see anything out of the ordinary. My innards were sore and protesting, but considering how aggressively we had sex, it was common for my feminine parts to be hurting. I couldn't tell if I'd been abused in some horrible fashion or not.

I probed my foggy memory, trying to recollect some hint of what had happened, but there was no flicker of awareness.

"Motherfucker," I muttered to myself, then I called, "Jordan!"

There was no answer, and I shouted for him again, but all was silent.

I didn't own a pair of jeans anymore — Jordan had pronounced them inappropriate attire for me — so I tugged on slacks and a blouse, then tottered out to search for him, but the place was empty.

"Bastard!" I seethed. "Bastard, bastard, bastard . . ."

I had to find that tape. I had to find it! I couldn't imagine what might be on it, and I absolutely had to know. I wouldn't rest until I did.

This was the last straw for me. I'd find that fucking tape, then I'd leave. I had no notion of where I'd go, or how I'd get there, but if I had to live on the streets, I fucking would. He would *not* be allowed to treat me this way!

Like a crazy woman, I went from room to room, methodically examining each nook and cranny, but I couldn't locate it. I ended up in his office, his sanctuary, his haven. He'd never told me to stay out of it, but I felt that I had no business prying into his affairs or snooping through his records.

I rummaged through every shelf, every cabinet, and as I prepared to poke around in his desk, I was frantic. It seemed so wrong to look inside that I glanced over my shoulder, worried that he had a hidden camera somewhere, that he'd know what I'd done.

I explored anyway, and in the bottom drawer, underneath all the junk, I found dozens of copies of the charity calendar in which I'd posed. Despite how Pam had once claimed otherwise, he always swore he'd never seen it or bought it.

I pulled them out and was shocked to also stumble on the publicity photo of me that had been in the *Oregonian*. It had been carefully cut from the paper, then laminated so that it wouldn't tear or fade. Below it was another string of photos, eight-by-ten color closeups of me from when I was still with Steve, when my hair was short, brown, and spiked.

In every shot, I was standing in the parking lot behind Mozart's and gazing at someone off to my right. I was laughing as if the other person had said something funny. I studied the pictures, hoping for a clue that would tell me when they'd been taken, but I'd been at the restaurant so often that it was impossible to guess. I couldn't recall the specific instance when

I'd been in that exact spot, or to whom I'd been speaking, and suddenly the information mattered very much.

When I'd initially met Jordan, I'd suffered from the constant and eerie impression that he'd sought me out for a reason, that crossing paths with him hadn't been an accident. Over the intervening months the feeling had waned, but with this discovery, I wasn't sure of what was true and what wasn't. My prior suspicions reared up and I was scared by the implications.

Had he seen me in the paper and become obsessed? Had he been following me? Had he hired someone to spy on me?

I remembered his sister-in-law's creepy remarks about how I should never let him dye my hair blond, which he'd just proposed I do the previous afternoon when I was trying on dresses. I'd ignored his suggestion, deeming it an idiotic comment made in passing, but now I was questioning everything.

Could he have murdered his first wife, Brittney? Her sister certainly believed that he had. What if she was correct? Was he a deranged psychopath who lured gullible females into his affluent world then killed them?

Maybe he'd killed scores of women. Maybe he'd kill me!

In my stressed condition, a thousand other terrifying and absurd scenarios coursed through my mind, and I gave them free rein. Every facet of our relationship seemed devious: the bizarre sex, my gradual isolation, the intense focus on me and my appearance.

I put the calendars and photos back in the drawer, nearly hysterical, convinced that I was about to be murdered. He'd latched on to me for a sick purpose that I couldn't unravel, and very soon my body would be floating in the Willamette River.

I was desperate to escape. Tape or no tape, I had to flee. I'd pack a bag, grab what cash I could scrounge, then vanish.

I raced to the hall when I heard the private elevator winging toward the apartment. Jordan was the only one who had a key to use it, was the only one who would step out of the carriage. My heart skipped so many beats that I was positive I'd drop dead.

The elevator stopped and he exited. I was paralyzed with fear, gaping like a deer caught in the headlights, while he strolled in casual and calm as ever, impeccably attired in a dark blue suit.

"Hey you," he greeted me as he paused to hang his coat in the front closet. "I'm surprised you're up. When I left this morning you were sleeping so hard, I couldn't wake you. I figured you'd be out of it till supper."

"Where's the fucking tape?" I hissed, ready to throw myself at him, to wrestle him to the ground and steal it.

At my furious question, he scowled as if a deranged stranger had sneaked in while he was away. "What tape? What are you talking about?"

"You fucking recorded us when I told you not to."

"I did not."

"You son of a bitch! Don't lie to me! The camera is right there!" I pointed to the bedroom.

He crossed to me, approaching cautiously as if I was a dangerous beast that might attack, and I have to admit that I felt a bit wild, that I could lunge for his jugular.

"I set up the camera but I never turned it on."

"Liar!" I screamed. "I know you did it! I know!"

"For Christ's sake, Meg, what's gotten into you?"

He came closer, closer, and I lurched away, calculating whether I could rush past him, whether I could make it to the elevator and have it whisk me off before he prevented me.

I didn't even have on shoes! How could I get away?

We were separated by only a few feet, and I warned, "Don't touch me."

He sucked in a shocked breath. "What is the matter with you? Have you gone completely out of your mind?"

"If you didn't tape me, what's with the camera?"

"I thought you might wake up, that I'd be able to coax you into it."

"You drugged me! That's why I slept so long. Don't deny it."

"God, what is up with you?"

"I found the pictures," I accused.

"Pictures of what?"

He was so confused, and his composure rattled me. He'd asked if I'd lost my mind. Had I? Were isolation and boredom driving me insane?

"You have copies of the calendar I was in. The newspaper, too!"

"So?"

"Why do you have them?" I shrieked.

"Because you're my wife and I love you. I collected a few copies."

"I want to go outside. Right now! I want to go shopping."

"So go." He shrugged. "I'm not stopping you."

"You never let me go anywhere."

"I've never said a word about any such thing."

Whenever I went out without him, he always seemed so upset. Was I imagining his displeasure? Was I imposing some weird and unnecessary restriction on myself? What was wrong with me?

My back was pressed to the wall, and I was trembling so violently that I was amazed I didn't collapse. I'm sure I appeared to have escaped from an asylum.

"You want me to dye my hair blond!"

"So sue me. I think some blond streaks would look good on you."

"You made Brittney dye her hair blond, too."

"Brittney . . . as in my first wife?"

"Yes!"

"I did not. She was born blond." He frowned, scrutinizing me. "Are you feeling okay? Should I call a doctor?"

"I'm not crazy!" I shouted, even though I sounded like I was.

He reached for me, circling his arms around me and pinning my hands to my sides. I was in a frenzied state, and I fought and kicked and cursed.

When I'd been snooping in his office, my suspicions had seemed rational and plausible, but as I hurled them at him, they merely seemed to be the rantings of a woman who was on the verge of a mental breakdown.

"Let me go! Let me go!" I demanded, but he wouldn't.

He dragged me to the bedroom and onto the bed, and he kept his arms wrapped tightly around me, his legs, too. I struggled and squirmed until I ran out of energy, and I fell to the mattress, my face buried in the pillow. Gradually he released his grip, and he eased away and went to the bathroom. I heard him rummaging in the medicine cabinet, then he returned and sat down.

"What's happening to you, Meg?"

"I don't know," I answered, too ashamed to meet his gaze.

"Should I phone somebody? Maybe if you talked to someone, you'd—"

"No." I didn't need a psychiatrist—or perhaps I did.

"For a minute there you acted like you were afraid of me. What brought this on?"

"I guess I'm tired."

"I guess you are." He leaned over and jiggled a bottle of prescription pills. "Why don't you take one of these?"

I stiffened. "What is it?"

"Jesus! It's just Xanax. I hurt my back last year and I had some left over." He paused, and I was fairly certain he was laughing at me. "It's a muscle relaxer. It'll calm you down."

He opened the bottle and shook two of the little pills into my palm. I studied them carefully, reading the tiny inscription, furiously pondering whether he could fake a pill, whether it might be something more hazardous disguised as something mundane.

He fetched me a glass of water, and without argument I swallowed the medicine, then I closed my eyes. I was exhausted from my outburst, so weary that I wondered if I'd ever crawl out of bed again.

He stood. "See if you can rest a bit."

"I will."

He walked around, shutting the drapes and dimming the lights, then he tiptoed out and I was all alone with my tormented thoughts.

Chapter Fifteen

ᚖᚖ

During one of my infrequent forays into the outside
world, I ran into Steve's mom on a downtown sidewalk.
I didn't recognize her until she'd passed me, and without hesitating I called out to her.

"Madge?" I said as she kept on in the opposite direction.

She halted and turned, her expression puzzled. Evidently
she had no idea who I was, which wasn't surprising. There
was nothing about me that resembled the Meg she'd known.

I was dressed in a pair of expensive slacks, a silk blouse,
and heels, a leather bag dangling from my shoulder. My
makeup was subtle but striking, my nails manicured, and my
hair was a longer brown, with fashionable blond streaks wo-
ven through it.

After my insane outburst at Jordan, I'd felt like a fool, so
on my own and with no prompting from him, I'd dyed it as a
quiet apology for the accusations I'd hurled.

As usual, he'd been correct about what the blond color

would do for my appearance: I looked fabulous. Different again, but fabulous.

"Yes?" Madge asked tentatively.

"It's me, Meg."

"Meg?" She frowned, not able to place me.

"Meg White, remember?"

"Oh, yes, hello, Meg. How have you been?" Her displeasure at seeing me was obvious.

"I've been great. How are you?"

"Fine." She thoroughly assessed me, taking in the pricey clothes, the chic hairstyle. "You've changed."

"I got married."

"I know."

The information had to have come through Steve, and at realizing that he was aware of what I'd done, I suffered a huge wave of regret. After all these months, it still felt like such a betrayal. I was still ashamed.

How had he learned of it? Was he saddened by the news? Did he have lingering feelings for me? Or had his fond memories been erased by the cruel way I'd left?

"How's Steve?" I couldn't resist inquiring.

"He's terrific."

"Well . . . good."

There was an awkward pause, then she said, "So tell me, Meg, has your husband's wealth bought you any contentment?"

When she'd previously been so friendly, I was aghast at the discourteous remark, and I insisted, "I didn't marry him because he was rich."

"Really?"

"No."

"Why did you, then?"

"I fell in love."

"I'm relieved to hear it. I'd hate to think that you'd done it for money." Her tone was scathing, indicating that she absolutely believed I'd wed him for his fortune.

I was desperate to defend myself. "I didn't mean for it to happen."

"Steve's a big boy. He's over it."

I was crushed. "I'm glad."

"He's engaged to Marie."

"Marie?"

"Yes, and they're a perfect match."

Her underlying message was loud and clear: She hadn't thought I was a suitable partner for Steve and was ecstatic that he'd moved on. My knees were weak.

"Are they happy?" I pathetically asked.

"Of course."

"I'm happy, too," I chirped like an annoying bird.

"I'm sure you are."

She evaluated my clothes and hair again in a manner that told me she didn't imagine I was happy at all. In fact, she looked as if she pitied me.

"It was nice to see you again," I offered.

"Nice to see you, too," she blandly responded, then she spun and continued on.

How dare she be so rude to me! I was tempted to go after her and let her have it. I'd enlighten her as to all the ways she was wrong, of how I was tickled with the choice I'd made, but I couldn't muster the necessary outrage for a confrontation.

Since that awful afternoon when I'd grown so unhinged,

I'd been regularly taking Xanax, so nothing rattled or upset me. I was absurdly calm, and I didn't care that I was. If I was feeling nervous or out of sorts, which was much of the time, I'd reach for a little white pill.

When I was in the apartment by myself for lengthy stretches, the walls would close in on me, my dread would rise, and I would self-medicate. If I decided to go outside, I'd be so anxious, on the constant verge of a panic attack, that I'd swallow one before I left and another after I got back.

I'd quickly gobbled up Jordan's old prescription. Full bottles—with my name on them—magically appeared without my questioning where they'd come from or why they'd arrived.

The drug had worked wonders. It soothed me, as it was supposed to do, but it also painted a fuzzy hue on the fringes of my life so that I didn't examine anything too hard or worry about anything too much. I was floating in a fog, the days and nights drifting by.

Madge had vanished, and I pulled myself away from staring at the spot where she'd been. I was only a few steps from home, and as I turned to enter our building, I saw that Jordan was down the block and coming home, too. He'd been watching me with a strange expression on his face, but as our gazes connected, he smiled.

He approached and linked his fingers with mine, leading me around the corner to his private elevator so that we wouldn't have to maneuver the security desk in the lobby.

The doors shut, and the carriage took off with a whoosh that always made me dizzy. I grabbed the handrail.

"I hate how fast this thing rises," I told him.

He chuckled. "You've pointed that out before."

"I'm just thankful it's enclosed, so I can't see how high we are."

"You're scared of heights?"

"Yes."

"You do pretty well in the penthouse."

"Haven't you noticed I never linger next to the windows?"

"No."

"Well, I never do."

To say that I was "scared" of heights was putting it mildly. If I stood in the center of the living or bedroom, I was okay, but if I went over to the glass and peered down at the street so far below, my vertigo was intense.

He kissed me, then he very casually inquired, "Who were you talking to?"

"When?" My meeting with Madge had been so stilted that I didn't consider it a conversation. I couldn't figure out to whom he referred.

"Down on the sidewalk. You were with somebody."

It was a sign of how the pills were working that I didn't pause to ponder my reply. "It was Steve's mom."

"Did the two of you have lunch?"

"No. I just bumped into her."

"And how is Steve?"

"She said he's great. He's engaged."

"Good for him. Is his fiancée anyone you know?"

Gradually, it dawned on me that candor was a mistake, and I wasn't about to mention Marie. "A mutual acquaintance."

"Any regrets?"

I laughed as if it was the funniest thing I'd ever heard. "No."

The elevator opened, and as we started into the apartment, he yanked me into his arms and studied my eyes.

"You wouldn't lie to me, would you, Meg?"

"No, never."

"Because I'd be very angry."

"I know you would be."

"Tell me again about Steve's mom."

Instantly I rippled with alarm, and I was positive I looked guilty as hell.

"There's nothing to tell," I insisted.

"You *bumped* into her."

"Yes."

"So I don't need to call her to find out the truth."

"Don't be ridiculous."

He nodded toward the bedroom. "Go take off your clothes and climb into bed."

"Why?" As if I had to ask!

"I want to fuck you."

I thought about arguing, about protesting that it was the middle of the afternoon and I didn't feel like it, but I knew better than to decline or disagree. Any perceived rejection would set him off.

"Should I put on some lingerie?"

"No. I want you naked."

"All right. Give me a minute."

As I walked away, my smile fled. I dawdled, removing everything slowly while I struggled to remember what it had been like at the beginning of our affair. I'd been so excited to be with him, so ready to try whatever he suggested.

Where once we'd been so hot, so together, his interest in me now seemed tedious and extreme. I was too weary to have sex all afternoon and into the night. When he was in the mood, he could go for hours, till I was bruised and sore and begging him to stop, and the more I complained, the longer he'd keep on.

His opinion was that I, as his wife, couldn't refuse him, which was bullshit. I could refuse, but it didn't do me any good because he never listened. The only result I garnered from resistance was more of what I didn't want in the first place, plus a dash of his temper thrown in.

I often wondered if he had any clue as to how my loathing for the sexual act was growing. Every time he demanded my participation, the notion was more abhorrent.

What would he say if he knew? How would he react if I flat out fought him and meant it? I couldn't bear to learn the answer.

Just as I'd gotten naked, he came in. He was naked, too, and he was very hard, his erection jutting out. He crushed me to him, cradling my face and stroking his thumbs across my cheeks.

"My beautiful Meg," he said, "do you have any idea how much I love you?"

"Yes."

"No. You couldn't possibly understand."

"I love you, too," I responded as was expected, though I was curious as to what the words were supposed to signify. How could our skewed interaction be described as love?

"Do you really?"

"You know I do."

Very sweetly, he kissed me, then he reached to the dresser and retrieved a bottle of lotion.

He held my palm and squeezed some into it. "Rub this on my cock."

I wrapped my fist around him and smoothed it all over. "Like that?"

"Yes. Now lie down on your stomach."

I hesitated, not certain of what he intended. There was a dangerous gleam in his eye that I didn't like. "What are you going to do?"

"You'll see."

"I want you to tell me first."

"Lie down!"

Anxious and wary, I scrutinized him, but ultimately I stretched out on the mattress. He climbed on top of me and stretched out, too, his slippery cock on my anus. He wedged a pillow under me so that my butt was a bit higher in the air.

"I'm doing this because I love you," he whispered.

"You're scaring me."

"Just relax," he said. "It will be over in a second."

"Jordan!"

I'd never previously been sodomized, so I didn't comprehend how much it would hurt or how unpleasant it would be, although I have to admit that he was very restrained when he could have been quite rough. He took his time, entering me inch by inch, letting me adjust to each increase in the awkward penetration. Eventually he was fully impaled, and as he thrust, I froze, my fingers clutching at the sheets. I prayed it would end as rapidly as he'd promised.

Luckily, he'd been honest—for once—and he finished and pulled out. Desperate to be alone, to come to grips with this new twist in our relationship, I curled onto my side, my knees hugged to my chest. I hoped he'd leave and was dismayed when he snuggled himself to my back.

I was relieved to be facing away from him so that he wouldn't observe my rage. At that moment, I hated him more than I'd ever hated anyone.

"That was very nice," he murmured.

"Yes, it was," I fibbed.

"I enjoyed it very much."

"So did I," I fibbed again, thinking that he had to sense my disgust.

"I may want to do it occasionally."

I took a deep breath, let it out, recognizing that it would be hazardous to disagree. "Sure."

"I was very gentle with you, but I could have made it painful."

"I realize that."

"If I was angry, it could be excruciating."

Was he warning me? Was he threatening me? He'd once told me that he'd sodomize me if he ever needed to hurt me, so I could only assume this was his way of proving that he'd been serious, and that he had enormous power over me.

He shifted away and off the bed, but he leaned over and caressed my hair, my shoulder.

"I've been very patient," he said, "about permitting you to go out on your own, but after today I can't allow you such freedom. I can't trust your judgment."

"What?"

"From now on, you'll have to request permission—after you've informed me of where you're going and who you're going to see. And I'll have to check up on you to guarantee that you've behaved appropriately."

So . . . my worries about his putting limits on my conduct hadn't been my imagination after all.

"It was an innocent encounter," I dared to retort.

"Perhaps. Perhaps not. But it won't happen again, will it?"

"No."

"I want to take a shower, then we'll have sex all night so that I can show you how much I love you."

He headed to the bathroom and turned on the faucets, and I rolled onto my back and stared up at the ceiling. I didn't know how I could keep pretending everything was fine. Something had to change, but how could it?

The thrill was gone, and the hot, torrid passion that I'd relished didn't seem so hot anymore. It seemed violent and demeaning, and I couldn't generate the necessary enthusiasm to continue.

If I tried to refuse him, he didn't exactly force me. I was always afraid of what he might do, so I'd end up acquiescing on my own. After, I'd be upset, but would carry on as if nothing odd had transpired, and the cycle would start all over.

How long could I persist before I was really and truly insane? How far and how hard could he push me till I simply went crazy?

I had to leave. But where would I go? And how would I get there? It was becoming obvious that the chances of him blithely letting me split were slim to none.

I was very still, listening as he bathed, as he finished and shut off the water. I sighed. It would be a very long night.

Chapter Sixteen

With a bland smile on my face and without divulging any of my true thoughts, I endured all the sex and bondage he chose to inflict. At dawn I fell into an exhausted sleep, and when I woke many hours later, I was alone, but miserable.

I had a bad sore throat and I ached all over. Imagining that a shower would cure what ailed me, I dragged myself into the bathroom, but I finished quickly and I crawled back to bed, trembling uncontrollably.

It occurred to me that I had a temperature, that I should take some Tylenol, but I was too sick to get up. Soon I was forced up by having to race to the toilet. I puked and puked, then stumbled to bed again, clutching a garbage can in case my stomach continued to rebel.

I was incoherent and delirious, my dreams tortured, my conscious moments confused. The apartment was empty and Jordan gone to who knows where. I could have phoned his cell and begged him to come home and nurse me, but we didn't have that sort of relationship.

I was so isolated. I desperately needed help, but there wasn't a single person I could ask to assist me. I felt invisible. If I vanished, no one would know. No one would miss me.

Vaguely, I heard Jordan enter the apartment, and I was lucid enough to recognize that it was night, that I'd passed the whole day and evening needing him, but having no idea where he'd been.

He fussed in the living room and kitchen, then eventually he tiptoed to the bedroom and peeked in to check on me. Instantly he was at my side, stroking and soothing me, holding me as I vomited, as I shivered with chills or baked with fever.

He stayed with me every second, leaving only to fill a water glass or wet a cool cloth. He was there as I napped or when I stirred. He contacted a physician, who actually made a house call and diagnosed me with a severe case of the flu. Then we were alone again, and another three days flew by in a haze before I started to feel remotely better.

As my condition improved, I was so grateful to him. He'd been so sympathetic, so devoted. I was like a shipwreck survivor he'd rescued, or maybe a beaten puppy that had been adopted by a kind master. Any disloyal opinions I'd previously had were washed away by my realization of how deeply he cared for me.

When the chips were down, when it really mattered, he'd stepped forward. Any other man would have fled in horror, but not him. He'd stood by me.

How could I fail to be indebted? How could I refuse to do the things that brought him such pleasure?

My illness had pitched me to a new level of dependency, had altered how I'd perceived his affection as slowly suffocating me. He demanded so little of me and he was so committed to my welfare. Why was I being so obstinate about giving him what he wanted?

It wasn't as if I hated the sex we had. I was merely uncomfortable with some of it, but I could swallow my dislike and forge on. For him. To make him happy.

Didn't I owe him? Hadn't I been proven wrong — repeatedly — about him and his motives?

The morning I finally felt well enough to get out of bed, I staggered to the bathroom, and as I stared at the mirror, I was stunned by my appearance. I was no longer a woman who could afford to lose any weight, yet for nearly a week I hadn't eaten. I was so malnourished that I looked to be on the verge of starving to death. I could count my ribs, my hip and cheek bones protruded, and my breasts were practically nonexistent.

For some reason, Jordan had broken down and bought me jeans and sneakers, and I tugged them on and went to the living room. He was in jeans, too, and an expensive pair of hiking boots. I smiled wanly and eased onto the couch. My knees were shaky, and I could barely keep down bland food.

"Are you going out?" I inquired, tamping down an irrational panic attack at the notion of being by myself.

"You can use some fresh air," he replied, "so *we* are going out."

"Where to?"

"I thought we'd head up into the mountains."

Despite my feeble state, I'd grab at any chance to escape the apartment, so I was thrilled. He stuffed my arms into a jacket and escorted me down to the street. His driver wasn't waiting, and we got into an SUV, with Jordan behind the wheel.

It was weird to be sitting next to him in the front seat of a car. I never had before, and it was so . . . so *normal*. I'd been chauffeured so often that it now seemed commonplace, rather than unusual, and I'd forgotten that ordinary people did such ordinary things.

Traffic was light, and very quickly we were out in the country and motoring toward Mount Hood. I dozed off and on, but I awoke when we steered off the highway and onto a bumpy gravel road.

We rumbled to a stop, surrounded by thick woods.

"Where are we?"

"East of the city. Up in the National Forest. I want you to see the view."

He circled to the hatch and retrieved some ropes and other gear, and he attached the items to an elaborate belt. He looked very buff, very fit, and I imagined this was how he'd appeared when he'd been a young surfer in California, when he'd drawn his first surfboard design.

He helped me out, then ushered me down a rustic trail. After a short walk we were spit out on a cliff. It wasn't that high—probably only a hundred feet to the ground below—but I hung back, content to peer out at the horizon without getting too close to the edge.

The scenery was spectacular, and I was tickled that he'd brought me, that he'd assumed I'd enjoy it. We were above the Willamette Valley, gazing down on Portland, the Columbia River meandering off to our right. For once the clouds were gone, the sky a fairy tale blue, and off in the distance I could see two snow-capped volcanoes.

As I dawdled, Jordan was busy with his ropes, tying them to a stout tree trunk. After checking knots, checking bindings, he came over to me and clasped my hand. Though I dragged my feet, he led me toward the cliff—as if he meant to jump over and take me with him. I tried to yank away, but he wouldn't let me avoid whatever dubious fate he'd concocted for me.

"I don't like this," I complained.

"I know you don't, but I want you to do it anyway."

"I'm scared of heights. I get too dizzy."

"It will pass."

"It won't!"

"It will."

He lugged me nearer, the drop-off approaching with disturbing speed. I started to struggle in earnest, but my poor health prevented me from putting up a decent fight.

"What are you doing?"

"I'm going to rappel to the bottom. And you're going to do it with me."

"I don't want to."

"You have to conquer your fears, Meg. You can't permit them to rule you."

"I think this is a perfectly legitimate fear, and I don't have any need to *conquer* it. I'm okay with it ruling me."

He chuckled. "I'm not. Come on."

He showed me some sort of harness and obviously expected me to climb into it.

"What's that?"

"I'll strap you to me the whole time. You can't fall."

"No."

"I don't like it that you're afraid. We'll work you through it, and when we're finished heights won't ever bother you again."

"But I don't care that I'm afraid."

"I do."

Ignoring my distress, he put the harness on me, ensuring it was secure. I stood in a trance, unnerved, but not sufficiently recovered to keep objecting. I was nauseous and weak, and I couldn't believe he'd presume I should engage in such a strenuous activity. From the tenacious set of his shoulders, I could see how determined he was, and unless I initiated a full-blown argument that I wasn't strong enough to conduct, I wouldn't be able to dissuade him.

Why would he deliberately frighten me? If I'd been feeling better, he couldn't have pushed me into it. Did he get off on the fact that my capabilities were diminished? Was he titillated by his ability to terrify me?

I was torn about how to proceed. I'd just decided that I'd try harder to make him happy. But wasn't there a limit? How far should I go in my efforts to please him?

Eventually we were hitched together, the rope looped through his legs and around his waist, and he was walking backward, taking me with him. I didn't participate, but I didn't resist, either.

"Shut your eyes," he suggested. "It will be over very fast."

When it came down to it, I couldn't leap off on my own. I was paralyzed with dread, trembling so violently that I couldn't move a muscle. No matter how he coaxed or cajoled, I couldn't take the final step.

He grew impatient and lifted me, carrying me over. We dangled in the air, swinging on the rope, our bodies careening toward the rock face, almost hitting it, then swinging away. My head was spinning, my vertigo severe, and my heart was pounding so intensely that I thought it would explode.

I squealed with alarm.

"Are you afraid?" he inquired.

"Very."

"Why?"

My response was primal and didn't need explanation, but I said, "I'm worried we'll fall."

"We won't."

"I realize that mentally, but it doesn't make this any easier."

"You have to rely on me, Meg. You have to accept that I'll always hold onto you. I'll never let you go. You understand that, don't you?"

"Yes, I understand."

He kept us there, suspended, for what seemed like an eternity, his disturbing words sinking in, then he lowered us inch by excruciating inch.

As my toes touched solid ground, my knees buckled and I collapsed, but we were still hooked together, his arms around me.

"I've got you," he said.

"I know."

"See? You were silly to be frightened."

He detached the harness and I dropped to the dirt, panting and shedding a few tears of relief. I retched into the weeds, but my empty stomach had nothing to heave up. While I caught my breath and my dizziness receded, he was surveying the cliff.

"Can we leave now?" I begged.

"No."

"Please? I'm really tired. I want to go home."

"We're going to climb up the trail and do it again."

"Again?" I was aghast.

"Yes. We'll keep on till I can tell that you're no longer scared."

I glared at him, trying to figure out what was swirling around inside his deranged mind. Was he crazy? Was I?

"We might be here forever."

"That's okay," he replied in all seriousness. "It's early. We've got all day."

"Oh, Jordan . . ."

"Let's do it. Up you go."

I felt too awful to let him torment me, but I was too sick and frail to stop him. How had I tumbled into such a mess? I'd just sworn that I'd be a more obliging wife. Why was I already reneging on my vow?

There didn't seem to be any answer that made sense. He was who he was, while I wasn't at all certain who I was. Not anymore. I'd become a needy, dependent female with no discernible personality. Apparently I was more content than ever to follow where he led.

Without a peep of protest, I slipped my hand into his and he pulled me to my feet.

Chapter Seventeen

❧

"Flex up on your knees."

"Like this?"

"Yes."

I was on the bed down the hall, the one that had never been remade after the red sheets arrived. I was wearing the black lingerie he'd bought when we'd fought over whether or not I would allow him to tape me.

He was peering at me through the camera lens, struggling to get the angle just right.

"Let me see your best pout," he directed.

I made a small moue with my lips. "How about this?"

"Perfect. You have such a *fuck me* mouth."

"I do?"

"Oh yes." He approached, leaned over, and kissed me long and slow. "That's why I like it so much when you suck me off. Every time I look at you, I get hard."

It was a crude comment, but it thrilled me all the same. I was still stupid enough to be tickled that he desired me, that he was never sated. I might be weary of the sex we had, but he always wanted more.

He puttered around, adjusting the lights, the pillows. Finally he was ready, and he shut off the lamps so that the room was dark except for where I was illuminated in the middle of the mattress.

He glanced through the viewfinder to be sure it was centered, then he hit *record*. The camera whirred.

"Give me that look again," he said. "Your pout."

I showed off for him, and he groaned with aroused pleasure, so I increased my vamping. I'd decided to do this, and if it killed me, I would make the most of it.

"God, you're good at that. Lower the strap on your bra." I did, and he added, "Now the other one."

I gazed into the lens, but my mind was a thousand miles away. I was remembering a beautiful spring afternoon when I'd lived with Steve. He'd played on a softball team, and I'd sat in the bleachers, cheering him on during a game. It was a nice memory, a solid memory.

I shifted from side to side. For over an hour, I'd been kneeling as he'd made his preparations, and I was stiff and sore. I wanted to lie down, but he said, "Don't move. You'll be out of the shot."

"My legs are tired."

"I'll be finished very soon." He pressed a button to zoom closer. "Unhook the front of the bra, then shake your hair off your shoulders."

Without thinking I obeyed, facing him, hiding any nerves or awkwardness. I was very opposed to the situation, but he'd asked so politely, had explained how much it meant to him, and I'd capitulated—after he'd promised I'd only have to do it once and never again.

He was eager to proceed, and I was naked with him ninety percent of the time anyway. How could it matter if it was in the flesh or on tape? I'd survive the episode and the contentious issue would be resolved.

"Squeeze your breasts," he instructed. I massaged them over and over, then he said, "Pinch your nipples."

I kept on and on, letting him watch, letting him record. It really wasn't so bad. When we'd begun, I'd been very anxious, so I'd taken an extra dose of Xanax. I was relaxed and serene, and none of it bothered me as it should have.

"Lick your finger," he told me, "then stroke it across your nipples." He studied me through the viewfinder, then murmured, "Yes . . . yes . . ."

He nodded toward the pillows. "You can sit back now."

"Thank you."

I flopped down, relieved to stretch out. I wasn't completely recuperated from my bout with the flu, and I was starting to worry that I'd never return to full health. Before I'd gotten sick, I'd been terribly run down, and it was taking me a lot longer to recover than it should have.

"Slip off your heels and work your stockings down."

I complied, flashing plenty of skin, being overly effusive. I wanted to be certain he was satisfied with the end product so that he could never tell me I hadn't given it my all, that he needed me to do it again.

I stripped till I was dressed only in the garter belt, and very slowly I slid it off, making the moment last. I was reclined, staring up at the ceiling, and I casually caressed my breast. I was floating; I didn't care about anything.

"Open your legs."

I glared at him. "No."

"Do it. Don't argue."

"Aren't there any limits here?"

"No. None."

"It's gross. I don't want to."

"Meg, it's a raunchy, X-rated home movie. Let me see some cunt."

He zoomed in even closer, and very reluctantly I submitted. Eventually, he'd tie me up. If I refused now, he'd simply force me later when I couldn't stop him. Wasn't it better to do it on my own terms?

I spread my knees. "How's this?"

"Great. Now pull your lips apart."

I reached down and did as he'd requested, and I pretended it wasn't me, that he was filming some other, unknown woman. A prostitute, maybe. Or maybe Kimberly. I was positive a whore like Kimberly would revel in this type of act.

Luckily, it was over quickly. He shut off the camera to pour me some wine laced with the aphrodisiac he liked, and I didn't utter a word. I was accustomed to taking it, and it heightened the mood so that everything was more intense. Considering how blasé I was about having sex with him, any encouragement was welcome and necessary.

Surprisingly, I didn't recall much of what transpired after that. I don't know if it was a combination of the aphrodisiac and the Xanax, or if I had an adverse reaction after my being so ill, but whatever the cause, I passed out. As he secured my wrists to the headboard, as he laid down and fondled me, I was awake, but seconds after that everything was a blank. I didn't have time to ponder the implications of him having given me something else, something stronger.

I slept like the dead, and when I next stirred it was the following afternoon. I was in my own bed, nude and curled into a ball. I didn't remember how I'd gotten there, if I'd walked on my own or if Jordan had carried me.

The apartment was very quiet, and I listened for him but didn't hear him, so I figured he was out. I rolled over and my entire body protested. I felt as if I'd been run over by a truck or crushed by a steamroller.

I yanked at the covers and sat on the edge of the mattress. I was dizzy and nauseous, and I peered down at my torso, hunting for evidence of what had been done to me. Everywhere I looked there were new bruises and scratches. My insides ached, my anus was very sore, as if I'd been sodomized all night and someone had used a baseball bat.

I shuddered with dread. What the hell had happened?

I stumbled to the bathroom, feeling hung over—even though I wasn't—and swallowing down the urge to puke. I went into the shower and stood in the hot water, letting it sluice over me as I struggled to recollect details, but I couldn't focus on any aspect beyond his binding my hands.

That part was extremely vivid.

You always make the knots too tight, I'd objected.

You always complain.

You're just being mean.

It's more fun if you can't get away. You know that.

The rest was a blur.

I finished washing and put on comfortable lounging clothes then headed to the living room, determined to find the video. I'd been down this humiliating road once before and was alarmed about where it would lead me.

I'd never located the first tape and Jordan had sworn there wasn't one. I'd gone off like a lunatic while he'd been totally calm and rational, and I was still embarrassed over how I'd behaved. This occasion would be different. There was definitely a tape, and I'd see what was on it. Depending on what I learned, I'd proceed accordingly.

I didn't have to search very long or very hard. When I entered the kitchen to brew some coffee, it was on the counter. There was a bouquet of flowers next to it, and a note from Jordan that said, *Thanks for doing this. It's very sexy. Can't wait to hear what you think. At meetings all day. Will be back for supper.*

I stared as if the video cartridge was a poisonous snake. It hadn't occurred to me that he'd simply set it in plain sight, that he'd invite me to watch it. I was afraid to pick it up.

I fumbled around in the kitchen, making coffee, drinking it, drinking some more. I nibbled on a piece of dry toast, trying to quell my churning stomach.

Ultimately, I ran out of reasons to delay. I grabbed it, marched into the den, and slipped it into the machine.

It was a typical home movie, probably better than most due to the lighting and quality of the camera, but there was no question that it was porn. The beginning had shots of the bed, the sheets, then I appeared on the screen in my black lingerie.

As I saw myself, I was so stunned that I hit the pause button. I wasn't sure it was me. I understood that I'd grown very thin, that I had brown hair with blond streaks, that it was longer and parted on the side, but I hadn't realized the extent of how much I'd changed or how awful I looked.

I was most shocked by how wan and unhealthy I seemed to be. My hair was dull, my skin pasty and gray. My eyes were empty, like a streetwalker's or a heroine addict's.

First thing every morning and last thing every night, I gazed at myself in the mirror, so how could I have failed to notice the true state of my pallor and emaciation? I'd pictured myself as very slender but fit, happy and glowing, but obviously I'd blocked reality.

I was gaunt and haggard, and I had no idea why Jordan kept insisting I was attractive. When I'd deteriorated so completely, why would he still lust after me?

I hit *play* again and the video restarted. I observed as my clothes fell away, as I fondled my breasts, as I dropped onto my back and removed my garter belt and stockings. I even sat through the closeups he'd taken of my crotch, which I found to be gross and insulting, and I hadn't a clue why the obscene pose appealed to him.

Finally, I arrived at the mystery moment. He was tying my wrists and feeding me the laced wine. I was about to fill in the gaps of what had occurred, but my anxiety spiraled and I shut off the machine. I was sweating like a pig, my pulse racing. Fleeting images skipped through my mind, like someone darting about in my peripheral vision.

Jesus! Why was I so upset? What didn't I remember? Apparently, my subconscious had a flicker of awareness and it was bubbling to the surface.

Terrified but resolved, I forced myself to keep going. Initially Jordan and I had sex as we always did, with him continuing on and on, never having to come. He turned me and positioned me so that there was plenty of tits and cock, plenty of thrusting and arching up.

I was awake, which perplexed me. Though I wasn't exactly animated, I wasn't passed out either. Occasionally I made sarcastic remarks for the camera, but my memory of the content was a blank.

There was a break in the film, as if Jordan had stopped for a bit, and when it commenced again the action was focused on my mouth. I was giving him a blow job and the view was zoomed in. Gradually the lens panned out, revealing more and more of our torsos, and when it fully showed us, the man with me wasn't Jordan.

I didn't panic. I sat very still, assessing and considering. He was a younger version of Jordan, maybe thirty or so, but very handsome with Jordan's same dark hair and buff body.

But it wasn't Jordan.

I went over to the TV and knelt down and put my fingers on the guy's chest, as if the truth might magically wing its way through the glass and into my hand.

I had transient recollections of him—or I *thought* I did. It seemed that he'd been very friendly, very cute, and when Jordan had brought him into the room and introduced him, I'd grinned and said hello.

Or had I?

My God, was I crazy after all?

I was too astounded to do anything but watch to the end. He came in my mouth, he came in my ass, and then he was gone and I was alone in the bed and sleeping peacefully. The video clicked off, and it was over, the screen black.

I rewound and watched it all again, trying to decide if Jordan might have faked it somehow, or if it was real.

Would Jordan have done this to me? Could he have done this to me?

After the day he'd tormented me out on the cliff, I'd come to grips with the fact that he was capable of any treachery. He'd often mentioned that he was eager for me to have sex with others, and I'd always refused. Had he simply forged ahead?

The prospect that he'd drugged me and done this without my consent was so evil that I couldn't quite accept it had happened. Yet what else could I possibly believe? The evidence was right before my eyes. I couldn't ignore it.

I knew him so well now, so much better than I had in the early months of our relationship, and I'd developed a keen insight into his personality. There were things he wanted from me, things he needed from me, and when I wouldn't voluntarily give them, he'd take them. He could be ruthless in getting his way.

I returned to the kitchen and read his cheery note.

He had to be aware of how furious I'd be, but he'd proceeded anyway. Was he insane? Was I?

I had to do something drastic to escape from him, but what? Why hadn't I left already? What was the matter with me?

If I asked him about the strange man, he'd have a perfectly logical explanation. Like a good little wife, I'd listen attentively as he convinced me that nothing was wrong, that I was mistaken about what I'd seen.

His words on the cliff rang in my ears: *I'll never let you go.*

I shuddered, certain he'd meant them in a more dangerous

fashion than I could ever comprehend, so I had to be extremely cautious. I couldn't just pick up and leave.

I had to figure out how to vanish without a trace.

I took another Xanax, then poured myself some wine and sat down to wait. I was positive I knew what he'd say, but I had to hear a justification from his own lips. Then I had to start making careful plans.

Chapter Eighteen

❧

When I heard the elevator, I was very calm. After my meltdown over the previous tape—or nontape, depending on what I believed—I was determined to behave rationally during the pending confrontation.

As Jordan entered the apartment, I was mostly concealed in a chair in a dark corner of the living room. He was dressed in loafers and jeans, and I observed silently as he hung up his leather jacket, as he leafed through some mail on the table in the foyer.

He strolled past me to stand by the window and stare out at the city, the lights across the valley coming on as twilight waned. He looked rich and successful, a man in charge and in his element. He looked so freaking *normal*. When he seemed so ordinary, how could I accuse him of hideous conduct? Wouldn't a monster have horns or fangs?

He turned and saw me huddled in the shadows.

"Hey, you," he said, "it was so quiet, I didn't think you were here." He walked over and pulled me to my feet. "I missed you. I couldn't wait to get home so we could fuck all night."

He tried to kiss me, and I shifted away so that he bussed my cheek instead.

"Did you see the video?" he asked. "I left it out for you."

"Yes."

"You were so hot! After you went to bed I watched it over and over. I've been hard ever since. But I wish your breasts were bigger. We should consider a breast enhancement."

"A breast enhancement!"

"Yes. I like how slender you've grown, but your bust has totally disappeared. I'd love you to be bigger on top. Not huge—just bigger."

I pried his arms from around my waist and stepped away. "We need to talk."

"How about if we fuck first? Then we can talk till you're hoarse."

By now I was used to his crudity. If he wanted to have sex, he had a one-track mind and couldn't be discouraged. Initially I'd relished the extra dose of passion as much as he did, but I couldn't figure out how I'd persuaded myself that it was fun. I hated who I'd become since marrying him, and he was dragging me farther and farther into a void where I didn't care to be.

I was drinking too much, taking too many drugs, and letting myself go. Somewhere along the way, *I* had ceased to be important. It was all him, him, him. I had decided to work at making him happy, but no matter what I tried, it wasn't enough. I had to get the hell away from him, but I had no clue how to hide where he would never find me.

I moved behind the couch so that there was a barrier

between us, and I challenged him. "Who was the man in the tape with me?"

He was puzzled. "The man?"

"Yes. Who was it?"

"Ah . . . me?"

"Don't lie to me. Not about this. Who is he?"

"I don't have any idea what you mean."

"You fucking know who he is! Don't deny it!"

"I don't know."

Just that rapidly, we were at the same impasse where we'd been with the prior video. He was composed and concerned, seeming to have no hint of why I was upset, while I was ranting like a lunatic.

"You drugged me, then you brought somebody up here to have sex with me." I was so angry I was trembling. I had no memory whether that was what had actually occurred, but it sounded true. "I demand to know who he is."

He studied me, then he shook his head, appearing harassed and miserable, as if he felt very sorry for me. "Sometimes, Meg, you really scare me."

"Why is that?"

"Because you get these insane notions and there's no dissuading you."

"This is not *insane*. Who the fuck was it?"

He sat on the couch, a foot casually tossed over his knee. "Start from the beginning, would you? I'm trying to make sense of what you're saying."

"You know very well what I'm telling you."

"I don't." At my dubious scowl, he added, "I'm serious!"

His nonchalance rattled me. I knew what I'd seen and I knew

what he'd done, but when he was so unflappable, it was difficult for me to be positive I was correct.

If he was lying, how could he be so relaxed? Could anyone
be that cold?

"I watched the tape," I seethed.

"I take it you didn't enjoy it."

"There's another man fucking me. He looks like you, but
he's not *you*." I took a deep breath, struggling for patience.
"Who is he, and why did you do that to me?"

"You think there's another man on the tape?"

"I *know* there's another man on the tape."

"Where's the tape now?"

"It's still in the VCR."

"Are you going crazy on me, Meg? Because when you act
like this, it makes me worry about being married to you. I'm
continually asking myself: why am I?"

His glare was so condemning that all of a sudden I felt as if
I was in the wrong. I was speechless with fury, and there were
a thousand ways I wanted to shout at him that I was fine, that
he was the one who was deranged, but he'd stood and marched
out of the room.

By the time I realized he'd proceeded to the den, that he intended to play the video, I had to race after him. As I skidded
to a halt, he was at the TV, and peered at me over his shoulder.
He hit the eject button and the cartridge popped into his hand.

"Is this the tape, Meg?"

"Yes."

"Sit down."

I slid down onto the sofa, alarmed over what I'd set in motion.

He was livid, while I'd grown tentative and unsure. How had he turned the tables on me? I was the victim! At least, I'd thought I was.

He pushed the cartridge into the machine, and he sat, too, ignoring me, his thumb on the remote as he scrolled past the first section where it was just me on the bed. Ultimately he arrived at the pertinent scene, but when the camera zoomed out, I was with Jordan.

Jordan . . . Jordan . . . Jordan . . .

It was his cock in my mouth, his body stretched out next to mine.

I was so confused!

I frowned and rubbed my temples. "No, that's not right."

"What's not *right?*" he scathingly inquired.

"You weren't there before! I swear!" I was desperate to un-ravel the mystery, but my reasoning was muddled beyond be-lief. Had I completely lost my mind?

"Give me the remote!" I insisted.

He shrugged and handed it over, and I fast-forwarded to the end, then rewound. Frantically, I moved forward and back, forward and back, hoping in vain to confirm that there'd been someone else with me, someone other than Jordan, but there was no one but him.

I punched STOP and stared at the rug.

"Are you satisfied?" he asked.

"I know what I saw. He was there!"

"Why persist with this garbage?"

My trembling increased as I fought to find a plausible an-swer, and with each passing second I was more agitated.

I'd seen it, hadn't I?

"You switched the tapes," I finally muttered. "Before I entered the room, you switched them."

"What?"

"You're deliberately trying to make me think I'm crazy."

"If you keep saying idiotic things like that, I won't have to try very hard."

He rose, an annoying expression of sympathy flooding his eyes.

Pensive and disturbed, he observed me as I leapt up and began to pace.

What was happening to me? I had no idea. Perhaps the drugs and alcohol, coupled with my recent bout of the flu, had left me unbalanced.

"You know, Meg," he started kindly, "I mentioned this previously, but I dropped it after your last episode."

He pronounced *episode* as if it was a dirty word, and I halted and whipped around. "What are you talking about?"

"You need to see a psychiatrist."

"Are you nuts?"

"No, but I'm terrified that you might be."

"Fuck you!"

"We have to discuss this. We can't keep putting it off."

"I don't need a shrink!" I screamed. "I am not crazy!"

But of course the louder I shouted, the more unhinged I sounded.

"I'm wondering if I shouldn't check you into a hospital. Just for a few weeks or months. You've been under a lot of stress. It might help if you had a long rest."

"I don't need to go to a mental hospital."

"You couldn't prove it by me."

I stormed out and down the hall, to the extra bedroom where he'd done the filming, but all evidence of the event was gone. The bed had been remade in its regular cream-colored sheets and they were covered by the usual bedspread. A quilt was neatly folded across the end.

The camera and wires had been removed, the spotlights dismantled, and the cords he'd used to tie me to the headboard had vanished. The space was clean and sterile, like every other bedroom in the apartment, like every bedroom in the entire world.

He came up behind me and laid a palm on my shoulder, but I flinched away and walked farther down the hall. I pressed my forehead to the wall, liking how cool it felt against my heated skin. I was in anguish, overwrought, and sincerely questioning whether—as he claimed—I was out of my mind.

After a lengthy silence, I murmured, "I need to get a job. Maybe if I wasn't here alone all day, I wouldn't be so whacked out."

"I realize that you'd like to, but you're not in any condition to work."

"What do you mean?"

"You drink constantly. You're shitfaced on Xanax. Plus, you haven't fully recuperated from when you had the flu. I doubt you'd be up to it."

"I want to get a job!"

"Fine," he said, his capitulation almost too easy. "Do what you want. Do what will make you feel better, but I'm warning you that I can't take much more of this. The next time you go off, I'm calling a doctor whether you want me to or not. I'll have you hospitalized. Do you understand?"

"Yes, Jordan, I understand."

For a painful, charged moment, we were frozen in place, then he spun and stomped off. He went to the front room, grabbed his jacket out of the closet, climbed in the elevator, and it swept him away.

I huddled there, my cheek on the wall until I was sure he wasn't coming back, then I trudged to the den and crawled onto the couch. The tape was still in the machine, the remote on the cushion. I clicked the *play* button and watched, transfixed, not certain what I was hoping to discover.

I scrolled to the appropriate scene, but as the camera panned up my body, there was no strange man having sex with me. It was just Jordan. Just Jordan all over again.

Chapter Nineteen

⚭

Despite what Jordan wanted me to believe, I wasn't crazy. I'd simply gotten myself into an awful mess and I had to get myself out of it. The first moment I was alone in the apartment, I went into his office, desperate to locate the original tape he'd made, as well as any other evidence that would tell me more about the man I'd married.

With hardly any searching, I stumbled on an entire folder about the incident in which his wife, Brittney, had died. I read the official reports, surprised that I'd waited so long, that I hadn't been more curious.

The facts seemed very straightforward. He and Brittney had been sailing near the Columbia River bar, a hazardous spot in northwest Oregon where the large river spills into the Pacific Ocean, which creates dangerous currents and swells. According to the Coast Guard, Brittney had been washed overboard by a huge wave that swamped their boat.

Jordan had been pitched into the frigid water, too, and they hadn't been wearing life jackets. She drowned, while he was rescued by a passing ship. Her body was found the next day.

I remembered her sister, Ashley, who was convinced that Jordan was a murderer. The evening I met her, I'd assumed her accusation was merely grief talking, that she blamed Jordan for something that wasn't his fault. After assessing the details of the accident, I was confused by her rage and couldn't figure out why she felt Jordan was responsible.

But I had to ask her. She was a bit high-strung, but she wasn't stupid. There had to be a reason why she was so adamant, and I had to learn what it was.

Her last name and number were listed in the file, and I memorized them as I started plotting how I could escape the apartment so I could speak to her.

Jordan and I had reached an uneasy truce. We had sex constantly, the rough sessions not waning in length or intensity, but there was little pretense remaining that we were doing it out of passion or affection. There were specific behaviors he expected me, as his wife, to perform, and I couldn't imagine what he'd do if I refused. Actually, I *could* imagine, so I kept participating.

I'd finally accepted that his attachment wasn't normal. His obsession and coercive tactics terrified me.

We hadn't discussed the tape or the anonymous man again. Nor had he raised the prospect of a mental hospital, but when I thought about him putting me in such a place, I shivered with dread. I understood that his mentioning it had been a sly and cunning threat, his goal wedged between us like a hangman's noose. If I angered him or if he grew tired of me, he'd follow through.

I wasn't familiar with the commitment process, and I didn't

know what authority he had over me as my husband, but I was afraid that it might be more than I wanted him to have. If he tried to have me sent away, I'd have to save myself. No one else would.

Day by day, I was more isolated and frightened. My credit cards had disappeared from my wallet, the phones had suddenly quit working, and the cash he had once stashed in a drawer for me—which often amounted to hundreds of dollars—had vanished.

I'd asked him about the phones. He claimed he hadn't liked the calling plan he'd purchased and was changing it, but the new account was never activated. The reality was that after the night of my meltdown, I'd forged ahead and mailed out several job applications, and the lack of phone service guaranteed that I couldn't be contacted by a potential employer.

He'd given me a cell phone instead, but that way he could track every call, as the bill would reveal what numbers I'd dialed. I wasn't positive, but I suspected he could probably use it to discover where I was, too, so I tried to leave it off unless I was in a spot where I didn't care if he found me or not.

As to the credit cards, he'd bluntly told me that I was spending too much money, which was a bald-faced lie. I never charged anything, but he said I was going through a depressive phase so it wasn't a good idea for me to have them, that I couldn't cure my boredom and unhappiness by shopping.

I hadn't uttered a word of complaint, but I realized that he was narrowing my world, making me more dependent on him, ensuring that I didn't have the means to run away.

I'd persuaded him to let me visit the library once a week, and apparently he felt it was a safe venue, one where I couldn't get into too much trouble. Sometimes he accompanied me, but other times, if he was busy, I walked there by myself. I enjoyed being outside, being around others, but I always sensed that I was being watched, as if he'd hired a private detective to spy on me.

Occasionally he showed up while I was perusing the stacks. He'd pretend that he'd merely stopped by on a lark, but I understood that he was checking on me, making certain I'd really gone where I said I was going. He was also subtly emphasizing that I couldn't get away from him.

He hadn't been violent again, but still, I was extremely spooked. Out on the cliffs, he'd warned me that he'd never let me go, and in the interim he was slowly driving me mad.

I couldn't comprehend why I didn't just sneak off. Portland is a large city, and I could have slipped into a crowd and been swallowed up. Or I could have marched over to the ramp on the freeway and hitchhiked away. I could have been hours away before he learned that I'd split, but I never acted.

I kept telling myself that I needed a smarter plan, and I kept waiting to think of one. It seemed too haphazard to simply take off, and I was sure I'd fail—especially if he had someone following me. It was a sign of his power over me that I feared he'd find me and bring me back, and if that happened I'd be in grave danger.

If I was going to flee I had to consider all the angles, had to calculate all the risks.

There was a pay phone next to the bathroom in the library, and it took three separate trips before I dredged up the courage to dial Ashley's number, and two more after that before she was home and picked up.

She hadn't sounded particularly surprised to hear from me, nor had she been curious as to why I requested a secret meeting, why she would have to sneak to the library and never tell anyone we'd spoken. She seemed to know why—which was definitely unnerving.

Without my suggesting it, she arrived in disguise, a scarf covering her hair, sunglasses shielding her eyes. She'd worn nondescript clothes, dark slacks, a gray jacket, plain loafers. She might have been anybody.

We huddled in a corner on the main floor behind the reference section, where I was mostly concealed but could observe the entrance, and there were no windows where someone on the street could snap a picture with a telephoto lens. Yet whenever the front door swung open, I flinched, convinced I would see Jordan crossing the threshold and about to catch me.

"Thank you for coming," I whispered as she approached.

"You're welcome."

The moment was so surreal. She pulled a book from the shelf and leafed through it, pretending to read it, while my attention was glued to the door. It felt as if we were actors in the middle of a bad spy movie.

"I wanted to talk to you about your sister."

"He killed her," she declared without hesitation. "As sure as I'm standing here, it was murder."

"But I saw the reports and—"

"I don't care what the Coast Guard said. He killed her and he got away with it."

Her voice had risen with emotion, enough so that a patron in a nearby chair flashed us a censorious glance. We drew closer together.

"Why do you say that?" I pressed.

"She was terrified of him, but he had her head so screwed up that she was afraid to leave. The last time she was able to contact me, she'd decided to ask for a divorce, and the next thing I knew she was dead. He drowned her, then tipped the boat somehow and claimed it was an accident."

"But it *was* an accident!" I protested, playing devil's advocate. "Everybody said so. Even the experts."

"Jordan is a world-class swimmer. He even went to college on a scholarship. Were you aware of that?"

"No."

"For years, as a teenager, he worked as a lifeguard in Southern California. He's comfortable in the roughest ocean waves, but Brittney couldn't swim a stroke. She was scared of the water and she'd told him that she was. He used to torment her over it. The bastard always made her go sailing when he knew it scared her to death."

I thought about confessing my fear of heights, about how he'd forced me to rappel off the cliff, but I didn't mention it.

She retrieved two photos from her pocket and laid them on the page of the book she held in her hand. "Here. This is her when she graduated from college, and then later, after she'd been married to him for a while. It was taken just before she died."

The first picture showed a pretty, plump, smiling brunette, but the second didn't seem like it could be the same woman. She was scrawny and pale, appearing anorexic. Her eyes were haunted, too big for her thin face. And her hair was blond.

I looked exactly like her, except for the fact that my hair was still mostly brown with a few lighter streaks. Jordan kept pestering me to go all blond.

"Jesus," I murmured, and I shuddered.

"You've become her." She pulled out another photo. "This is his mother."

It was a grainy shot from a newspaper, but the resemblance to me and Brittney was uncanny. She was an emaciated, frightened-looking blonde, too.

"You think he's turning us into his mother? That's sick."

"He killed his mother—"

"He did not!"

"He did, and most likely, he's doing it over and over again with the women he meets. I doubt you and Brittney are the only two."

Her comment was so over the top that I began to suspect *she* was the crazy one, that Jordan was correct in supposing her personal hatred of him had left her slightly unhinged.

"His mother is in a mental institution," I insisted.

"No, she's dead, from a drug overdose. She fell asleep and drowned in her own bathtub when Jordan was twenty. The police considered it to be suspicious, but they couldn't prove anything."

"How do you know all this?"

"I hired an investigator after he murdered Brittney."

I was uneasy and regretting that I'd called her. "You're wrong about his mother."

"I'm not." Her certainty was disturbing. "Has he started taping you while you're having sex?"

"No."

I couldn't figure out why I lied, and I frowned as if it was the most bizarre question I'd ever heard. I was embarrassed and ashamed by the things Jordan made me do. I wanted to understand why he was torturing me, but I wasn't about to admit that it was the very reason I'd sought her out.

"He will, very soon," she said. "He has this friend who's — well, I wouldn't say *gay;* maybe *bisexual* is a better word — but he'll come over to the apartment, and you'll have to do it with him while Jordan videotapes you. He won't let you refuse."

My knees were weak, my stomach roiled. "He did this to your sister?"

"She told me all about it. Of course, by then I didn't have many chances to speak with her, and I *never* saw her. She was so isolated. He kept her away from me so she couldn't tattle."

"If she was so opposed to participating, how could he make her?"

She shrugged. "He'd simply tie her down and proceed. Or he'd drug her. It would happen when she was passed out."

"You're sure?"

"Yes. He's probably done it to other women, too, some who liked it" — Kimberly instantly sprang to mind — "or some who were too afraid to come forward or who weren't positive about what had occurred because of the drugs. I bet that if you searched the apartment, you'd find some of the tapes. He's such a pervert; he'd keep every one he ever made."

I was aghast. "You really believe he'd keep them?"

"He's a psychopath. He'd never get rid of any of his little trophies."

My head spinning, I stared across the library. What was true? What was real? I couldn't decide anymore.

"I should be going," I finally said, too disordered for further discussion.

"You need to contact the police," she urged before I could step away. "Don't wait."

I scoffed. "What would I tell them?"

"That he killed his mother, and he killed his first wife, and he's about to kill you, too."

"Did your sister go to the police?"

"She was too frightened, so I went for her."

"What did they do?"

"Nothing. They thought I was crazy."

"And afterward?"

"It was ruled a drowning, so they wouldn't investigate. They claimed my filing a complaint and her sudden demise was a co-incidence."

I nodded. If I spoke to the authorities, they'd assume I was nuts, too. If I later died under mysterious circumstances, I was a nobody, so they'd save their energy and write it off as a fluke. I had no proof that Jordan had taped me, no proof that he regularly drugged me.

As to kinky sex, was that a crime? I didn't think so.

Besides, he'd be able to make a good case that I was a lush who was addicted to Xanax.

I was silent, pondering her remarks, when the heavy door at the front of the building opened and Jordan strolled in. He paused, gazing around as if he knew I was with Ashley, as if he knew I was doing something wrong.

My heart skipped several beats, and I was shaking so hard that I was amazed I didn't fall down. I cowered behind the enormous bookshelf, wondering if he hadn't slipped a tracking device into my purse or shoes.

"Oh, my God," I whispered as I lurched farther out of sight.

"What is it?" she hissed in reply.

"Jordan just walked in."

"Good-bye," she said. "Be careful, and please don't ever call me again."

"But . . . why?" At that moment, she seemed my only link to the civilized world, my only connection to a life away from the one where I'd been ensnared.

"Because I'm scared of him, too, and of what he might do to me if he ever found out we'd met."

She rushed away down another aisle, and stupidly I yearned to run after her, to beg her to take me with her. She could validate my perception that something bad was about to transpire.

I looked at the quiet, studious people who were serenely focused on their books. What if I went up to one of them and screamed, *Help! Help! My husband is here! He's about to kill me!*

There'd be a huge ruckus. The cops might even be summoned, but why would they intervene? Jordan carried himself like a rich movie star, and I had no evidence that he was other than what he appeared to be. My ridiculous anxiety would seem absurd.

As if he had a honing beacon, he turned directly toward me. He started down one side of the bookshelf, while I skedaddled down the other, only the rows of books separating us. I was flushed and panicked, obviously in a heightened state of agitation, and if he saw me he'd know I'd been doing precisely what I shouldn't have.

I hovered, waiting as he rounded the far end of the stack, then I raced away and out the door, down the stairs, and onto the sidewalk. It was summer, but it was a cold, wet afternoon, and I stood in the mist, letting it cool my heated face. Despite the gray sky, I put on my sunglasses, then headed toward our apartment.

I hadn't taken ten steps when my cell phone vibrated. Merely to piss him off, I let it buzz a few times, then I answered.

"Hello?"

"Meg, I thought we might go have some coffee, so I stopped by the library. Where are you?"

"Oh, I just left. I'm on my way home."

He sounded so fucking normal, just an ordinary husband dropping by to surprise his ordinary wife, while I was trembling and terrified beyond belief.

What would come next? I couldn't begin to guess.

Chapter Twenty

✿

I'll be gone for a few hours," Jordan said. "I'm meeting some people."

"Okay."

"I don't want you to go anywhere while I'm out."

"Why?"

"Do I need a reason?"

"Yes, actually, you do. The sun's shining. I thought I'd walk down by the river."

"If you still want to later, I'll take you then."

"Why can't I go now?"

As if I was a heavy burden, he sighed. "You know you're not healthy enough to be out on your own."

"Stop worrying. I'm completely recovered."

"Are you?"

He assessed me in a way that told me he didn't think so, that told me I looked like shit, which was true. My eyes were dull, my hair stringy, my skin blotchy, and I was more emaciated than ever, fatigued and too run down to focus on personal hygiene. I didn't mind that I wasn't caring for myself. The deeper I fell into a funk, the more content I was to wallow there.

"Take off your shirt," he ordered.

"What?"

"Your shirt! Take it off."

I was wearing a knit top with no bra underneath. My breasts had shrunk so much that support was unnecessary. I shrugged, drew the shirt over my head, and tossed it on the floor. Judging weight and size, he smoothed a hand over my chest. Finally, having reached a decision, he nodded.

"You're too skinny," he chided. "You look like you're starving."

"Haven't you heard?" I countered. "Thin is *in*. It's very chic to be this slender."

"Bullshit. I'm phoning a plastic surgeon tomorrow. I hate that your tits are so small. When we're having sex, it's like I'm screwing a boy."

"Thanks."

"You have to have implants."

"My breasts are fine!"

"Just like the rest of you?"

His tone was scathing, and instantly I felt terrible, as if I'd failed him in a whole new way. I don't know why I kept suffering from such stupid urges to please him. Long ago I'd learned that it was impossible.

He clasped my nipples, pinching them hard enough to make me wince.

"We're having them fixed, Meg. Don't argue with me."

He spun and left, and I followed him to the living room,

suddenly desperate for him not to go. I was like a torture survivor: I'd fallen in love with my captor. I detested having him home and underfoot, but it was so quiet when he was away. Most days he was my only contact with the outside world, and I was pitifully grateful for the slight connection.

As he put on his jacket, I asked, "Where will you be?"

"Does it matter?"

I wasn't really curious about his plans, but I liked having some idea of when he'd return, of having some warning before the stressful moment of his arrival.

"What if I need to get hold of you?"

"Call my cell. I'll answer if I'm not tied up."

"What will you be doing?"

"Fucking around."

I couldn't guess if he meant it literally, but I was far beyond the period when the notion could make me jealous. I wasn't concerned about who he saw or what he did. If it was other women, I simply wished they would sate some of his massive sexual drive, but they never gave me any help in that department.

"Sounds fun," I lied.

"It will be, and I'll be very aroused when I get back, so be ready to fuck me all night."

In previous months I'd have been thrilled to have him say something like that, but now the prospect merely made me tired. "I'll be waiting."

"Good. And remember, don't go anywhere."

"I won't."

"I'm serious, Meg."

"I know you are."

He stepped into the elevator, and as it whisked him away I

sagged with relief. I couldn't figure out what was wrong with us. His conduct was rarely alarming, but whenever we were together, the tension was enormous, our discord escalating.

I gazed at the elaborate penthouse. How could such a lavish residence have become such a prison? I wandered about, unnerved by the silence, then I tiptoed into his office. I sat at his desk and swiveled in the fancy chair. Whenever I came into the room, I had the feeling that I was being watched, and I often wondered if he'd installed a camera, if he was taping me.

Perhaps he never actually left the building. Perhaps he was hiding somewhere nearby and studying me on a monitor. At this point, I wouldn't have put anything past him.

I opened the top drawer, then the next and the next. I don't know what I was hoping to find. The copies of the calendar and the photo from the newspaper weren't there, which had me questioning whether I'd really seen them. Was it part of some game Jordan was playing? Was it one more petty attempt to have me believe I was crazy? Or had I lost it? I was too confused to tell if I was nuts. Did that in and of itself make me crazy?

In the bottom drawer there was a new file with my name on it, so of course, I had to snoop through the contents. The fact that it was in plain sight made me think that he wanted me to stumble on it, that he'd placed it there specifically for me to see.

To my surprise, it contained a prenuptial agreement between me and Jordan. Both our signatures were on it, but I'd never previously seen the document and I certainly hadn't signed it, even though it was an excellent forgery of my handwriting.

Prior to our wedding, he'd never mentioned his fortune or

what my rights were to any of it. When we'd married, it had been such an intense time, the ceremony so hurried, that I'd never considered his wealth in relation to me. Obviously Jordan had, but why couldn't we have just discussed the situation like two rational adults?

I wasn't stupid. I comprehended that he was rich, that we'd entered the union with him having everything and me having nothing. If he'd set the proposal in front of me, I'd have consented to it in a heartbeat, so why all the subterfuge?

My signature called out to me, and I traced a finger over it. I recognized that he was sending me an important message, that there was a threat here I should decipher, but I couldn't solve the riddle on my own, and I didn't know who could explain it to me. Probably I should have chatted with a lawyer, but I wasn't acquainted with one.

On the surface, the terms seemed very straightforward. If we divorced, I would get a pittance, a ten-thousand-dollar settlement. If I died, my heirs would get nothing. By signing it—which I hadn't—I swore that I fully understood my position, I was lucid and stable, and I freely relinquished any claims against him.

I didn't want his money. Once I found the courage to split, I'd gladly return to the sort of existence I'd had before meeting him. He had a ton of cash and luxurious possessions, and they gave him a lot of power, but he was so unhappy. I shared in his wealth and what it could buy, but I was miserable, too, so I couldn't see what good the money did for either of us.

But . . . why would he go to such lengths to guarantee that I couldn't have any of it?

It had to be another subtle threat that he'd never let me

leave. Maybe he imagined I sat around all day plotting our divorce and how I could end up rich and single at his expense. Maybe this was his method of ensuring it didn't happen. Or maybe it was an indication of imminent danger, but I was too much of an idiot to dodge whatever bullet was coming.

Suddenly I felt as if the walls were closing in on me. I had to get out of the apartment, had to talk to somebody who would listen. Who would?

I stuffed the file back in the desk then. With no regard for Jordan's admonition about staying home, I grabbed a sweater, sunglasses, and purse, and headed downstairs. I exited the lobby and dawdled on the sidewalk, gaping at my surroundings as if I was an alien on a new planet. I had no idea which direction to go, so I started strolling aimlessly.

After a few blocks I stopped at an old mansion that had been refurbished into offices. There was a discreet gold plaque on the stately porch that said "Attorneys at Law," and I debated for an eternity, then thought, why not? Why not march in and ask their opinion?

I'd never contacted a lawyer about a legal issue, so it was a daunting decision, but I climbed the stairs and went in. The plush carpet sucked up all noise, making it seem as if I'd stepped into a vacuum. A coffee table had *Forbes* magazine and the *Wall Street Journal* arranged for clients to peruse while they waited.

There was a beautiful, immaculately dressed receptionist behind an ornate reception desk. A leather couch sat across from her. She smiled at me. I was dressed in stylish clothes, too, so I looked like I belonged in such an exclusive place.

"May I help you?" she inquired.

"What would I have to do to meet with an attorney?"

"Simply make an appointment."

"Oh, okay." I frowned. "Could I speak with someone now?"

"Now?"

"If anyone's available."

"Let me see." She studied her computer screen, then said, "I have some time with Mr. Gray, right after lunch. Would that work for you?"

The slot was ninety minutes away. Did I dare risk it? "How long is an appointment?"

"That depends on what you need to talk to him about."

"I have some questions about a prenuptial agreement."

"Is it already drafted? Or are you thinking about drafting one?"

"It's already drafted."

"Do you have a copy with you?"

"No." And I was positive I never would have a copy.

"Well . . . how about if we schedule you at one o'clock, then you can tell him what you need." She assessed her computer again. "What's your first name?"

"Meg."

"And last?"

I stared at her and the computer as panic set in. What if Jordan found out I'd been here? What if he learned that I'd discussed our private business with an outsider? What would he do to me?

Beyond Jordan and his feelings on the subject, what would I say to a lawyer? He'd want to see the document, and I'd have to explain why I couldn't show it to him. If he advised me to

bring it by later and I went to Jordan's office to retrieve it, I was
certain it would have disappeared, as the calendars and newspaper photo had disappeared.

If by some magic stroke of luck it was still in the drawer,
I'd have to convince the attorney that my signature had been
forged. How could he believe me? Jordan was very rich, and
it was only logical and appropriate that he'd have a prenuptial
agreement in effect.

I'd sound like a lunatic.

And I'd have to pay for the visit. How would I ever come
up with the money? I had exactly two dollars in my purse and
couldn't imagine how or when I'd get my hands on more.

It had been foolish, assuming I could approach a stranger
and beg for assistance.

I sighed. "I better not."

"Are you sure?"

"Very."

I spun to depart, and as I reached the door she said, "If you
change your mind, just let me know. I'll fit you in."

"I appreciate it, but I won't change my mind."

I loitered on the sidewalk, wondering what to do, where to
go. A clock was ticking in my brain, warning me to hurry home.

Jordan scarcely ever gave me explicit instructions to stay in
the apartment, and when he did he was serious. I had to get
back before he discovered that I'd left. Each passing second
was dangerous.

There was a pay phone on the corner, and I went to it and
picked up the receiver. Without pausing to reflect, I put in some
coins and punched in Marie's number. I had no idea if she lived

at the same address, but I was desperate to hear a familiar voice.

She answered on the third ring. "Hello?"

I was so stunned that I didn't reply, and she had to repeat herself.

"Hello?"

"Marie?"

"Yes . . . ?"

It was obvious she didn't recognize me, and I was crushed. I rested my forehead against the glass of the phone booth.

"It's me, Meg."

There was a lengthy, awkward silence as she tried to place me. "Meg . . . White?"

I still never thought of myself as Meg Blair. "Yes."

Her tone was bored and cold. "What do you want?"

What *did* I want? "I decided to see how you are."

"I'm fine."

She didn't offer anything more, didn't ask how I was doing in return. Another silence ensued. Finally I said, "I heard you and Steve are together. I heard you guys are engaged."

"Yes, we are."

"That's nice. I'm happy for you."

Again, she didn't seize the opening for further conversation. I could picture her in her apartment, ambling around her kitchen, gazing out the window, down the street toward Mozart's.

"Why'd you call, Meg?"

"I wanted to talk to you."

"It's been six months. Why now? What's going on?"

"I miss you."

She chuckled wearily. "No, you don't. After all this time, don't pretend."

"I'm not pretending."

"What's the matter? Isn't your fancy marriage working out like you hoped it would? Are you wishing you had somebody to complain to? Well, I don't care to be the shoulder you cry on, and it's wrong of you to expect me to listen."

It had taken every ounce of courage I possessed to drop the quarters in the phone, but she had no means of knowing how hard it had been for me. She was so sarcastic, so unenthused, and till that moment I guess I hadn't truly comprehended the depth of what I'd done.

I'd selected my path, and I'd strolled down it with a callous indifference. I was reaping the bitter fruits of what I'd sown.

"No, I didn't want to complain," I insisted. "I just wanted to say hi."

"Now you have."

"Yeah."

"I'll let Steve know that you called."

"Thanks."

"He was so worried about you. In the beginning, after you first took off, he was frantic. He called and searched and asked people about you, but no one had heard anything. He was terrified over whether you were okay or not. Did you ever think about that?"

"No."

"I didn't suppose you had."

"Tell him . . . tell him I'm sorry, would you?"

"No, I won't. In fact, I don't believe I'll mention you, at all. Whatever your problems, they're your own fault. You've caused him enough trouble. He doesn't need any more on your account."

I'd never felt more humiliated.

I knew I deserved her censure, but it hurt so much! I tried to remember that rainy winter day when I'd blithely shed my old life for Jordan. At the time it had seemed like the only choice, the only direction I could go.

When had I grown so selfish? I'd been so intent on my own needs, and any distress I might have inflicted on Steve had seemed a small price to pay. But what had I gained? What had I lost?

"I understand," I mumbled.

"Good. Please don't contact me again."

"I won't."

I hung up. It was the same admonition Ashley had given me after we'd had our clandestine meeting at the library. Was I tainted? Was I poison?

Whatever I touched, whatever I did, it turned to shit. I'd simply forgotten how to reach out and connect, and I'd been yearning for support from the two women that they couldn't possibly supply. I was on my own, floating free, an invisible woman in a sea of strangers.

Defeated, disgusted with myself, I trudged away.

Something had to change. *I* had to change. I recognized my dire situation, but I never took any action to correct it. Everything seemed so difficult, out of my control. My mental processes were so jumbled that I couldn't pick a new course. The notion of formulating drastic decisions, then implementing them, was too difficult. It was easier to coast.

At our building, I signed in at the security desk and rode the elevator up to the top. I was inside the apartment and had put my sweater in the front closet before I noticed that Jordan was home, that he was sitting on the couch and watching my furtive entrance.

He was sipping from a glass of liquor, which he rarely did, and anger rippled off him in waves. We stared as I fiddled and shifted from foot to foot. He would expect me to provide an explanation, but I had no clue how to begin.

"Hello, Jordan," I ultimately said.

"Hello, Meg. Where've you been?"

"I ran out to get a mocha."

"Did you?"

Since I wasn't holding a cup of coffee, it was a ridiculous lie, but it was too late to retract it. "I was only gone a few seconds."

"Really? Would you like to know how long I've been waiting for you?"

I could barely keep from wincing with dismay. I started into the room, praying I looked nonchalant, but I was incredibly frightened.

I forced a smile. "It's so nice out. Would you like to walk down to the river with me?"

"I told you not to go anywhere today."

"I know."

"So why did you leave?"

"I just . . . just needed to get out."

"And I told you not to."

There was a bleak sense of finality in the air, as if we'd

arrived at the point where we'd been headed all along. He uncurled from the sofa, and as he stood I noted that he was clutching a belt. It was folded in half, and he tapped the dangling part against his thigh.

"You never listen to me, Meg."

"It was just a coffee, Jordan. You're making too much of it."

"Am I? You know, it's occurred to me that when I give you an order, you don't think you have to obey it."

I wasn't about to comment on the word *obey*. We were at a hazardous impasse, and I didn't want to enrage him more than he already was.

"I'm sorry," I said. "It won't happen again."

"Won't it?"

"No."

"I can see that you're lying."

"I'm not."

"You're playing some game with me and I can't allow it to continue." He gestured with the belt. "Go to the bedroom."

"Why? What are you going to do to me?"

"I'll tell you when we get there."

"Tell me now."

"Go!" he said very firmly, but he didn't raise his voice. He *never* raised his voice.

"Not till you tell me what you're going to do."

"You have to be punished. It's time you realized that there are consequences for your impulsive behaviors."

"You may be my husband, but you're not my boss and you're not my keeper."

"Are you sure about that?"

He lifted the belt and brought it down hard across my face, then he did it again and again. I fell to the floor and huddled in a ball, his message coming through loud and clear. He had a lesson to teach, and I was a fast learner.

Chapter Twenty-one

❦

"We're going to watch some videos."

"All right."

"You'll study what the women in the tapes are doing, then you'll do the same things to me."

"Whatever you want is fine."

After whipping me with the belt, he'd locked me in a closet for two days and two nights. At least, I guessed that was how long it had been. I was battered and befuddled, and I couldn't accurately judge how much time had passed.

When he finally let me out, there had been none of the sweet consideration he would have shown earlier in our relationship. By sneaking out after he'd specifically told me not to, I had crossed a line with him, and apparently my sin was too ghastly to be forgiven.

I couldn't predict what would happen now. No one knew where I was. No one would come by to check on me. I was totally alone, at Jordan's mercy.

For quite a while I'd planned to escape, but my senses had been dulled by narcotics and alcohol. I'd been too zoned to view my danger as urgent, and I'd procrastinated, had debated and questioned my options, until now it was too late to go. I still recognized that I had to get away, but I was beyond rational thought.

The entire period that I'd been imprisoned, I hadn't had anything to eat or drink, and I'd hardly slept. I'd been so terrified, I'd doze off only to jerk awake, certain I was about to be murdered.

After freeing me, he allowed me to shower and pull on a robe, but he hadn't fed me. I was too scared to ask for food, too scared to initiate any conversation that might throw him into another rage, so I was pretending to be very meek.

I had to buy myself some time so that I could regain my bearings and plot a course. He couldn't constantly be home to stand guard over me. I had to be patient, had to wait for an opening, then make a move once it arrived.

I was on the bed in the extra bedroom. The red satin sheets were back, cords tied to the headboard, sex toys arranged on the dresser. He poured what appeared to be liquor into a glass, then he held it out to me.

"Drink this."

"What is it?"

"Brandy. It will help you relax and do what you have to do."

"Could I just have some water?"

"No."

The chances were great that he'd laced the brandy, that he was about to drug me into a stupor, but I didn't care. I was so thirsty that I would have swallowed anything. I sipped it slowly, savoring the pungent flavor, though it landed like a bomb in my empty stomach.

There was a TV in the room and he walked over to it. On the shelf beneath it, I could see a row of homemade videos. They looked as if they'd always been sitting right there, even though I'd searched high and low to find them. He slipped one into the machine, then he came over to me.

With remote in hand, he climbed onto the mattress and crawled behind me. He lounged against the pillows, with me situated between his legs, and he yanked the robe off my shoulders so that I was naked.

"You shouldn't have disobeyed me, Meg."

"I didn't mean to, Jordan. I said I was sorry."

"I had you followed. I know that you went to a lawyer."

I hoped he wouldn't notice how the admission shocked me. I'd often wondered if he hired detectives to trail after me, but the notion had been so preposterous that I'd never given it serious credence.

My failed trip to the attorney's office seemed to have transpired in another life, to someone else. I realized I had to invent a good story, but my mind was so fuzzy that I could scarcely respond. "I was lost. I stopped to ask directions."

He grabbed my nipple and twisted it painfully. "Oh, Meg, when will you accept that you can't lie to me? I always learn the truth sooner or later."

At that moment I was so run down and so frightened, while he was so strong and in control, that he seemed omnipotent. In my fevered brain, it was perfectly logical that he was aware of everything I was thinking, everything I was doing. There was no way I could fight him and win.

"Who did you call on the pay phone?"

I wasn't about to tempt fate with another lie. "My old friend, Marie."

"I advised you not to associate with her."

"I know."

"You didn't listen to me."

"I was just confused."

"Yes, you were. You won't try anything so foolish ever again, will you?"

"No."

"Because now you see how angry it makes me." He was still wrenching my nipple. "You don't want me to grow even angrier, do you?"

"No."

"You can't ever leave me, Meg. You have to understand that fact and come to grips with it. Have you? Do you understand it?"

"Yes, Jordan."

"You must remember the vows you spoke at our wedding: 'Till death do us part.'"

"Yes."

"You can't ever break them. I won't let you."

"I won't try."

I sounded like a puppet, and that was precisely how I felt. I was beyond argument, beyond defiance. Until I had an opportunity to eat and rest, I could only nod and agree. Besides, in light of my predicament, I suspected that I would never escape. I couldn't imagine how it would be possible. He had all the power, while I had none.

"I'm going to spend tonight showing you what it will be like for you from now on. Your world has changed completely. Since you've proven I can't trust you—"

"You can trust me! I swear it."

"No, I can't, and it's all your own fault, so you can't ever be left to your own devices. *I* will handle everything. *I* will guide you in all your decisions and behaviors."

"That's fine."

"If you refuse to do as I say, you'll have to be punished."

"I don't need to be punished."

"Yes, you do. I've been entirely too lenient, and I had too much faith in your ability to act as you should." He pointed the remote at the TV and hit the *play* button. The video scrolled in the machine. "Let's watch for a bit."

He poured me another brandy and made me gulp it down. In silence we waited for the action to begin. When it did, I was disgusted to see Kimberly, at his beach house, in his hot tub. She vamped and preened, giggling seductively as she massaged her breasts and finger-fucked herself. He'd filmed it all, the lens zooming in on her shaved privates, on her pink pussy.

"Do the same thing, Meg," he commanded. "Touch yourself the same way."

I caressed my chest, and he studied my movements but wasn't satisfied. He took my hand and forced it down to my crotch, and he held it there till I slipped a finger into my vagina and worked it back and forth.

The scene faded and new ones commenced: Kimberly on the patio furniture, Kimberly in the kitchen, Kimberly in the living room in numerous lewd poses. Eventually it was Kimberly with Steve, my sweet, chubby, endearing Steve, but I was so detached that it seemed as if I were gazing at people I didn't know.

I observed the two of them screwing in the water, and I was disheartened to discover that I'd been correct, that they'd started in immediately after they'd gotten in the tub together. I'd once been curious as to how long Steve had lasted before yielding to temptation, and it was depressing to learn that it hadn't been very long at all.

We sat for an eternity, assessing how my old boyfriend fucked Jordan's favorite prostitute, and it was very creepy. I wanted it to be over, but I didn't dare ask him to shut it off. If I said anything, he'd make me watch it for hours; he might make me watch it for days.

The camera followed them through most of the rooms on the ground floor of the house, then upstairs to a bedroom. Ultimately Jordan joined them. Kimberly was on the bed going at it with Steve while Jordan took her from behind.

"Get up on your knees," he ordered me now, and I complied.

He gripped my hips and fucked me just as he was fucking Kimberly on the tape. He'd clasp me in the same places on my body, would match his tempo and mutter the same comments. He knew the sequence so well, had memorized every detail, which provided eerie evidence that he'd seen it dozens—or even hundreds—of times.

The tape clicked off, and Jordan pulled out of me and walked over to the VCR to insert another. It was the one I couldn't recollect, when I'd originally viewed it and thought I'd had sex with another man.

I was dispassionate, disengaged, as Jordan went through the same motions with me again. His knowledge of the content was staggering, alarming, downright sinister. He'd turn me and talk to me in all of the same ways as he was doing on the screen.

On the video I was giving him a blow job, which was what he had me mimic exactly. It was the most demeaning, uncomfortable episode of my life. My stomach was so upset, the liquor burning a hole, my appetite raging, but without complaint I sucked him to the end.

When the tape stopped, I'd hoped we were finished, that he'd made whatever absurd point he'd intended, but he went over and put in a third one. By then we'd been through four hours of porn, with him fucking me and fucking me. I was dazed, exhausted, starving, and deprivation had me on the verge of collapse.

"Can't we take a break?" I finally begged. "I'm so hungry. If I could have a bite to eat, it would be easier to keep going."

"You can't eat until I say so."

"Please?"

"No."

The tape began, and it portrayed a woman I didn't initially recognize, but as it continued, I concluded that it could only be his first wife, Brittney. How sick was that? She had blond hair, which wasn't a surprise—Jordan obviously favored blondes—but it was scraggly and limp, her eyes too big for her thin face. I was witnessing her in a deteriorated condition, after she'd been extensively tormented by him.

She was emaciated, slow, and confused. Her speech was slurred, and she was a tad unsteady, as if she was very drunk or very high.

Jordan had her tied to a bed.

"Is that Brittney?" I inquired.

"Yes," he admitted after a pause. "How did you know?"

"I guessed. She was very pretty."

"She could be when she made an effort."

"She looks like me."

He chuckled. "She certainly does."

"Did you love her?"

"She always disobeyed me," he said, which was and wasn't an answer.

"Did you kill her?"

"Lie down, Meg."

"Did you?"

"Lie down!"

I was so miserable, thinking I might vomit, thinking I might simply faint dead away, but without argument I let him secure my wrists to the headboard.

He had sex with me, the video humming in the background, and I stared at a spot over his shoulder, my reflections a thousand miles away. Over the past few months he'd worked very hard to rattle me, to make me believe I was crazy, and maybe I was.

My mind was so detached from what was happening to my body that I didn't feel the two were connected anymore. I was two separate beings—a mental one and a physical one—and I was positive I'd snapped. This had to be how torture victims survived, by drifting off to a netherworld where nothing mattered. I could be beaten or psychologically abused, but it wasn't particularly grueling, and the void where I'd gone wasn't such a bad place to be.

In step with the video, Jordan pulled out another length of rope and wrapped it around my neck. He would tug at it just enough to scare me, to convince me he was about to strangle me. Then he'd loosen it and I would gasp for air, trying to suck in as much as I could before he started in again.

He tightened it over and over, for a very long time. I was too bewildered and weary to focus on much of anything, so in spite of the danger I showed very little reaction. Just as I'd decided I was about to die, he quit and moved off me. He stood, glaring, his gaze cold, his expression lethal.

"Do you understand how it's going to be?" he asked.

"Yes."

"Do you have any questions?"

"No. Everything is crystal clear."

"Good."

He spun and left, and I closed my eyes and drifted off, praying that I would never awaken.

Chapter Twenty-two

❦

"I n here."

Jordan gestured, and I stepped into a stairwell that was steep and dark, with no handrail. I teetered on my high heels, and he placed his palm on my back to steady me.

"Where are we?" I asked.

"We're meeting an acquaintance of mine."

He'd mentioned that we were going out, and I'd been so happy to get out of the apartment, to see other people and breathe fresh air, that I'd agreed. But when it had come time to leave, he'd dressed me in lingerie and stockings, in a pearl necklace and heels, then he'd put a coat over the top. Anyone looking at me wouldn't have guessed that I was practically naked underneath.

I had tried to refuse my lack of clothes, but not very hard. My mind was muddled, my thoughts chaotic and unreliable, and often I didn't comprehend what was transpiring. When

I struggled to figure out why, it occurred to me that I was being drugged, but I was in such a relaxed stupor that I didn't care.

I didn't know how he was accomplishing it, and I supposed he was adding narcotics to my food or beverages. He had me thoroughly tranquilized so that I never raised a fuss, so that I never argued or complained. Like a complacent, malleable doll, I was easily led and coerced into doing whatever he suggested.

The stairs ended at a door on the fourth floor. Jordan knocked while I leaned against the wall, huffing with exhaustion after the short climb. He kept me on a minimal diet, and I no longer engaged in strenuous activity—never even took walks—so the least exertion drained me.

After a few seconds the door opened, and I was amazed to be greeted by the mystery man from the video. He was wearing tight jeans, no shirt or shoes, and with his dark hair, blue eyes, and toned body, he might have been Jordan's wilder, younger brother. He had an earring in his ear and a rose tattooed on his forearm.

"I didn't think you were ever coming," he told Jordan as we entered the living room of an apartment.

"Sorry," Jordan answered. "We're running late."

The man pointed to me and addressed me as if we were old friends.

"Hi, Meg."

"Hello."

He reached out and traced a finger down my cheek, and it was a sign of how languid I'd grown that I simply stood there and let him do it.

"Meg," Jordan said, "this is Adrian."

I frowned. My speech was slow and deliberate, and I had to concentrate to form words. "Adrian, do you know why Jordan brought me here? He won't say."

"Well, yes, Meg," Adrian replied. "You know, too."

"I do?"

"Yes."

They both chuckled and exchanged a heated look, as I realized what was about to happen. There was a tiny voice in my head, screaming that this was wrong, that I shouldn't proceed, but I couldn't muster the outrage necessary to protest.

"Come with me."

"Okay."

Adrian steered me down a hall and into a bedroom complete with a king-size bed and the same type of red sheets Jordan occasionally put on our extra bed at home.

Jordan followed us, and he was very comfortable, as if he visited regularly. He went to a cupboard and poured me a drink. When he prepared something for me to ingest, I always scrutinized him closely, hoping I'd catch him furtively dropping in a sedative, but I never noticed anything unusual and this time was no different.

He held out the glass, and I couldn't make myself decline. My brain wouldn't cooperate. I was thirsty and hungry, and I greedily seized it. I took a few sips, decided it tasted like straight brandy, and gulped it down. He poured me another and I gulped it, too.

He stepped behind me and removed my coat while Adrian nestled himself to my front, so that I was trapped between them. They gazed at each other over my shoulder, and as Adrian saw my skimpy lingerie, my black net stockings, he beamed with approval.

He cradled my face in his hands, then he trailed down my neck and chest to massage my breasts and play with my nipples. He continued on, encircling my narrow waist, my slender hips. He clasped my butt and hugged me to him so that his loins were pressed to mine.

"Have you figured out what we're going to do?" he inquired.

"No," I lied. Even in my trancelike state, I couldn't help but understand.

"We'll have sex while Jordan watches. He likes to watch. Did you know that?"

"Yes."

"This will make him very happy."

"Good," I murmured, though I recognized that what Adrian had said wasn't true. There wasn't any way to make Jordan happy.

I glanced around at Jordan. "Are you sure about this?"

"Yes, very sure."

"I don't want to do it."

"You have to, Meg. You don't have a choice."

"Are you filming a video?"

"Yes, but I'll start with some still photos so I can study them later, when we're home."

Adrian had reclined on the bed, and he was clutching my wrist, drawing me down to him, and with only scant resistance I joined him. Jordan pulled up a chair and sat next to us, settling in to observe for a while before getting out his camera.

In the end, it turned out to be easy, and in light of some of the things Jordan made me try, not that unpleasant. Adrian was very attractive, the sort of guy I once would have drooled over, once would have dreamed of having as a boyfriend.

He was a skilled lover, too—a tad rough, a tad demanding, but adept all the same. I was accustomed to harsh treatment, so in comparison to Jordan, much of it was extremely tame.

Adrian dealt with me as if I was a date he was seducing, as if he'd picked me up in a bar. Gradually, he stripped me so that I was naked, and he nibbled and caressed, pinched and fondled. He went down on me, and he spent an inordinate amount of time licking and stroking, his fingers in my vagina and ass.

Though I was too out of it to become aroused, I appreciated his efforts, and it was really quite erotic. If I hadn't been so numb, I probably would have had several orgasms. As it was, my senses were too dulled for me to react.

Suddenly he hovered over me and was thrusting away, though I wasn't aware of when he'd changed positions and entered me. His fabulous blue eyes were intently focused on me, and he kept on forever, his muscles tensed and straining toward release.

My subconscious allowed a moment of recall, and I saw how we'd previously done exactly this.

I asked, "Have we had sex together before?"

"Don't you remember?"

"No."

"You blocked the entire thing?" He laughed. "You've crushed my ego, but then I'll console myself by recollecting that you were a bit out of it."

"Did I like it?"

He considered, then shrugged. "I don't know."

"What did we do?"

"Mostly what we're doing now. Didn't Jordan show you the tape?"

"No."

He smiled at Jordan, and it was a secretive lover's smile. "Shame on you, Jordan. You should have let her see it."

"I did," Jordan replied. "She just forgot. Sometimes she gets mixed up."

Adrian rolled me over so that he could fuck me from behind, and finally Jordan unpacked his camera and photographed us. After that, it became more of a modeling session. Adrian would do something Jordan enjoyed, and Jordan would say, "Hold it right there."

He'd take several shots, then Adrian would start in again, only to pause when Jordan wanted to capture a specific pose. We kept on through many varied scenarios, including a blow job that I didn't have to do all the way to the end—for which I was grateful—but I was on my knees, with my mouth stretched wide, and when Jordan pronounced us finished, I was very miserable.

Adrian ushered me into the bathroom. He adjusted the water in the shower and helped me in. I thought I'd have some solitude, but he climbed in, too. Before I realized what he planned, before I could protest, my back was braced against the tiles, my legs wrapped around his waist, and he proceeded to have sex with me again.

He was more physical than he'd been in the bedroom, when Jordan had been with us, and he pounded into me and came with a wrenching groan. I was balanced on his thighs, his cock throbbing deep inside, and he bit at my nape, hard enough to break the skin.

He pulled away and guided me down till my feet hit the bottom of the tub and I could stand on my own.

"You have the greatest mouth," he said. "God, it was torture, holding off while Jordan snapped all those pictures."

"Do you have sex like this a lot? With you doing it and him taking photos?"

"Not a lot. Just when he bumps into a woman who might be interested, and occasionally *he* has the sex and I take the pictures."

"Which do you like better?"

"It depends on the woman. I might feel like fucking her or I might not."

"Does Jordan let you decide?"

"Not always."

At the enigmatic response, I wondered about the situation regarding me. Had it been Adrian's idea? Or Jordan's? I was too worn out to inquire, plus I didn't care to know any details of their peculiar association.

The shower door opened, and Jordan surprised me by joining us. The two men were tender and concerned, washing me as if I were a princess. They soaped and rinsed my torso over and over, as they kissed and licked all my intimate spots, then they lifted me out onto the rug.

Adrian left, and Jordan dried me and dressed me in my lingerie and coat. Then he escorted me to the living room and seated me on the couch.

"You did very well, Meg. I'm proud of you."

"I'm glad."

"Stay here. I'll be out in a few minutes."

He went down the hall to the bedroom and shut the door.

He and Adrian were sequestered, and it was so quiet that I suspected they were having sex, though with the two of them and their strange relationship, I couldn't be positive. For all I knew, maybe Jordan was paying him, or maybe they were checking their calendars to arrange another appointment.

It was the first instance I'd been alone since my foolish trip to the lawyer's office, so I should have seized the chance to sneak away, but instead I dozed off, succumbing to a lethargy that was too heavy to fight. I closed my eyes and napped until Jordan awakened me with a gentle shake.

Dizzy and disoriented, I stood, reeling as Adrian walked us out. He kissed me on the lips. "Thanks, Meg. That was very fun."

"Yes, it was," I answered politely, as if we'd merely stopped by for supper rather than an evening of pornographic endeavor.

"It was nice to see you again."

"You, too."

"We'll have to do it again very soon."

"I can't wait." Was that really me speaking?

He grinned at Jordan. "We were so busy that we didn't get out the video camera."

"It gives us something to anticipate for next time," Jordan replied.

"It definitely does."

Adrian stared at Jordan so keenly, appearing as if he'd lean over and kiss him good-bye, too, but he didn't. The moment passed. Had I imagined it? Were they in love? Were they lovers? With Jordan it was impossible to guess, but anything seemed likely.

I followed Jordan down the stairs and out into the cool summer night. His car was sitting by the curb, and we climbed in and headed home.

Once inside, Jordan locked himself in his office while I stumbled into the bathroom. For an eternity, I dawdled in front of the mirror, studying myself, evaluating the odd, eerie face that gazed back at me.

I was so thin, so sluggish and detached. What had happened to me? I couldn't marshal the concentration to be alarmed, nor could I identify my precise problem. My world was so fuzzy, my focus so narrowed.

After what I'd just done with Adrian, I couldn't believe that I didn't look different, but I was exactly the same. Nothing had changed. How could that be?

Other than a bruise on my shoulder where Adrian had bit me in the shower, there were no marks to indicate that a foul incident had occurred. I wasn't battered or cut, wasn't maimed or injured.

I didn't feel ashamed. I didn't feel disgusted or shocked. I wasn't even angry at them, when some flicker deep within told me I should be. My emotions had been blunted so thoroughly I simply wasn't able to suffer indignation.

Slowly, I removed my clothes and dragged myself to bed. Jordan came in and glared down at me, exhibiting no hint of affection.

"You behaved yourself tonight," he complimented.

"I tried my best."

"I was pleased." With one hand, he offered me a glass of liquor. With the other, a large white pill.

"What is it?" I asked.

"It's your medication, remember? It calms your nerves and helps you rest."

"I'm pretty tired. I don't think I need it."

"Yes, you do."

"I'm sure I'll fall asleep without any trouble."

"Take it anyway," he pressed. "You know the doctor said you have to."

Had I been to a doctor? I didn't recall such a meeting, but he seemed so certain. I shrugged, grabbed the liquor and the pill, and swallowed both.

Chapter Twenty-three

꧁꧂

W hat do you think?" the beautician asked me.

"It's fine," I lied, feeling sick.

She smiled at Jordan. "How about you?"

"It's perfect," he said. "Just how I wanted it."

"Great." She began gathering up her supplies.

"When should we have you back for a touch-up?" he inquired.

She riffled her fingers through my hair. "Maybe in a month? We'll have to see. Her original color is very dark, so any growth will be noticeable right away."

"We'll call you."

"I love private appointments." She gaped around at the lavish furnishings, her envy blatant and embarrassing to witness. "Do you have my card?"

"Yes. Thank you."

Jordan escorted her to the elevator and sent her on her way.

I stayed in the bathroom, disturbed by how blond I was.

The shade was wrong for me, particularly with my skin now so pallid and blotched. It highlighted the poor state of my health, the emaciated condition of my body.

Jordan hadn't bothered to inform me that the beautician was coming, so I'd been extremely shocked when he'd ushered her into our bedroom.

Mute and stunned, I'd sat through the procedure, not resisting, not complaining, for what could I possibly have said? If I'd claimed that the dye job meant Jordan was about to murder me, I'd have sounded like a lunatic. Yet with each swab of her brush, I'd felt as if she was marking me for a death sentence.

I heard him returning, and as he joined me I stiffened, scared to have him so near. He stared over my shoulder into the mirror, both of us studying my reflection.

He petted the limp strands, sniffing the harsh smell of the chemicals. "I've wanted you to be blond for so long."

"I hate it," I dared to reply.

"I love it."

"I don't."

"So? *I* like it, and that's all that matters. Your opinion is irrelevant."

"Are you going to kill me now?"

"What?"

"Now that my hair is blond, are you going to kill me?"

He frowned and shook his head. "Meg, you say the strangest things. I'm so worried about you. I really believe that you've leapt over some ledge of sanity."

"No, I haven't."

"You're completely out of your mind. I've thought so for some time."

"I'm not!"

"We need to phone that psychiatrist we discussed, to talk about hospitalization. A short visit might be a big benefit for you."

"I'm not crazy!"

"Aren't you?"

He stuck his hand in his pocket and pulled out a pill. "Here. You're due for your medication."

"I don't take medication."

"Yes, you do. You're always forgetting."

Was I? I was so confused. Could I have been on a prescription that I didn't remember?

He wagged it under my nose, the pill beseeching me, seeming to demand that I swallow it. I glared at it, at him, then I seized it and choked it down without any water.

"There!" I jeered. "Are you happy?"

"Yes, Meg. I'm very, very happy. Why don't you lie down and rest."

"I'm not tired. I want to stay up."

"Well, you can't. Adrian invited us over. He's excited to fuck you again. Especially now that your hair is different."

"I don't want to go to Adrian's."

"It's not up to you. It will *never* be up to you. So take a nap because we'll be up very late."

"I'm not tired!" I protested again, gnashing my teeth.

"You will be very soon. Your prescription helps you relax."

As if I was a small child, he urged me toward the bedroom, and I went without argument. I plopped down, and he tucked an afghan around me.

"See?" he said. "It's easier when you simply do as you're told."

"You're not always right."

"That's where you're wrong. I know what's best for you. I know better than you do yourself."

The pill had a potent and immediate effect and I could feel myself drifting off. My eyes kept closing, but I could sense him watching me.

"Promise that you won't murder me while I'm sleeping." My speech was slurred and slow. "I'd like to be conscious when you do."

"For God's sake!" he grumbled. "I should record some of your comments so I'd have evidence of how irrational you've become."

"If you try to convince people I'm crazy, no one will believe you."

"Won't they? You're a drug addict, a sex addict, and an alcoholic. When I married you, you seemed like such a normal girl. How could I have made such a horrid mistake?"

I was sure he was chuckling, almost gleefully, but I was too zoned to look over and see if he was. He walked away, and I fell into a deep, peaceful sleep. Much later, I awoke with a start. It was dusk, so I'd been out the entire day.

My heart was hammering with alarm, and I lay still, wondering what had roused me. I focused very hard and realized that a phone was ringing. Though the noise was very faint, my world had grown so isolated and silent that it seemed jarring. I was delighted that there was a person who'd contacted us, and I was flooded by a huge wave of nostalgia for the sound and what it represented: friends, work, socializing.

Intrigued, eager to know who it was, I crept off the mattress and sneaked to the door. I opened it just a crack as Jordan picked up.

He listened to whoever was on the line, then he asked, "How did you get this number?"

He listened again, then snapped, "My answering service has notified me every time you called, but I didn't see any reason to call you back." A pause. "No, she's not here. She's at our house in Colorado for the summer."

There was another pause, a lengthy one, then he scoffed, "No, I won't tell her. I showed her your last message, and she said she's moved on and wishes you'd quit pestering her. Now you really need to give this up. It's not appropriate for you to speak with her. If you keep bothering us, I'll talk to my attorneys and find a way to stop you. Good-bye."

Very quietly, he placed the receiver in the cradle and I sagged against the wall.

Someone had called for me! Someone wanted to know where I was! Whoever it was had tried more than once! Who could it be?

There were only three possibilities: Steve, Jeffrey, or Marie, although after learning how aggravated she was, I couldn't imagine her relenting. Or Jeffrey. Could either of them have had a change of heart?

Jordan rose from his chair and tiptoed to the hall. I scurried back to the bed and faced the far wall, my eyes scrunched tight as I steadied my breathing and pretended to be asleep. He came in and stared down at me, checking to see if I'd stirred, but I must have fooled him. He spun and left.

As his footsteps receded, I wept with relief. For so long I'd felt invisible, positive that no one missed me and no one cared that I'd disappeared. Suddenly I was reborn, raised from the dead.

I was so comforted by the news, and impatient to have the identity of my secret champion revealed. In fact, my life might depend on it. Despite what Jordan kept intimating, I wasn't crazy. I was terrified, run down, and constantly being medicated into a stupor. In my more lucid moments, I suspected he was poisoning me, too, and I desperately needed help.

I had to figure out how to break the cycle. When Jordan fed me drugs and I swallowed them without complaint, I wallowed in a fog where I wasn't concerned about what was happening to me.

I had to discover who was searching for me, then devise a method for contacting him or her. I spent my days nearly comatose or being abused, so I couldn't function clearly enough to rescue myself. I had to have someone guide me out of my quagmire. Most of all I needed someone to be aware of where I was and that I was still alive. It would give me a reason to continue holding on.

The powerful narcotic I'd taken earlier must have worn off, because as I gazed out the window, watching the evening sky fade to indigo, I was more alert and coherent than I had been in months. I reached out mentally, trying to picture Steve, to picture Jeffrey or Marie, hoping one of them would sense my attempt at connection, would perceive how urgently I had to speak with them.

Eventually I went into the bathroom. I took a leisurely shower, and when I finished, Jordan was waiting for me.

"I didn't think you'd ever wake up," he said.

"I guess I was more tired than I realized."

"I told you that you were. You never listen to me."

"Yes, I do."

"Let's get you dressed."

He dried me, then led me into the bedroom. Black lingerie and stockings had been laid on the bed. On seeing them, I frowned.

"We're meeting Adrian," he reminded me. "Did you forget?"

"Yes. I forgot."

"We're late. You need to hurry."

"I don't want to go over there."

"Actually, he's coming here. I expect him any minute."

"I don't want him in our house."

"It's not *our* house, Meg, it's mine, and he's here a lot. You just don't always see him."

Jordan pushed me onto the mattress and knelt in front of me to pull on the garter belt and stockings. Once he had them secured, he widened my thighs so that my privates were exposed, and he looked his fill, his fingers probing inside me. I studied the ceiling, feeling like a patient on the table at the gynecologist's office.

I tried to recollect the sexual thrill this man had given me in the beginning, tried to ignite a spark that would carry me through whatever deed he'd insist I perform, but I couldn't summon that hot, early passion. I had been so wild for him, so eager to do whatever he'd asked, but now I only wanted to be alone. How had the ember of desire been snuffed out so quickly and completely?

He massaged my breasts, fondling and poking at them, then he stood and yanked me up so that I was sitting.

"Adrian agrees with me about your breasts," he claimed. "They need to be bigger."

"I'm certain he's an expert on the subject."

"I've made you an appointment with a plastic surgeon."

I shrugged, not interested enough to press for details and recognizing that it was futile to protest. If Jordan was determined that I have surgery, I would.

"I get so excited," he said, "just from imagining you and Adrian together."

"I'm glad you find me entertaining."

"Oh, I'm definitely amused by you. If I wasn't, you wouldn't be here."

Another woman, a *normal* woman with an ordinary husband and marriage, might have assumed Jordan was referring to a divorce. I, on the other hand, was convinced he meant he'd kill me once he grew weary of tormenting me. In his world, unwanted wives were expendable.

"Then I'd better give you a good show with Adrian."

"He plans to sodomize you."

"Sure," I consented. "Whatever the two of you want is fine with me. I'm happy to do it."

I didn't believe Adrian wanted any such thing, and Jordan likely made the outrageous suggestion merely to frighten me. I feigned nonchalance and ignored the threat.

He clasped his cock and stroked it across my lips, demanding I open for him, and I did. I was in no mood for the beating I'd receive if I didn't obey. He fucked my mouth till my jaws and neck were aching, but he never came. He simply stopped and drew away, and for the first time ever I conjectured about his disinclination toward orgasm.

Initially I'd been impressed by his stamina, and I'd viewed it as an indication of his lust for me, but now I was positive it was a mark of problems down below. It dawned on me that this was a warning I should have heeded at the outset of our affair, though I didn't necessarily understand what signal was being sent. I didn't know if he couldn't get sufficiently aroused, or if he was so controlled that he never felt the urge, or if the lack was caused by some weird psychological hang-up.

I suspected it was the latter situation.

Jordan ran a thumb across my lips, now chapped and stretched beyond their limit.

"I love giving it to you in the mouth," he said. "I love making you take me that way."

"I know you do."

He left for a minute, going into the other room and returning with a glass of wine that he shoved in my face. I scowled, recognizing that I should refuse it, but not able to decide how I could. If he ordered me to drink it, I had to, even if he forced it down me.

I was sober enough to grasp that it was probably laced with a narcotic. If it was something strong, I'd never recall that someone was looking for me or that I had to learn who it was. I would drift off to that contented spot where I seemed to linger so frequently, and I wouldn't remember.

Not certain what to do and not disposed to provoke him, I sipped it, but it tasted like regular wine. Was there a drug that had no flavor? Shouldn't there have been a bitter tang or residue at the bottom? I didn't know.

He held out the large, white pill and I stared at that, too. As opposed to the wine, I had no doubt about its effects. After I took it, I would glide off into the void, and I might be there for a long time.

"I don't want it," I complained. "I don't need it."

"Of course you *need* it, Meg. Your nerves are shot."

I cradled it in my palm, and it felt as if it weighed a thousand pounds. I couldn't muster the strength to place it on my tongue.

"Swallow it!" Jordan commanded, growing irked. "Adrian will be here any second. I don't want to keep him waiting."

I'd forgotten about Adrian.

In light of what the next few hours would bring, was it wise to be conscious? Did I wish to be lucid and cognizant of what transpired? Wasn't it better to be numb?

Still, I couldn't do it. I shook my head, which angered him. He clutched my neck and rammed the pill far back in my throat, then he poured wine into me till I was choking. I couldn't keep from swallowing, and as the pill slid down, he nodded with grim satisfaction.

"Stay in here," he said. "I'll let you know when we're ready to begin."

"Okay." I was coughing and sputtering.

"Fix your makeup. It's all smeared."

He stomped out and I collapsed onto the bed, quiet as a mouse till I heard him in the living room, turning on some music.

The medicine would work very fast, and I couldn't risk that it might cloud or erase my memory. I opened the drawer in the nightstand and was thrilled to stumble on a notepad. I ripped off a sheet of paper, and took it and a pen into the bathroom and shut the door.

Across the top, I jotted the date and time that the phone

had rung. Then I wrote: *Someone called for me. They were worried and trying to check on me, but Jordan lied and said I was in Colorado and that I didn't want to talk to them. They've called before, too, and he keeps hanging up on them. If I wonder later, or if I'm confused, I really heard it. It really happened. It wasn't my imagination and it wasn't a dream. I have to find out who it was and tell them I'm in trouble.*

Considering my level of terror and disorientation, it was probably the bravest thing I'd ever done. My emotions careened between fear and excitement. I folded the paper in fourths and buried it in the bottom of my cosmetics case. Then I started applying lipstick and blush as if it was an ordinary evening.

The drug was rapidly kicking in, the fog creeping over me. I rested my hand on the lid of the case, glad I had the hidden message, relieved and soothed in knowing it would be there whenever I needed to be reminded of what was at stake.

Chapter Twenty-four

ॐ

"Y ou didn't do very well, Meg. You should have made more of an effort."

"I know, Jordan. I apologize."

"Too much of it is slow and boring. You needed to be more spontaneous."

He was watching the new video of Adrian and me. He'd filmed it days earlier, and he was still absorbed with deciphering every detail, which was hilarious since I appeared nearly comatose in every shot. He had me study it as he indicated what he viewed as my mistakes and advised me as to what he wanted me to do differently next time.

He was so freaking insane!

There were a few sections where I'd been roughed up, but for the most part it wasn't too bad. Adrian was a good lover, very thorough and concise, but not brutal or sadistic as Jordan could be. He was handsome, too, his smile dazzling, his body fantastic, so there was nothing distasteful about seeing him go through the motions.

In true porn style, my face usually wasn't visible. I was merely the naked woman Adrian was fucking, so I might have been anyone. In my disoriented state, I wasn't concerned over my participation, and I could observe dispassionately. I suffered no bouts of panic or shame.

The tape ended, and Jordan stood and walked over to put on his jacket. I was surprised. It was the middle of the afternoon, and it had been weeks since he'd left me on my own. He'd taken to working at home, sealing himself in his office for hours while he had phone conferences and answered e-mail and correspondence.

Adrian visited occasionally, food and liquor were delivered, but when they were, I was locked in the closet in the bedroom. Jordan never gave me a chance to speak with anyone, to slip someone a note or beg a stranger for mercy. Not that I would have. I was so wasted and unkempt that I could have been an escapee from a mental ward. I was a frightening sight, and I was too demoralized to attempt an approach that would be rebuffed. I couldn't live through the humiliation.

"Where are you going?" I asked.

"It's beautiful outside. I need some fresh air."

"May I come with you?" The pleading tone in my voice was mortifying.

"You're not up to it."

"I am!" I insisted, though feebly.

"You're awfully ill. I'd be embarrassed to be seen with you."

I wasn't *ill*. At least, I didn't think I was. I simply looked like shit after surviving months of being drugged and poisoned. "I'll wear a scarf. And sunglasses. No one will be able to tell."

"What if you cause a big ruckus? What if you collapse or make a scene?"

"I won't. I promise."

He sighed, but nodded. "All right, but if you misbehave it will be the last time I let you out. Do you understand me?"

"Yes."

"I mean it, Meg. I can't figure out what's wrong with you. I've given you everything you could ever need, but you've fallen to pieces. I'm revolted by you."

"I'm sorry. I don't know what's wrong with me either."

"I feed you," he nagged, "but you get thinner and thinner. I buy you medicine to calm your nerves, but you're a wreck. What should I do? I wish you'd give me a hint."

"I can't explain it."

"I've decided that I should have other lovers—women who are sexy and interesting enough to arouse me. I can't bear fucking you anymore. You disgust me."

"I know."

Absurdly, I was at my lowest point. I felt that I'd failed as a female and as a wife. He'd crushed my self-esteem until I was an empty shell, but I was such a mess that I couldn't see how he was manipulating me.

"I'm going to start bringing other women home."

"Please don't."

"I realize that it will be difficult for you, but I don't dare leave you alone so I can go out to have sex. I can't imagine what kind of trouble you'd get yourself in if I was away too long."

"You can leave me. I won't be a problem. I swear."

"No. I'll invite them here so you can see them. You have to be reminded of how a female grooms herself. You need to remember how much I like to fuck a partner who has the stamina to do it."

"Couldn't you . . . you . . . meet them somewhere else?"

"No, it has to be in the apartment. I've been planning to phone Kimberly for a while now. I'll have her stop by. Perhaps if you see her again you'll recollect how you used to be. Don't you have any pride in your appearance?"

"I'll try harder," I said, shamed beyond measure.

If I'd thought his screwing others would keep him away from me, I wouldn't have cared what he did, but I knew him too well. Despite how repulsive he deemed me to be, our intimate relations would never diminish. He enjoyed tormenting me too much. His having dates in the apartment would be another ordeal for me to endure, another way he could humble and degrade me.

He sighed again. "If you're coming with me, you have to make yourself presentable."

"I will."

"Go change your clothes and put on some makeup. And for God's sake, brush your hair."

"I will. Right away."

Like a trained rat, I scurried to the bedroom and did what I could to rectify my condition. I pulled on baggy slacks and a bulky sweater that would hide my emaciation. Then I went into the bathroom and swabbed on some blush as I stared in horror at my reflection.

Was I dying? Maybe it wasn't poison. Maybe I was as sick as he claimed. After having the flu, I'd never really gotten better, but that had been months ago. What was the matter with me? Why couldn't I recuperate?

Jordan called to me, telling me to hurry. I turned to go, but at the last second I riffled through my cosmetics case and ran my finger across the note I'd written, checking to ensure it was still there. I read it at least once a day, sometimes two or three times. Whenever I touched it, my heart would pound.

Someone missed me. Someone was searching for me. I had to find a way to contact them.

I closed the lid and joined him in the living room.

"Here." He held out a pill.

"I don't need it. I'll be fine."

"I don't want you to have a nervous attack while we're out on the street."

"I won't. I'm looking forward to being outside."

"You have to take it or I won't let you come with me."

"Okay."

I grabbed it and went into the kitchen to fill a glass with water. He followed and observed as I stuck it in my mouth, as I began drinking the water. When he was satisfied that I'd downed it, he spun away and headed for the door, and I sneaked the pill from under my tongue and stuffed it in my pocket.

We rode down in the elevator and exited onto the sidewalk. It was a pleasant autumn afternoon, and I couldn't believe how fabulous the air smelled or how fast everything seemed to be moving.

I'd been trapped inside for ages, so I was very skittish. I jumped at sounds and shied away from people. I felt as if I was out when I shouldn't be, as if I was doing something wrong, and I feared that at any moment I'd be spotted and forcibly dragged to the penthouse and locked in.

I tagged after Jordan, quickly out of breath from trying to keep up. I stayed in the background as he entered a liquor store, as he stopped at a florist's. He was purchasing things and placing orders, providing me with proof of how his regular life was proceeding without me. I'd been his captive for so long that I'd forgotten he had an entire social world that didn't include me.

We went into a bar, and I blinked and blinked as my vision adjusted to the darkness. He led me to a stool and had to help me climb onto it. I was that frail.

The bartender asked what we wanted, and Jordan requested a beer for himself and wine for me. With a whispered threat for me not to leave my seat, he sauntered off, and I didn't even think about disobeying him. Where would I go? I didn't have a penny to my name, and I was so run down that I could barely walk. If I tried to escape, he'd chase me down before I could make it a single block. If I pleaded for assistance from others, he would easily convince them that I was ill and out of my mind.

I was content to enjoy the noises and odors, the murmur of conversation. I was always isolated, so the rumble of civilization was very exciting.

There was a mirror behind the bar, and I could see into a back room complete with pool table and video games. Jordan was in a booth in the corner, talking to a pretty girl who resembled me from the days when I'd been Meg White.

She was younger than me, and she had short, spiky brown hair, black clothes, and clunky earrings. Jordan was focused on her in the intent way that had once thrilled me, and she was soaking up his attention. I assumed they were lovers or were about to be, and I suppose I should have been outraged, but I wasn't capable of such a fierce display of sentiment.

If I'd been feeling stronger, I might have stomped over and warned her to be wary.

Don't be fooled, I imagined myself blithely saying. *He's a psychopath and a liar. He doesn't mean any of it.*

I ignored him, not caring enough to speculate as to why he was hitting on somebody and wanting me to watch. Was he hoping I'd be upset? That I'd pitch a fit? Man, was he in for a surprise! I'd lost the gene necessary for jealousy, or perhaps he'd drugged it out of me. He could do anything and it wouldn't bother me a bit.

I gazed around at the handful of customers, at the jukebox.

Over by the door, a woman sat by herself, smoking a cigarette. Her purse was on the table, her cell phone next to it. I couldn't keep from peeking at that phone, couldn't quit pondering how easy it would be to pass by unobtrusively and steal it.

Had I the temerity to carry it off? Was I that stupid? That brave?

What if I was caught? What would happen? Both with the police, who would certainly be notified, but also with Jordan, who would know why I'd taken it and who would be very angry.

I had never been a religious person, but suddenly I prayed harder than anyone had ever prayed in all of history. I wanted that phone. I wanted it! I was too confused to figure out how else to make my call for help. There were phones in the apartment, but whenever I picked up a receiver there was no dial tone.

I was never allowed out alone, and even if some miracle occurred and I was, I didn't have any coins to use in a payphone.

I stared, I prayed, I stared, I prayed.

Jordan's flirtation had ended, and he returned to my side. He gulped his beer.

"Let's go."

"Can I finish my wine?"

"No."

"You can chat with your friend some more," I urged, "while I drink the rest of it. I don't mind."

"She and I have said everything we need to say."

I didn't waste any energy wondering what he meant. I'd seen the adoring gleam in her eye. If he'd suggested a sexual rendezvous, I'm sure she'd agreed. She'd been glancing at me, checking me out. Who had he told her I was? His dying sister?

He guided me off the bar stool, steadied me on my feet, then he started out. I lagged a few steps behind. As I neared the door, I decided God must have been feeling sorry for me. The woman with the cell phone rose and headed to the bathroom, taking her purse, but imprudently leaving her phone unattended and in plain sight.

I walked by the table and trailed my hand across the wood. In a smooth, casual gesture, as if I stole things all the time, I scooped it up and slipped it into my pocket, then I followed Jordan outside.

I was weak with fear. I braced, waiting for voices to raise, for accusations to be hurled, for fingers to point, but no one noticed what I'd done.

I kept on, the phone a heavy weight against my thigh.

Chapter Twenty-five

When we arrived home, I headed straight to the bath-room to bury the phone in my cosmetics case, next to what I thought of as my sanity note.

Shortly, Jordan came in and changed his clothes, donning the sexy-guy outfit he'd been wearing when I first met him: tight jeans, loafers, leather jacket.

"Are you going out?" I inquired, excited that he might be, that I'd be left alone.

"Yes."

"When will you be back?"

"I don't know yet. I'll have to see what happens."

Was he hooking up with the girl from the bar? So soon? The prospect had me worried—for her, but for myself, too. Had he found my replacement? If so, I was in greater danger than I'd realized.

He went to the kitchen and returned with a pill and glass of water.

"I just took one not too long ago," I complained.

"You're due for another."

Was I being too lucid? Could he sense that I hadn't swallowed the one earlier? I had to be more careful.

"I don't feel nervous."

"I can't risk that you'll have a meltdown while I'm out."

"Jordan!" I protested, but since I was supposed to be drugged, I sounded too exasperated.

"I don't like how you're acting so I'm locking you in the bedroom."

"You don't have to. I swear I won't go anywhere."

"It's for your own good. If you got into mischief, I'd be very angry and you'd have to be punished."

"So you're saving me from myself?"

"Yes."

I knew he couldn't be dissuaded, and I grumbled, "All right."

He held out the pill. "Take it."

I did, trying to be sly and hide it under my tongue, but he never glanced away.

"Did you swallow it?" he asked.

"Yes," I lied.

"Show me. Open your mouth."

I stood there, mutinous, so he stuck his finger inside and easily located it tucked next to my cheek. I panicked, not sure what he might do, but certain it would be very bad.

"Do you see why I can't trust you?" he demanded. "I have to watch you like a hawk. Why must everything be such a battle with you?"

He gripped my neck and shoved the pill down my throat,

reaching so far back that I gagged. Then he dumped in the water till I had no choice but to ingest it or choke.

It slid down; I couldn't stop it, and he pushed me away in disgust. I fell onto the bed.

"Don't fight me, Meg," he seethed. "You can't win."

He stormed out and I huddled in a ball, listening as he locked the bedroom door and exited, the elevator whisking him away.

The instant he was gone, I raced to the toilet, and I tried and tried to make myself puke, but I simply couldn't do it. I'd never previously forced myself to vomit, and I didn't know how it was accomplished. The pill was like a lead weight in my stomach, and very quickly its narcotic effect would kick in and I'd be comatose.

I dug into my cosmetics case and pulled out the cell phone. I didn't think I'd have many opportunities to use it before the owner realized it was missing and had it disconnected or—God forbid!—had the phone company trace it to me.

Could they do that? Could they discover that I'd made one tiny call from Jordan's apartment?

I was becoming incredibly devout. I murmured another prayer, begging that I be allowed this link that might save my life. Until I'd met Jordan, I'd always been a decent person, a caring person. Didn't I deserve a second chance?

I looked at the clock. It was late afternoon, so Steve would be at work, on the road, and using his own cell. Still, I dialed our old apartment for some reason, comforted by the notion of my message winging its way there. The phone rang and rang, then finally the machine picked up. It was Marie's voice. "Hi. This is Steve and Marie's. Leave a number."

Up to that moment I hadn't fully grasped that they were a couple. Perhaps they were already married. Marie wouldn't want me pestering Steve. Without a word, I hung up and tried Steve's cell.

I had no idea what to tell him or how to explain my predicament. What precisely did I want him to do for me? After how I'd treated him, why did I feel he owed me any assistance?

I thought he'd be kind, that he'd be kinder than Marie had been, but how could I be positive?

Self-doubt and apprehension ate away at me. Hands shaking, heart pounding, I waited till his voice mail clicked on, and I was paralyzed by the fact that he hadn't answered. The silence was deafening. It went on and on. What should I do?

I clutched the phone as if it was a lifeline, which it was, and I stared at it, wishing a solution would be revealed. I was dying to talk to him, to convince him that I'd married a madman, that my husband was about to kill me, but I hadn't seen Steve in nine months. How could I persuade him in a short recording?

He'd assume I was as crazy as Jordan always said I was. Maybe I was! I was so mixed up!

With a groan of despair, I hung up again. As if it was too hot to hold, I dropped the phone on the counter.

Frantic, I paced. I was a coward, a fool. I was so immobilized by terror that I no longer knew how to function. I needed someone to advise me how to save myself; I was too befuddled to figure it out on my own.

Tears of frustration stung my eyes. I couldn't do anything right, couldn't even make a fucking phone call to an old friend. How could it matter if Jordan murdered me? I was too stupid to live.

Rapidly, I was growing sleepy, the narcotic oozing through my veins until every inch of me would be polluted. I paced faster, refusing to succumb, desperate to stay awake.

Suddenly the cell rang. In the small bathroom, in the quiet apartment, it seemed very loud, and I jumped and gaped at it. I crept over, certain that it would be the phone's owner, demanding to be apprised of why I'd stolen it, but as I saw the number on the screen, I nearly collapsed with relief.

"Steve?"

"Meg?"

"Yes." I braced myself against the wall.

"I knew it was you!"

"How?"

"I just knew. Where the hell are you?"

"I'm in Jordan's penthouse. It's downtown."

"I know where it is. I made it a point to find out. I came down there a bunch of times, but I couldn't get past security."

He came for me . . . He came for me . . .

"They're very fussy about who they let in," I absurdly mentioned.

"I'd prowl around, hoping you'd walk by, but you never did."

"Jordan doesn't permit me to go out very much."

"Why not?"

"He has to keep an eye on me."

"What?"

It was the first conversation I'd had in so long, and I sensed that I was mucking it up, but how could I describe such a bizarre quandary in a coherent way?

"I've been trying to contact you forever," he said, "but the bastard won't let me. Are you okay?"

"No, I'm not. I'm in terrible trouble."

"That's what my mom told me. I guess she bumped into you one day, and you looked awful. It's . . . it's had me worried. I decided I should check on you, but if it's none of my business, tell me to butt out and I will."

"Do you think I'm crazy?"

"No." He chuckled. "A little impulsive, maybe, but not crazy. Why?"

"Jordan claims I'm crazy, but I don't know what's real anymore."

"Jesus," he muttered. "Your words are all slurred together. Are you doing drugs?"

"He gives them to me. He says I'm too nervous. They make me sleep all the time."

"What the fuck! You don't have a *nervous* bone in your body."

"I don't?"

"Oh, Meg," he sighed, "what's happened to you?"

"I'm afraid of him."

"With valid reason. He's not a normal guy. There's something creepy about him, you know? It's like he's not all there."

My head was starting to pound, the narcotic making me dizzy. "I'm so confused."

"Do you want to get out of there?"

"Yes."

"How about if I come for you right now? I can be there in half an hour. Meet me down in the lobby."

I surged with a rush of genuine excitement, but it quickly faded.

"I can't."

"Why?"

"I can't go anywhere. He locked me in and he has the key."

"Is he there? Put that stupid fuck on the line. I want to talk to him."

"No, he left."

"And you're locked in?"

"Yes."

"He can't treat you like he would a bad dog!"

"It's wrong for him to do that, isn't it?"

"Yes, it's very wrong. Jesus!" he muttered again.

"He has me take all these drugs, and then I can't think straight. And I was really sick, but I never got well. I'm so tired."

"I'm coming down there! I'll figure out a way to get in, even if I have to beat the shit out of the security guard."

"I'm scared to leave."

"Oh, honey," he murmured, "you'll be fine. He's just screwing with your head. He's an asshole. Don't pay any attention to him. Don't let him frighten you."

"Once I escape, I have to hide where he can't ever find me. If he knew where I was, he'd kidnap me and put me in a mental hospital."

"Why would you say that?"

"He warns me constantly, but I don't want to go to one."

"You won't ever have to. I promise."

"But if I run away, he'll kill me."

"Has he threatened to?"

"No, he simply says that he won't ever let me leave, and I'm pretty sure he means it literally."

"Does he hit you?"

"Only when I do something wrong."

He whistled softly. "You are so fucked up."

"His first wife fell out of a boat and drowned, and he insists it was an accident, but it wasn't. He made her blond and thin, then he made me blond and thin, too."

"Okay . . ."

I could hear his hesitation. He was beginning to question whether it had been such a good idea to offer his assistance.

"I'm not making this up!"

"No, you're just so whacked. I can't believe it."

"Ask her sister what happened. Her name's Ashley. She'll tell you."

"I'm certain she would," he said as if soothing a lunatic. "Listen, my mom invited me over for supper, and I'll discuss this with her and get her opinion about what we should do. My sister went through some of the same shit a couple of years ago. I'm wondering if I should hire a lawyer or something."

"When are you going to your mom's?"

"Now."

"Please don't hang up!" I had this insane feeling that once we were disconnected, I would really and truly disappear.

"I have to for a bit, but I'll call you right back."

"When?"

"An hour or two? I'd like to contact the police, but I'm not sure if they can take you out of there or what. My mom will know."

"Jordan is so sneaky. He'd persuade them that I like to be alone, or that I'm sick and resting, and they'd side with him."

"But you're not his prisoner. He can't hold you against your will."

"He'll say I'm under a doctor's care. He swears that I'm on medication, but I don't remember if I am."

"Then maybe we need some sort of court order to keep him away from you. And maybe we need to hide you in a women's shelter for awhile. I'm not positive what's best, but I'll ask my mom. Then I'll call you and tell you the plan. Should I use this same number?"

"Yes, but I can't have the phone on where he might hear it ring. So leave me a message."

"Give me two hours max," he vowed. "And if you don't answer, I'll just show up. I'm not fucking around with him anymore."

"I'll be waiting."

"In the meantime, don't panic. My mom will know exactly what to do. I'll bring her with me. Everything will be okay."

"I know," I replied. He sounded so confident that I actually believed him.

"Hang in there."

"I will." He was about to go, and I said, "I always felt bad about how I left last winter. I was such a bitch."

"Ah, Meg, it's all in the past. Don't worry about it."

"I never said I was sorry."

"I knew you were."

The line went dead and I shut off the phone. The plastic case was warm from being cradled in my palm, and I held onto it till it cooled, then I slipped it into the bottom of my cosmetics case.

I gazed into the mirror and smiled, but it felt unnatural, my facial muscles out of practice.

He was coming for me! He'd speak to his mom, then they would both come! They weren't afraid of Jordan like I was, so he wouldn't be able to browbeat or intimidate them.

I wanted to pack so I was ready, but I couldn't start. With the conversation ended, I was swiftly losing the energy I needed to stay conscious and focused. I'd forgotten about the pill Jordan had forced down my throat. I was getting drowsy and sluggish, and soon I could barely stand.

My head was spinning, and I had to lie down so that I didn't fall down. I decided to rest for a bit, then check for a message. I hoped Steve would arrive before Jordan returned. That would be the best way. I would run off, and Jordan would walk into an empty apartment. I'd be gone without his being aware of where or how. There'd be no threats, no fear, no chance that he'd follow me. I'd vanish into a black hole.

I was nauseous and woozy, and I crawled onto the bed and closed my eyes.

Just for a few minutes, I told myself. *My vertigo will pass, then I'll get up and Steve will be here.*

Steve had promised, and he wouldn't let me down. He wasn't that kind of person. He'd come through for me. I had no doubt.

Chapter Twenty-six

When I woke up, I was groggy and achy, sure I was coming down with the flu again, but then I felt the same every morning. My stomach was churning and I wondered if I might puke. I peered out the window, trying to focus. I was certain I was supposed to be doing something, but what?

I glanced at the clock, the red digits flashing nine fifteen, and it was bright daylight outside.

I could hear Jordan speaking softly, and I also heard a female voice. She was giggling and cooing, but shortly she left in the elevator.

Had Jordan brought someone home with him? Had he carried on while I was passed out in the next room? Where sex was concerned, nothing he did would surprise me. Still, it seemed extreme, even for him.

I remembered telling Steve that . . .

The entire discussion with Steve came rushing back to me. I hadn't imagined it, I hadn't dreamed it, and I was frantic.

He'd called around four the prior afternoon, and he'd said he was going directly to his mom's for supper. He was to have arrived in about two hours.

Oh my God, had I missed him? Had I been unconscious and not able to respond? Had he pounded on the door? Had my stolen cell phone rung and rung but not been answered? Or had he decided not to intervene after all?

I pictured him at his parents' house, sitting at the table in their cozy kitchen. He'd have told his mom how crazy I'd sounded, how desperate. She might have persuaded him not to assist me. *Don't get involved,* she'd likely have said. *You can't win against a man like Jordan Blair.*

Or perhaps Marie had been opposed. Perhaps both women had felt it was a stupid idea and had urged him to forget it. If he'd agreed that I wasn't worth the trouble, I couldn't blame him.

What was I to him? I was no more than an old girlfriend who'd behaved badly. He had a new life, a new fiancée, and a wedding on the way. He didn't need me reappearing like a ghostly apparition. I was such a mess that not only would he have had to fend off Jordan, he'd have had to house me, feed me, and help me get back on my feet.

I'd been so selfish, had demanded too much, but I couldn't bear to assume that he'd abandoned me to my fate. I convinced myself that he hadn't. He wouldn't leave me all alone; he wasn't that kind of guy. There must have been a change of plans.

I envisioned him at the courthouse that very moment, asking a judge for a protective order to keep me safe from Jordan once I was free. Or maybe he was racing to the police department, the legal document clutched in his fist, so that he could show the officers why they had to rescue me. Any second now, the security desk might call to inform Jordan that the cops were coming up.

Suddenly Jordan was walking down the hall. He unlocked the door and tiptoed in. I could sense him standing by the bed, staring down to see if I was still asleep. I could smell cigarettes, perfume, and alcohol on him.

He went to the bathroom and took a hasty shower, emerging only minutes later. He stomped over and shook me, so I rolled to face him. He was naked.

"Get up!" he commanded.

"All right, all right. Calm down."

"You're taking a shower with me."

"No, I'm too tired."

"Meg!" He was tugging on my hand, hauling my legs over the edge of the mattress. "I want to fuck you, and I intend to clean you up before I do."

"I won't have sex with you." I tried to wrestle away, but I didn't have the energy to put up much of a fight. He'd always been much stronger than me, and currently it was no contest.

"It's not up to you."

"You've been having sex with someone else," I complained.

"Yes, I have," he replied without a hint of remorse, "and now I'm going to have sex with you, although I have to tell you that the woman I picked up last night was a hell of a lot prettier than you, and she was a lot more fun. Fucking you has become such a chore."

"If you detest it so much, go fuck yourself. You'd probably enjoy it more anyway."

It was the only genuinely discourteous thing I'd ever said to him, and he chuckled. "My, my, you have a bit of backbone left. I must be losing my touch."

He yanked me to my feet and half-carried and half-dragged me into the shower. I was kicking and cursing, my fevered brain certain that Steve would knock while the water was running, that I wouldn't answer and he'd go away and never return, but Jordan was determined to wash me and he wouldn't be dissuaded.

The water was scalding hot, and I cried out as he pushed me under the jets. He lathered me with soap and grabbed a rough brush and scrubbed my skin until it was raw. When he was finished, he drove me to my knees, and he fucked my mouth, keeping on and on, the water sputtering over my nose so that I couldn't breathe.

Slowly, I was being suffocated. I wished I would die. The word *suicide* flitted through my head, and it comforted and sustained me through the ordeal. I started calculating how I might do it, which method would be least painful and quickest. The simplest route would be to hoard the pills Jordan forced on me. Considering their potent narcotic effect, I wouldn't need very many to kill myself.

I would give Steve a day or two, but if he didn't appear I'd proceed on my own, would end it as soon as I was able.

Surprisingly, after I reached this decision, I grew very serene. There was a conclusion in sight and I wouldn't have to go on like this forever. I could deal with Jordan and his psychotic conduct. It was nearly over.

He pulled away and helped me to rise, then he dried me very carefully, fussing over me as he had at the beginning of our relationship.

He dried himself, too, then he led me to the bed, and we had straight, missionary-style sex, with me on the bottom and him on top. As he thrust, he gazed down at me, and absurdly his look was almost tender.

"You'd never leave me, would you, Meg?"

"No."

"And you still love me."

"You know I do," I lied. Had I ever loved him? I didn't think so. I'd lusted after him, had been charmed and fascinated by his wealth and maturity, but I had confused those emotions as being indications of something more.

"If you tried to sneak off, I'd find you."

"I know that."

"There's nowhere you could hide."

"I'm sure that's true."

"I'd search and search, and when I located you I'd bring you home—even if you didn't want to come."

"But I'd never go in the first place," I insisted, recognizing it as the safe reply, "so it's silly to talk about it."

"If you did, I'd be very angry."

"Yes, you would."

"I've been kind so far. Haven't I been kind to you?"

"Yes."

"Haven't I fed you and clothed you and loved you, too?"

The man was so friggin' delusional. How could I not have seen it right off the bat?

"Yes," I repeated. "You've been wonderful."

"If I learned that you didn't appreciate it or that you weren't grateful, I'd be justified in being upset, wouldn't I?"

"Yes, you would, but I'm here and I'm yours. I'm very happy."

He studied me, then nodded. "Good. Very good."

The intercourse became rougher, his penetrations more violent. He rolled me and urged me up, my palms braced on the headboard, and he fucked me until my knees were weak and my insides sore.

Finally, he drew away without having an orgasm, and he let me slide down onto the mattress. He climbed to the floor and went to the kitchen, and when he returned he was holding not just the big white pill, but numerous others, too.

I wrinkled up my nose. "I'm not taking all those."

"You have to, Meg. You need them."

"What are they?"

"Energy vitamins."

"I don't need vitamins," was my response, although I secretly agreed with him. I needed *something*, but I couldn't guarantee that what he was giving me was actually what he claimed.

"We have to work on your health and stamina. You're too frail. Your hair has started falling out. We have to halt your downward spiral."

"Fine. I'll take the vitamins but not the other one. It makes me too sleepy."

"You can't."

"Why not?"

"The white one's very addictive. If you suddenly quit taking it, you'd be more of a mess than you already are."

"What do you mean?"

"Don't you remember? Your doctor said we have to wean you off it. You can't simply stop."

How freaking great! I thought to myself. He'd addicted me to a major narcotic, then pretended a physician had prescribed it. I had no memory of any such appointment, no memory of any such discussions.

He shoved the entire pile under my nose, along with a glass of wine to wash it down when I hadn't had breakfast yet. "Swallow them one at a time. The sooner you begin, the sooner you'll be finished."

"I need some food in my stomach or they'll make me nauseous."

"So? I'll take care of you. Don't I always take care of you?"

"Yes, you always do."

But I remained adamant, and he relented and let me have an egg and toast. After eating them, I felt sicker than ever, and I went back to bed without consuming any pills. I drifted off, and when I awoke it was evening. My door was open, so I figured Jordan was out in the apartment.

Steve hadn't come, so something must have happened, and I was desperate to see if he'd left a message on the cell phone. I had to risk looking at it. Though I was unsteady, I rushed to the bathroom.

I lifted out the tray in my cosmetics case and fumbled through it, frantically searching under the compacts and eye shadows for my sanity note, for the stolen phone, but they weren't there!

I took everything out, put it all back in, took it out again. I ran my fingers over and over the edges and bottom, but the phone and note had vanished.

I slumped against the wall. By hiding them as I had, I'd presumed I was so clever, so sly. Where was the goddamn phone? Where was my note?

Jordan had found them. It was the only possibility. He wouldn't have allowed anyone into my bedroom — not when I was a captive inside it — and no one else had access to the bathroom. I pictured him snooping around when I was comatose, checking my dressers and pockets as if I was a misbehaving adolescent.

The bastard!

I was weak with fury and fear as I calculated what the discovery indicated for my safety, for my future. So far Jordan hadn't said anything, but he would. He'd retaliate in a vicious manner. It wasn't in his nature to ignore such an affront to his authority.

Had he prevented Steve from coming for me? Was that why Steve hadn't arrived?

I repacked the case, placing every item in its exact spot so there was no hint of my hysterical examination of the contents. Then I stepped into the shower, plotting, considering my options. I hadn't taken the white pill in many hours, so my mind was fairly clear and I could see disaster approaching like a train wreck.

Jordan would be more focused on me than ever, so my chances for escape would be even more limited. We were now engaged in a game of cat and mouse. I wouldn't admit that I knew he was slowly killing me, while he wouldn't admit how fervently he would work to imprison me to the very end.

If I was to survive, I had to be more cunning, had to use my lucid moments to better effect. Though suicide had appealed the prior night, I didn't really want to die. I wanted to live! I had to keep from ingesting the pills, had to accumulate them for a terrible decision later on. In the meantime, I had to investigate other avenues of rescue, had to lay out varying strategies.

Most of all I had to be on guard, lest he murder me before I realized what he was about to do.

I dressed and went to the kitchen, and I made myself tea and toast. I was at the table when Jordan entered and sat across from me. He was holding a newspaper, and we stared at each other, the silence awkward. I ignored him and finished my food.

I was at the sink and rinsing my plate when he asked, "Do you remember your old boyfriend? What was his name? Steve?"

I shuddered with dread. "Yes, why?"

"Have you heard from him recently?"

The question was a minefield I had no idea how to navigate. Since Jordan had stumbled on my phone, he already knew the answer. If I told the truth, I was dead. If I lied, I was dead.

I chose denial. I would go to my grave insisting we'd had no contact.

"I haven't spoken to him since that day I moved out of my apartment last winter."

"Really?"

"Yes, really!" I was snide, forceful. "Why?"

He shrugged. "I had some news I thought I'd share with you, but I don't know if I should."

"What *news?*"

"You don't care about him anymore, do you? I'd hate to throw you into a relapse. Given your delicate mental state, it might be too much for you to handle."

"Just fucking tell me what it is!"

He slid the newspaper over to me. He'd circled a small story buried in the Metro section. I traced my finger across the headline: PORTLAND MAN MURDERED IN APPARENT ROBBERY.

Steve had been killed with a stab wound to the chest. It had happened when he was getting out of his car in a dark parking garage down the street from our building. His phone, wallet, CD player, and CDs were missing. There was a quote from a police detective about random, senseless violence being on the rise in the city.

I had to read the article five times before the significance sank in. Steve had talked to me, had promised to rescue me, and he'd been murdered as he'd arrived to follow through. I didn't think for a single second that it was random or senseless. In fact, I was positive that it had been meticulously planned and carried out so that I would understand the danger of asking others for help.

Jordan had repeatedly advised me that he would never let me go, that I would never be free. I'd believed him, but I hadn't comprehended how dire the stakes were, and I'd lured Steve to his death. As sure as I was breathing, Jordan had killed him. I had no doubt. I would never prove it, would never find evidence to confirm it, but I knew it all the same.

Too troubled to continue looking, I folded the paper and pushed it away. I glared at him, searching for signs of guilt. His face was an inscrutable mask, but so was mine. He showed no emotion, no concern or sympathy, and I was equally blasé.

He had killed Steve, and it had been my fault, but my stupidity had taught me a valuable lesson: I was totally alone. I would never approach anyone again for I couldn't risk having another person hurt by Jordan. I was extremely distraught, but I wouldn't give him the satisfaction of witnessing my sorrow. I wouldn't let him know that I suspected anything at all.

I sighed. "Poor Steve."

"Aren't you the least bit upset?"

"Why would I be?"

"I thought the two of you used to be close."

"He was an okay guy, when he wasn't getting blow jobs from your favorite prostitute."

In light of what a fine man I'd always considered Steve to be, it was a horrid remark and I was ashamed to have uttered it, but I had a pretense to maintain. If Steve was watching over me from heaven, I hoped he'd forgive me.

Jordan stood and rounded the table so that he hovered over me. He seemed very large and menacing, his greater size and strength more obvious than it had ever been.

He brushed his thumb over my bottom lip, then he trailed down my chin and neck so that his palm was across my throat. He squeezed, not tightly enough to cut off my air, but sufficiently that I would recollect how easily he could.

"You're mine, Meg."

"I know."

"You'll never get away from me, so it doesn't do you any good to suppose you might." He nodded toward the bedroom. "I want to fuck you. Go in and take off your clothes."

It was the most repulsive, most hideous suggestion anyone had ever made to me.

"No, I won't."

I shoved him away and rose and stomped off, aware that he'd never let me refuse. I was so cold, my fingers and toes like ice, but I didn't mind. If I was frozen, the next few hours would be more bearable.

I'll kill him, I vowed. *I'll kill him for Steve. And if I can't do that, I'll kill myself instead.*

I heard him down the hall, coming after me, and I braced, ready for anything.

Chapter Twenty-seven

❧

"Drink this."

"What is it?" I asked, but I knew it wasn't anything I should ingest.

"It's an aphrodisiac."

"I don't want it," I protested, though refusal was pointless.

"I don't care."

I was completely reliant on him for sustenance, though meals were infrequent and I was slowly being starved. I couldn't *not* eat, so when he brought me food I gobbled it down. When he brought me water or wine, I drank it, as I did now. I'd stopped worrying over what was in any of it. I was like a rabid animal, desperate for any nourishment that was offered.

The wine coursed down my throat, and soon I'd feel either heightened sexual effect or I'd start having delusions. There was a fifty-fifty chance that one or the other would transpire, and I couldn't decide which was worse.

He'd cut back on administering the white pill, so I wasn't as groggy and zoned as I'd been. In its place, he was slipping me hallucinogens, so I was more confused than ever, paranoid, and having trouble distinguishing reality from fiction.

He made no pretense about the fact that I was being held against my will, and he'd taken to whispering sly comments about what had happened to Steve, what might happen to me if I was too disobedient. I was rarely out of his sight. If he had to leave the apartment, I was bound, gagged, and locked in the bedroom closet.

"You're doing much better, Meg."

"Yeah, right."

"You are! Your skin is smoother. Your hair is healthier."

He was so totally lying. My condition continued to deteriorate, my weight in particular beginning to alarm me.

"I'm glad one of us thinks so."

"It makes me want to fuck you more than ever. I have some great fun planned for tonight."

"Is Adrian coming over?"

"No, not Adrian."

He went to the living room, and I struggled to decipher his response. Did he simply mean Adrian wasn't going to visit? Or did he mean that it would be someone besides Adrian?

There wasn't any use fretting about it. Whatever he'd set in motion would occur, and short of racing to the kitchen, seizing a butcher knife, and stabbing him to death—which I was too physically drained to accomplish—there was no way to prevent it. I merely had to do whatever I could to survive another day.

He was fussing with the stereo, selecting music for our sexual encounter, so I had a few minutes on my own. His jeans were tossed across the end of the bed, his wallet in the pocket, which was a mistake he never usually made. I sneaked over and took it out. It contained close to a thousand dollars, and I removed a twenty that I was positive he'd never miss, then I put the wallet back and arranged the jeans in the same haphazard manner in which they'd lain before.

I walked over to the drapes, located the slit I'd made in the hem, and wedged the money inside. Over the past few weeks, I'd stolen small amounts, and I had nearly three hundred dollars stashed in various locations in the apartment. If he stumbled on one cache, I had more in other spots.

In my lucid moments, which were few and far between, I observed and plotted. He was a very smart, determined, and organized man, but it had to be difficult to watch me constantly, to never leave me alone, to relentlessly conceal my existence from others. Someday he'd screw up, and when he did I'd tiptoe out the door with my hoarded cash.

I was no longer immobilized by his threats. At the first opportunity, I'd vanish, and I would spend every second hiding. For a time I'd be invisible, I'd be gone and safe till he tracked me down, but the brief interlude of freedom would be worth any price.

The drug he'd given me was swiftly kicking in, and I was disturbed to note that it was a hallucinogen. Tiny pricks of light were winging on the edges of my vision. I kept seeing someone creep up on me, but when I'd whip around, no one was there.

I went to the nightstand and opened the drawer, wanting to learn what sex toys he'd brought home, wanting to have some idea before he actually pulled them out and started using them.

There were ropes and creams and dildos, as well as other tools I couldn't name. I wondered—as I often did—who he fraternized with that he'd been taught such disgusting practices.

At the bottom of the pile were two cell phones nestled side by side, and I stared at them, curious as to why they were there, why I hadn't previously noticed them. I peeked over my shoulder, certain he was out by the stereo, and reached in and picked one up.

It was just a phone, with no identifying marks, but it was similar to the one I'd stolen. I turned it on, but it didn't work so I put it back. I grabbed the other one and as I studied it, my heart skipped several beats. There was a business card taped to it. *Steve's* business card was taped to it.

It was Steve's phone. In Jordan's nightstand.

I strained to figure out what I was witnessing, what I was really holding, but I was confused by the narcotic. I sifted through the remainder of the contents and discovered a CD player and a case of CDs. I remembered the newspaper article about Steve's murder, about the items that had been taken during the supposed robbery.

They were in Jordan's drawer . . . in his drawer . . . in his drawer . . .

Steve's phone was in my hand. Kind, sweet, loyal Steve, who'd never done anything to me but be my friend.

I began to tremble, and the shaking grew until my entire body was quivering with shock and rage. My temper was exacerbated by the drug. Sounds were amplified, colors streaming behind my eyes, the furniture moving and floating.

I could hear Jordan coming, his strides pounding like a giant's. I lumbered toward the door, the phone clutched against

my thigh, and as he stepped across the threshold, I lashed out
and hit him alongside the head as hard as I could.

"Bastard!" I hissed.

"What the fuck?" he muttered.

I swung again, but he lurched in surprise, so the blow was
wide. He lunged for me and I leapt away.

"You killed Steve!" I charged, finally saying it out loud. "You
killed him! You motherfucker! You killed him! You did it!"

"Are you out of your mind?"

"I'm going to tell! I'm going to tell everyone it was you!"

He dove at me, wrapping himself around me like a vise as
he wrestled me over and down onto the bed. I fought as if my
life depended on it, as if this was the very last thing I would
ever do. I kicked and screamed, scratched and bit, as he bat-
tled to gain control.

Though I brawled valiantly, it was no contest, and soon my
wrists and ankles were bound to the bed frame, a gag in my
mouth. I was crying, yanking on the cords, cursing him even
though my exact words were stifled.

I was pleased to see that he was winded, that our skirmish
had been more than he'd bargained for. He sat on his haunches
and ran his fingers through his disheveled hair. He was wearing only his jeans, his chest rapidly rising and falling, a sheen
of sweat glistening.

He leaned over me, his hulking form terrifying, his fury
unleashed.

"You're crazy, and you're more deranged every day." He
smiled, delighted with how completely I was breaking down,
that I'd arrived where he'd planned for me to go from the outset. "I should have had you locked up months ago."

I glared at him, my hatred and malice unveiled even as I spiraled out to the fringe of sanity. I was desperately trying to hold on to what I recognized as real, but the drug was extremely potent. His hair sprang out from his head like thick ropes, the individual strands wiggling as if they were snakes. His face was distorted, his eyes glowing red, and he looked like the devil escaped from hell.

I glanced at the nightstand, and he glanced at it, too, and chuckled. "I don't know what you think you saw, Meg, but there's nothing there. You've jumped off the deep end and you're drowning there. When will you realize it?"

He opened the drawer and showed me various objects. I couldn't peer fully inside, but there didn't seem to be a CD player, any CDs or phones, when I knew that I'd seen them. I'd attacked him with one clasped in my hand. He had a welt on his temple from where I'd struck him.

He crawled off the mattress and started out. "We have a guest. I'll be right back."

I grappled with the restraints, tried to spit out the gag, but I couldn't free myself. I was so angry, but I was gradually losing my grip on why. The drug was smoothing over the rough spots, making me forget, making me uncertain.

It seemed like he was gone for an eternity, or it could have been just a few seconds. I thought others entered the room with him. Or perhaps not. I wasn't sure of anything, and in my last cogent instant, I hoped that, whatever he'd given me, the drug wouldn't waste too many of my brain cells. I'd heard stories of people who'd taken LSD or PCP, who'd soared off into madness and never recovered. What if he had done something similar to me?

The hours passed in a blur. Occasionally I assumed I was awake, but then I'd decide I was dreaming. When I managed to concentrate, the walls were heaving, monsters and demons dancing by. I couldn't breathe and constantly felt as if I was choking to death.

I saw Kimberly, and I saw Adrian, too. Maybe both of them were present, or maybe neither of them were. I was fairly positive that someone had sex with me, over and over, but it could have simply been Jordan, although I recalled him as being behind the camera and taping me.

I was beyond knowing, beyond caring, and as night faded to morning, it was a blessed relief when the world stopped spinning, the furniture stopped moving, the noises stopped screeching, the bizarre visions fizzled out.

It was very quiet, and I fell into an exhausted sleep.

Chapter Twenty-eight

❦

When I woke, it took me many minutes to figure out where I was. I stared at the ceiling, at the shut door. The room was tiny, empty of anything but a chair, me, and the narrow cot on which I was lying.

I decided it was the storage room off the kitchen. Jordan must have cleaned it out and placed me in it. Was this to be my cell?

Visions of the previous night—at least I hoped only a single night had passed—flashed through my head. I pushed them away, scared to look too closely at the images that kept trying to break through to the surface. Much of it had a nightmarish quality, so I didn't want to remember what had happened.

I was in pajamas, and I had been given a pillow and a blanket. I didn't smell like sweat or sex, and I supposed I'd been bathed.

Very slowly, I sat up and braced my feet on the rug, thankful for the steadying effect of the floor. I tiptoed to the door and spun the knob, but as I'd suspected it was locked. I pressed my ear to the wood, but I didn't hear any sounds on the other side.

I went back and fell onto the lumpy mattress, and I curled into a ball, the blanket pulled to my chin.

The silence frightened me. I didn't like what occurred when Jordan was home, but what if he left? What if he took off on a month's vacation, and I starved while he was away? What if he was hit by a car while walking down the street? No one knew I was imprisoned in his penthouse, so no one would rush to find me.

I struggled not to panic, to remain calm and rational. I recollected what I could about the newspaper article that had described Steve's murder, about my locating his stuff in the nightstand. I was positive I'd seen his belongings. They had been real. I could still sense having the plastic phone case cradled in my hand as I'd whacked Jordan with it.

Of course, there was always the possibility that the items hadn't actually been Steve's, that Jordan had deliberately planted them in the drawer even if they had no connection to Steve at all. Jordan might have been simply trying to alarm me or make me admit I was crazy, but I was confident they were Steve's.

Jordan had them, and he wanted me to know that he did. It was another means of terrifying me, of wearing me down.

I rested for hours, dozing, then jumping awake. Eventually voices rumbled down the hall and soft footsteps approached. I took a deep breath. I was at the end of my rope. If Jordan shoved pills down my throat, if he refused to let me eat, if he forced me to have sex, my mind would snap. He wouldn't need hallucinogens.

He opened the door and loitered in the threshold with another man I didn't recognize. As if I wasn't present, they whispered about me, the terms *schizophrenia* and *manic-depressive* being mentioned. The man said I was too old for the onset of either but that with mental illness one could never be certain of what the brain would do.

I wanted to laugh. Had I already been diagnosed? Had a person I'd never met proclaimed me insane?

Finally they skulked over. Jordan had a bruise on his temple and scratches on his cheek from our brawl, and I was pleased that I'd fought hard enough to leave marks.

The man with Jordan was probably in his sixties, chubby and balding, dressed in a gray suit. He carried a black bag and he had a stethoscope around his neck. He had a kind face and observant eyes, and he quickly and thoroughly assessed the barren room, the cot, my hunched form.

Jordan stroked his fingers across my hair. He oozed concern, was all solicitous, generous empathy. I flinched away and he sighed with resignation, the beleaguered husband, the unappreciated spouse.

"Meg, there's someone here to see you."

I glared but didn't answer.

The man came forward and introduced himself. "I'm Dr. Theodore Swenson. My friends call me Dr. Ted."

He smiled, trying to warm up to me, but I didn't smile in return.

"Meg," Jordan murmured, "Dr. Ted is the psychiatrist I've been telling you about. I know you've been opposed to the idea, but after your . . . well . . . your episode yesterday, I decided we couldn't wait any longer for you to talk to him."

I gazed at Swenson. "I don't care what Jordan said to you. I didn't have any stupid *episode*. I was drugged against my will. *He* drugged me. He does it all the time."

The doctor and Jordan exchanged a conspiratorial glance that was filled with nuance and indicated that they'd had lengthy discussions about me. Swenson would have accepted Jordan's version without question, would assume Jordan had spewed the truth, so I had very little chance of swaying him. Still, I had to try.

He was my only hope, and with how my world had narrowed, he might very well be the last human being besides Jordan with whom I ever spoke.

"How does this . . . this . . . *drugging* occur?" he inquired, clearly humoring me.

"He slips it into my food and beverages, or he flat out forces me to take pills that contain strong narcotics. I sleep for days."

"Really?"

"And when I'm unconscious, he brings people into the apartment and lets them have sex with me."

"While you're unconscious, you say?"

"Yes. He tapes it. He has these weird fetishes, and he likes to watch others having sex—more than he likes having it himself."

"I see," Swenson mused. "Why does he act this way toward you?"

"In the beginning I thought it was love, but it's not. It's obsession. I don't know why he became fixated on me, though. You should analyze him and find out. I'm betting it has something to do with his mother. You could spend the rest of your career unraveling what it is that makes him tick. He's a lunatic."

He and Jordan shared another significant look. Whatever lies Jordan had told about me, I was merely confirming a diagnosis Swenson had already formed.

"Mr. Blair"—Swenson gestured to the door—"why don't you step into the hall so Meg and I can have a moment alone."

"Sure," Jordan cordially agreed.

He brushed a hand down my shoulder and arm, and I stiffened, hating to have him touch me. At my petty rejection, he frowned and sighed again.

"I just want you to get better, Meg. You understand that, don't you?"

"Yeah right," I sneered. "You're going to murder me any day now. Don't pretend otherwise, you sick bastard."

"Do you have any idea how it hurts me when you make accusations like that?"

"You killed Brittney, and you killed Steve, and you'll kill me, too—as soon as you can figure out how to do it and not get caught."

"Who are Brittney and Steve?" Swenson asked.

"Brittney was my first wife," Jordan explained. "She drowned years ago in a boating accident."

"And Steve?"

"Her old boyfriend. He died recently, during a robbery. The news sent her into a downward spiral."

I scoffed. "Steve wasn't robbed. I'd managed to contact him and beg him to help me escape, so Jordan murdered him."

Jordan scowled at the doctor. "See what I mean? These absurd notions lodge in her head and she can't shake them. They're driving her insane."

"Delusions can seem very real," Swenson replied, "to the individual suffering from them."

"We don't have a life anymore," Jordan complained. "We can't even go out for a walk because I'm so panicked about what she'll say to strangers on the street. I can't continue to put up with it."

"No, definitely not," Swenson concurred. "You shouldn't have to."

I hadn't realized Jordan was such a marvelous actor. He appeared so oppressed, the patient, selfless husband with the ridiculous, impossible wife, and Dr. Ted was eating it up.

"I can't bear it when she's like this," Jordan said. "Something has to give."

"That's why I've offered my assistance, Mr. Blair."

"Don't talk about me as if I'm not here," I protested.

"We're not, Meg," Swenson declared, and he eyed the door, eager to rush Jordan out so my therapy session could commence in earnest. "Why don't you wait outside? We'll call if we need you."

"Tell him everything, Meg," Jordan urged. "I can't get through to you, but maybe he can."

"Meg and I will be fine," Swenson beamed.

Jordan left, though I was positive he wouldn't go far. He'd hover nearby so that he could eavesdrop, and once the doctor departed he'd use my remarks as an excuse to punish me. The prospect of incurring his wrath made it dangerous to have a frank discussion, but I was determined to forge ahead.

I sat up, and I was freezing. I tugged the blanket over me like a shawl.

Swenson was across from me in the chair. He studied me,

his concern evident as he stated the obvious. "You're not feeling very well, are you?"

I snorted with laughter. "No. I feel like shit."

"Why would you suppose that is?"

"Because my husband has been starving me and drugging me. He's probably poisoning me, too. Ask the coroner to check it out during my autopsy, would you?"

"I will." He nodded in sympathy. "Why would your husband do these terrible things to you?"

"How should I know? He's a fucking psychopath."

"He'd like to check you into a hospital."

"I just bet he would."

"I'm curious as to your opinion on the subject."

"He wants to convince you that I'm crazy, and he wants it on the record. After he murders me, he'll fake it so it looks like a suicide, and it will be an interesting footnote in the police report."

I could practically see the officer's notation: *Wife was previously under intensive psychiatric care.*

"I'm a fairly smart guy. I don't think Mr. Blair could *make* me believe anything."

"From how you're evaluating me, it's pretty clear that he's already succeeded."

"How is it that I'm evaluating you?"

"Like I belong in a loony bin."

"You hardly belong in a loony bin, as you put it." He smiled reassuringly. "You're tired and a bit confused. That's all."

"Isn't that enough?"

"Tell me about the attack last night."

"What attack?"

"Mr. Blair advised me of how you assaulted him for no reason, that you scratched his face in the altercation, and he had to wrestle you to the ground to stop you."

"He sure did."

"Can you describe the incident for me?"

"Would it do any good?"

"It's not a question of good or bad, Meg. I'm merely trying to understand what's going on with you."

What was the point of saying anything? How could I expect him to aid me in any fashion that mattered? I could temporarily flee to a mental hospital, but there had to be a catch. Jordan would never let me evade him so easily, so if he was pushing for hospitalization, there was an ulterior consequence. I simply wasn't shrewd enough to figure out what it might be.

Then again, why not confide in Swenson? At least I'd die with the satisfaction of knowing that somebody had been alerted to what Jordan had done to me. It hadn't all been in secret, and maybe the information would prevent him from doing it to another woman later on.

"Okay, listen, this will seem preposterous, but here it is: he chose me. I don't know how or why. He just did. He lured me into his life, and he's been torturing me and trying to do away with me ever since."

His frown deepened. "It must be terrifying to constantly feel that way."

"I'm used to it. He's very devious, very controlling. He tormented his first wife, then he murdered her, too."

"So you've claimed."

"He's held me prisoner for months. Once, after I begged and

pleaded, he let me go outside with him, and when he was distracted I stole a woman's cell phone and called Steve with it."

"Steve is your old boyfriend?"

"Yes. I told him how scared I was and that I couldn't get away on my own. He was coming for me, but Jordan killed him so he couldn't help me. It happened just down the block."

"I realize that you truly believe all this, Meg, but do you comprehend how irrational it sounds?"

"Yes, but you said you wanted to understand."

"I do. I do."

"When I attacked Jordan, it was because I'd opened the drawer in the nightstand and Steve's things were there."

"What things?"

"The items that were taken during the robbery."

"Hmm." He assessed me, pondering his responses, then he offered, "Would you like to look in the drawer with me? Would you like to show me what you saw?"

I chuckled miserably. "No. Jordan would have emptied it by now."

"How about if I take a peek for you? Just to be certain."

I hated him for indulging what he plainly viewed as a bizarre whim, but I waved toward the hall.

"Whatever turns your crank, Dr. Ted. Be my guest."

He patted my hand in commiseration, then rose and went out. As I'd suspected, Jordan was perched by the door, playing the troubled spouse. They conferred in whispers, then proceeded to the bedroom. They were gone a long time, then Swenson came back, shutting Jordan out once again.

"Find anything interesting?" I inquired.

"Not really, Meg. It was just a drawer."

"What? No dildos? No whips? No erotic creams?"

He pursed his lips, his gaze narrowing. "You have quite a fixation on sexual matters."

"Don't I, though?"

"Have you recently noticed your carnal appetite increasing?" He was nearly salivating at the prospect.

"Actually, Jordan makes me do such disgusting things that if I never had sex again, it would be fine with me."

He nodded vigorously, as if I'd finally said something relevant, then he opened his bag and took out a syringe.

I recoiled with alarm. "What's that for?"

"It's a sedative. It will help you rest and it will calm some of your paranoia."

"I'm not paranoid. I know what's real and what isn't." It was a small lie, but I felt it deserved uttering.

"I can't risk that you might try to hurt yourself again."

"What do you mean?"

He tsked. "There's no need to pretend with me. I can see the bruise marks around your neck."

"The bruise marks?" I placed my palm on my throat, wincing when I discovered a tenderness I hadn't noted. "What the fuck . . . ?" I mused to myself more than to him.

"You tried to hang yourself. Don't you remember?"

"You think I tried to hang myself?"

"Your husband told me all about it, but we'll get you settled down. We'll get you the treatment you need."

We engaged in a staring match as I weighed my options. I yearned to decline the medication he was determined to provide, but how could I? How could I fight him? How could I fight both of them? Why dither over the shot? I'd been abused for so long that it scarcely seemed worth the fuss.

I shrugged and held out my arm. "Sure. Do whatever you want to me. Everybody else does."

"Oh, Meg, I wish you'd consider me a friend."

"Best buds, Dr. Ted. Absolutely."

I closed my eyes, flinching as the needle poked me, but he finished quickly. When I glanced over, he was scrounging in his bag again. He pulled out a file folder.

"These are commitment papers," he explained.

"If I sign them, will I go directly to a mental hospital?"

"No. We'd simply like to have them in case we need them."

"And if I refuse?"

"Then your husband and I will pursue other avenues."

"You'd commit me? Against my will? Is that what you're telling me?"

"We'd like to avoid proceedings that would cause a scandal, so we're hoping to care for you at home. If we can keep your situation private, you won't suffer any social ramifications."

"How convenient for Jordan," I mocked. "A public commitment hearing would be so awkward. People would know he'd driven two wives crazy instead of just one."

"Let's not worry about what might be. Let's focus on what *is*, which is the fact that you're ill and you require some assistance with recuperation."

"I'm not fucking *ill!*"

He ignored the remark and continued on. "After I leave, you can discuss the document with Mr. Blair, and I'm certain the two of you will come to the appropriate decision."

"I'm certain we will," I echoed, oozing sarcasm.

"Now, the medicine will work very fast and you'll fall asleep. When you wake up, you'll be less anxious."

"Great. The more I'm comatose, the more I like it."

"And I'm giving a prescription to Mr. Blair so he can have it filled for you. I'll apprise him of the proper dosages. It will keep you stable till our next appointment."

"Thank you," I meekly consented, aware that with Jordan in charge of any pills, I wouldn't have a choice about taking them.

He stood and smiled down at me. "I'll stop by tomorrow."

"I can't wait," I lied.

He walked to the door and I imagined he'd never see me again, that when my name was next mentioned in his presence, it would be because I was dead. He seemed like a good person who genuinely wanted to heal me, and it wasn't his fault that he'd never previously encountered a psycho like Jordan. He had no idea with whom he was dealing, and I didn't blame him for being skeptical of my wild stories.

In light of Jordan's suave demeanor and large bank account, who could peer through the façade to the maniac lurking beneath the surface? I'd been easily taken in.

"Hey, doc," I said.

"Yes, Meg?"

"If you're informed that I died—that I hoarded the pills and committed suicide with them, or that I hanged myself or something like that—don't believe it, okay?"

"Meg, you mustn't fret so much. Everything will be fine."

"I want to live," I insisted. "Remember for me, would you? And . . . and . . . when you learn that I supposedly committed suicide, talk to Ashley."

"Ashley?"

"Brittney's sister. She'll tell you what happened to me. To both of us."

"Meg . . ."

"Promise me."

"I will, I will," he soothed, but he was humoring me again. In his eyes, I appeared stranger by the second.

"I wouldn't expect you to go to the police or anything. I just want someone to realize what he did to me."

He scowled, perplexed by my attitude. "Try to rest, Meg. Some of these new drugs can work wonders. We'll have you feeling better in no time."

He left, and I could hear him conferring with Jordan, could hear them moving into the living room, could hear him exit the apartment.

Jordan returned and spun the key in the lock, sealing me in. At seeing how right I'd been, how wrong the doctor had been, I gazed at the ceiling and cackled with mirth. I sounded mad as a hatter and every bit as demented as Jordan claimed.

Chapter Twenty-nine

✦

We were back where it had all started.

I was standing in the living room of Jordan's beach house, gazing out the window to the ocean off in the distance. The blue sky and billowy clouds made it appear to be the kind of autumn morning where you could tug on shorts and play Frisbee on the sand, but looks were deceiving. It was very cold and blustery, too windy even for flying kites.

Jordan had driven us out in the night when I was too sleepy to complain. I hadn't inquired as to why he'd done it, and I didn't care why. Any place was better than being locked in the storage room, and I was hoping to use the change of location to sneak away.

I didn't have a penny in my pocket, didn't have an ID or a phone, but I could see stretches of Highway 101 meandering through the mountains. I pictured myself on the shoulder, my thumb stuck out to passing cars and trucks. There had to be someone who would stop and whisk me away without asking too many questions.

Jordan walked up behind me, his unwelcome palms on my shoulders, and he stared out at the ocean, too.

"Are you still afraid of heights?" he taunted.

"No, you cured me," I lied.

He chuckled, knowing it wasn't true. "I think we'll try some climbing."

I remembered that awful day after I'd been so sick, when he'd terrorized me by having me rappel down the cliff. I elbowed him in the ribs and stepped away.

"I'm not climbing with you. Not ever again."

"You will if I say so."

"You can beat me to a pulp if you want to. I won't do it."

He nodded in an enigmatic way that sent chills down my spine. He had successful methods of forcing me, of making me do whatever I swore I wouldn't, but surprisingly he dropped the subject.

"Fine," he relented. "Let's take a ride instead."

"Fine. Let's do."

If he wanted to go somewhere, I wasn't about to protest. I had so few opportunities to be around others, so few opportunities where he might be distracted and I could flee without his noticing.

He retrieved my coat from the closet, and as he held it for me I dared to goad him. "If you allow me outside, aren't you worried that I'll run away?"

"Why would I worry about that? You're a grown woman, Meg, and I'm not your nanny. Why would I restrict your behavior?"

"You are so full of shit. Why did you bring me here?"

"Don't you know?"

"I haven't a fucking clue."

"I abhor your foul mouth. When I married you, I didn't realize you were so common."

"And when I married you, I didn't realize you were such a deranged asshole."

He sighed, acting as if I was the greatest burden in the world. "I've been so patient."

"Really? What is it that you wanted from me that I didn't give you?"

"I wanted everything."

"And I gave you everything."

He frowned. "No, you didn't. You never gave me anything at all."

His answer made no sense, but I was beyond the time where I would have expended any energy trying to decipher it. "So if it was all such a waste, just divorce me. Why torment me to death?"

"Because it's so fun."

"It hasn't been very *fun* on my end."

"Well, it's been an absolute blast on mine."

"Has it?"

"Yes."

Was he serious? Was he joking? His mind and his motives were and always had been a complete mystery to me, so as usual I had no idea if he was sincere or not.

We went to the SUV and proceeded down to the highway. I watched dispassionately, understanding that the scenery was beautiful but not caring that it was.

Eventually we passed a sign to a State Park, and Jordan slowed and turned off. The smaller road wound through the forested hills, up and up, until we came to an isolated parking lot. Ours was the only vehicle in it. We were hundreds of feet above the water and clouds had moved in. The sky was now gray, the ocean, too, and there were rain squalls out on the horizon.

The coast stretched for miles to the north and south. There were no towns or telephone poles, no houses or radio towers, just trees and jutting cliffs. We were stranded at the edge of the earth, the last two people left.

The wind was stronger than ever, rattling the car, and I didn't want to get out. I hated being up so high, and I didn't have a good feeling about why Jordan had brought me to this spectacular, desolate spot.

He climbed out and shivered against the cold. From the rear seat he grabbed his jacket, then he circled around and opened my door. He extended his hand, expecting me to take it.

"Come on, Meg."

"No."

"You have to see the view."

"I can see it okay from here."

"It's better from over there."

He pointed to some interpretive signs. "This is a historic area. Come with me. You'll enjoy it."

I continued to balk, so he dragged me out and pulled me across the asphalt. I'd assumed we'd stop at the signs, but we went past them and out onto a trail. In one direction it made a sheer and treacherous descent to a remote, rocky beach. In the other it zigzagged to a scenic promontory that was quite a distance away and exposed on all sides. It was reached after many perilous twists and turns of the path that led to it.

There were numerous warnings posted: *Dangerous Cliffs Ahead! Do Not Leave Designated Trails! Hikers Should Exercise Extreme Caution!*

I dug in my heels, not inclined to go any farther, which only caused him to yank more persistently.

"Where are you taking me?" I asked.

He indicated the promontory. "Out there."

"I won't go."

"It's not up to you."

I jerked away and started back to the SUV, and instantly he was on me. With an arm around my waist, he picked me up and carried me to the trail. Though I kicked and fought, I couldn't escape, and within seconds we were out of sight of the parking lot and out on the cliff.

Huge, ancient trees towered above us, the wind pummeling our hair and clothes, the surf roaring as it crashed into the rocks below. There was nothing between us and the open air, no fence, no guardrail. It was straight down, the drop so steep that I was queasy merely from glancing at it.

I was terrified that my skirmishing would make him lose his balance or loosen his grip and we'd plunge over the edge, so I ceased my struggles. He was satisfied with my capitulation, and he allowed me to put my feet on solid ground.

I collapsed against a nearby boulder, holding on for dear life, trying to quiet the frantic pounding of my heart.

"Are you afraid, Meg?"

"Fuck you."

With finger and thumb he clasped my chin, and he squeezed

hard, forcing me to look at him and nothing else. "I love it when you're scared."

I slapped him away. "You're sick. I've always thought so."

"Not *always*," he countered. "There was a time when you thought I walked on water, when you thought I hung the moon."

"That was before I realized you were a deranged lunatic."

"Do you think I'm crazy?"

"I don't *think* so. I know it for a fact."

"Why is that? Because I've demanded more from you than you were prepared to give?" He grinned, appearing evil and ominous. "What's a little sex and drugs among friends? If you didn't want to participate, you should have said something."

He'd insinuated himself between me and the parking lot, and I was eyeing the width of the trail, calculating how much space I'd need to skirt by him and run to safety. "Is that how you rationalize all this? Have you convinced yourself that I didn't refuse frequently enough or vehemently enough, so it's my own fault?"

"Precisely."

"How convenient."

"Yes, isn't it? I explained your peculiar sexual tastes to Dr. Ted, too, and he agrees with me that your incessant need for carnal stimulation is amazing. He's very intrigued by your case; he'd like to study you."

"So *I* am the one with the sexual problems?"

"Yes, and now it's been fully documented."

I scoffed. "Does your demented mind ever stop hatching plots?"

"You shouldn't be so focused on *my* mental shortcomings. You should be more worried about your own."

"Those being . . . ?"

"*You* are crazy, Meg. I had you examined by a noted psychiatrist and he recommended a lengthy hospitalization. You're certifiable."

"Very clever, Jordan."

"Yes, wasn't it?"

"Why didn't you check me in right away?"

"As your devoted husband"—he oozed sarcasm—"I decided you should have a final weekend of freedom before I followed the doctor's orders and locked you away. I took you to your favorite spot, where we spent our honeymoon."

"So the insane asylum is still approaching? When? When we get back to Portland?"

"Maybe. Maybe not. If you were to commit suicide—say, for example, you were to throw yourself off this cliff in a moment of hysteria—it wouldn't be a surprise to anyone."

I was saddened to realize that he was correct. He'd isolated me from the real world, and I couldn't guess what stories he'd told people about what had become of me. No one had seen or heard from me in a very long while, except Dr. Ted, and during our brief conversation I'd been at my worst. He'd had no doubt that I was a danger to myself. I'd had the bruises on my neck to prove it.

"I hate you," I seethed.

"You *hate* me?" He chuckled, the sound eerie and unnatural. "I can't permit you to feel that way."

"It's not up to you!" I said, tossing his annoying phrase back at him. "I'll feel however I please. It's none of your damned business."

"You keep trying to leave me."

"I couldn't have. Your prison is too secure."

"You called Steve. He was coming for you and I couldn't let him."

"You're wrong. He didn't care about me. He wasn't coming." It alleviated my guilt to pretend that Steve hadn't been serious, that he hadn't actually planned to help.

"No, he was delighted to be your knight in shining armor. Why turn to him, Meg? You had to know I wouldn't like it."

"I want a divorce," I bravely declared. "I want to be alone, to be away from you."

"When you married me, you swore you'd stay with me till death parted us."

"I didn't mean it."

"But you're not allowed to lie to me, Meg. When will it begin to sink in? You're mine and you'll be with me forever."

I didn't intend to be with him for even the next few seconds if I could figure out how to knock him down and race for the parking lot. "It's over, Jordan. It was a mistake for us to get together. You have to accept it. I don't want anything from you. I don't need anything from you. I'll simply disappear and we'll both move on."

"It's not over, Meg. Although I enjoy your petty attempts to flee, you have to quit fighting me. It's pointless. You can't win."

As if I hadn't spoken, he stepped in and trapped me against the boulder. The disgusting asshole had an erection, and he flexed it on my leg.

"You're going to fuck me out here while you're scared and wondering what I might do."

"Like hell I am."

"If you're frightened, your senses will be more potent and alive, so the sex will be fantastic."

"I won't do it. You can't make me."

"Is that what you suppose? You know, Brittney refused me that last day, too. She couldn't swim and she was afraid of the water. She wouldn't have sex when I told her she had to."

"You were about to fuck her when she was . . . was . . . terrified?" I stared at him, desperate to fling a remark that would wound him, but I couldn't conceive of an insult that was horrid enough to describe what he was.

I inadequately accused, "You're a monster."

"Brittney said exactly the same thing to me and look what happened to her. You haven't learned your lesson, Meg. You haven't learned how hazardous words can be—but you're about to."

He leaned down and kissed me very hard, his tongue in my mouth and gagging me. He slipped his fingers into my coat and brutally squeezed my breast. I wrestled away, but he was still positioned between me and the car. There was no room to evade him. I was hemmed in by the cliff on one side and the boulder on the other, with not a single inch remaining to maneuver.

"Let me go!" I fumed.

"No."

"Let me out of here!" My alarm and my voice were rising.

"No," he repeated, calm as ever.

I peered over his shoulder toward the SUV, wishing I'd see hikers coming down the trail after us. But as had been my situation for months, there was no one to rescue me. I had to rescue myself.

"If you touch me again, I'll kill you!" I vowed.

"Really? You would? I doubt you have the nerve."

He stepped in again, crushing me to the rock, and he gripped my hips, his torso pressed to mine all the way down. "I'm going to fuck you," he warned, "while you're so close to the edge, while you're positive I'll let you fall."

He was fumbling with the button on my slacks, with the zipper, and he was about to have them loosened. I absolutely wouldn't have sex with him in this awful place. I absolutely wouldn't!

I started brawling in earnest, not concerned if we lost our balance, if I plunged to my death. Fury and panic gave me strength I was astounded to possess.

"Yes," he whispered, grappling to control me. "Fight! Fight for your life! Surrender to the fear. It will be so much more arousing if you do."

He had me clutched tightly to him, and I bent in and bit him on the chest, latching on so violently that I was certain I felt skin tear. He lurched away in pain, but I didn't let go, and he had to slap me in order to free himself.

We stood, glaring at each other, and his hatred was unmasked, his true sentiments visible. I saw such loathing and contempt, such malice and malevolence, that I stumbled away, frightened of him in a fashion I hadn't yet been.

"Why did you marry me?" I demanded.

"Because I could. Because you were all alone. There was no one who cared about you in the entire world, so I could do anything to you." He gestured at the barren landscape, laughing at how exposed we were, how high up and secluded. "You're mine and you always will be. I brought you up here, and I can fuck you or I can murder you and no one will ever know. Now do you understand?"

"Oh yes," I said, "I understand."

There could only be one ending for us. In the split second it takes for a heart to beat, I reached out and shoved him with all my might. He was gloating, triumphant in his power over me, and I caught him when he hadn't expected that I would. He staggered and tried to grab onto me. I wasn't sure if he was hoping to right himself or to pull me down with him, but I leapt out of range.

Gravity dragged him off, and it occurred so swiftly that I scarcely had time to grasp the enormity of what I'd done. With an expression of extreme astonishment but no audible comment, he toppled over the edge, his body hurtling away, vanishing in the blink of an eye.

I dawdled there, stupefied, gaping at the spot where he'd been. My head reeling, my mind screeching in shock, I meant to peek down, but I was too much of a coward to lean over and see where he was. I didn't know if he'd survived by simply dropping, broken and battered, to a ledge somewhere below me, or if he had fully plummeted to the turbulent water and drowned.

If he'd cried out, if he'd bellowed my name as he bashed and tumbled on the way down, the pounding of the surf was so intense that I couldn't have heard it.

I was trembling, dizzy and disoriented, weak from fatigue and hunger, and wondering if I might faint. I groped around, trying to get my bearings, to figure out how to proceed. My natural and initial human instinct was to have him rescued, but if he was still alive—I was probably damned for thinking it—I didn't want him saved.

I glanced up, and there was finally a group of hikers approaching. They hadn't noticed me yet, though, and I cowered behind the boulder, needing to compose myself so that I didn't look and sound like a madwoman.

What should I say? What should I do? I had to tell them that something had transpired, but what should my story be? I'd just pushed Jordan off a cliff. Most likely he was dead, but he could have been severely injured and hanging from a precipice—in which case I had to stall and delay while I prayed that he perished before aid could arrive.

How could I persuade anyone that my handsome, rich husband had lured me out to this horrid location so he could murder me? How could anyone believe that he'd been about to shove me over, so I had shoved him first?

The truth was ridiculous and implausible. *I* was the one with a documented history of mental illness. *I* was the one with drug and alcohol problems. *I* was the much younger, poor girl, who'd seemingly materialized from nowhere to wed a millionaire.

I jumped into view and ran toward the hikers, screaming and waving my hands in the air.

"Help! Help!" I wailed. "Help me! Oh God, help me! Jordan fell! Jordan fell off the cliff!"

I reached the stunned man at the front of the line and collapsed into his arms, acting every bit the distraught widow I would have to be from this point on.

Chapter Thirty

❧

T ell me again what happened."

I peeked over at the sheriff. At first glance, with his stomach bulging over his belt, his thinning hair and sagging jowls, he resembled my idea of a typical small-town cop. I could have easily mistaken him for an idiot or a buffoon, but I'd learned my lesson and I wouldn't be duped by a deceptive appearance.

"I told you," I said. "One minute, he was standing there and the next . . ." I shrugged, adding nothing further.

"It's a long way down," he casually mentioned.

"It certainly is." The men in the rescue crew on the rocky beach were so far away that they could have been ants. "Is he . . . he . . . dead?"

"Oh yes." He studied me, his astute gaze digging deep. "A fellow couldn't survive such traumatic injuries."

"It's so dreadful." I covered my mouth, not having to pretend I was ill. My nausea was very real.

I was so glad to hear that Jordan had been killed, but I hid my elation. If he'd lived to condemn me for what I'd done, I couldn't have defended myself in a thousand years.

"Let's go over this again," the sheriff needled.

I shivered, sighed with anguish, and lied. "It was an accident. A terrible, terrible accident. He was near the edge, talking to me, and the ground gave way. It was over in an instant."

I snapped my fingers to indicate how quick it had been.

"I bet," he mused. "Did you say anything to him?"

"As he fell?"

"No. Before."

"Of course. I warned him not to stand so close."

"He didn't listen?"

"Well, yes, he listened, but he laughed and said the Park Service wouldn't allow people out this far if it wasn't safe. He thought I was worrying for nothing."

"What were the two of you doing out here?"

"We were sightseeing. What do you suppose?" I pointed down the trail. "We were hiking to the overlook. He wanted me to see it."

"Show me exactly where he was."

"There."

"And you?"

"Here."

Luckily for me, there were scuffle marks in the dirt to suggest that it might have occurred precisely as I'd claimed. Still, the sheriff was very shrewd, and he evaluated the cliff, the angle, the sheer drop to the water, hundreds of feet down. He didn't miss a single twig or stone, and though outwardly he seemed calm and relaxed, I could sense his mind racing, taking it all in.

My own mind was careening between trepidation and relief, and I was amazed by my composure. I yearned to run back to the parking lot, to hop in the SUV and speed away, but I couldn't arouse suspicions. The sheriff was determined to linger on the precipice, so I had to be the grieving widow and linger with him. I had to act as if I was concerned and willing to help.

The rescue team had managed to drag Jordan out of the pounding surf, and he'd been stuffed in a body bag. They were wrapping ropes around him, beginning the arduous task of lugging him up the hill. The scene was gruesome.

"Do I have to keep watching?" I inquired, and I slumped against the boulder.

"Are you all right?"

"No, I'm not!" I snapped. "I'm cold and tired, and I just want to go home and lie down."

He assessed me, then nodded. "Let's get you to your car."

At his words, I almost hugged him. "Thank you."

I started down, focusing on the rugged terrain and not glancing toward the ocean for any reason. It took an eternity to leave the trail and firmly plant my feet on the pavement. I nearly collapsed in gratitude.

The sheriff accompanied me to the SUV, stopping me before I could climb in.

"I need to ask you a few more questions."

"Can't it wait? Please?" Tears flooded my eyes, and they weren't faked. I was desperate to escape so I could break down in private.

I reached to open the door, but it was locked.

"Shit!" I muttered, my frustration spiraling.

"What?"

"Jordan had the keys in his pocket."

"I can have a deputy drive you. Where would you like to go?"

Now there was a dilemma for the ages. Where was I to go? To the beach house I hated? To the penthouse that had been my prison?

I didn't have any other connection, didn't have money, family, or friends, but I wasn't about to explain my quandary. My twisted relationship with my dear, departed husband was none of the sheriff's business.

"To our beach house, I guess. It's just down the road."

"Do you live in Portland?"

"Yes." I lived there as much as I lived anywhere.

"How long will you stay out here on the coast?"

"I don't know!" I was exhibiting more exasperation than it was wise to display. "I'm sorry, but I'm exhausted and confused. What happens next?"

"We'll have to talk again."

"Fine. Give me a number and I'll call you."

"That's not how it works," he said. "You give me one where I can call *you*."

I glared at him, certain I appeared guilty as hell. I didn't know our fucking phone number. Was there one? How could I account for my not possessing such simple information?

I rattled off the old number, what it had been before Jordan had had our service terminated.

The sheriff retrieved a notebook from his pocket and jotted it down. Vaguely I wondered what he'd think when he dialed it and learned that it hadn't been operational in months. Hopefully I'd have vanished by then.

"May I go now?"

"Sure." He gestured to a deputy, instructing him to escort me home then return to the scene. I was walking with him to his cruiser when the sheriff said, "Hey, Mrs. Blair, aren't you the least bit curious?"

It took me a few seconds to realize that *I* was the Mrs. Blair to whom he was speaking. I whipped around. "What do you mean?"

"Well, about your husband's body."

"Okay, I'll bite. What about the body?"

"There'll be an autopsy."

"Why?"

"To establish cause of death."

"He fell off a cliff! I imagine you'll find plenty of cuts and bruises. Maybe even a fractured skull and some broken bones."

"I imagine I will, too."

"And then he'll be released to me?"

"Yes, so you can hold a funeral and have him buried or whatever. I'll be in touch."

I recognized that I should feign more interest, that I should be more inquisitive or appreciative, but I couldn't muster the appropriate amount of distress.

"Is there anything else?"

"After I get the autopsy results, I'll advise you as to how the investigation is proceeding."

"What investigation?" He'd finally made me angry and I stomped over to him. "He fell off the goddamn cliff. Are you claiming he didn't?"

"Nope. Not claiming that, at all."

Yet, he seemed to say.

It was obvious he didn't believe my story, that he figured Jordan's demise had transpired with a little help from me. I smiled, a knowing, confident smile. He could conjecture all he wanted. The other hikers had only seen my frantic race toward them, but they had no clue of what had occurred prior, so I was the sole witness. I would take my secret to the grave.

"You think I pushed him?" I dared to inquire.

"Did you?"

"You're a very suspicious man, Sheriff."

He shrugged. "It comes with the job."

"I loved my husband very much," I lied. "We were very close."

"Were you? You don't seem all that disturbed to me."

"That's because I'm in a state of shock!"

"The reality hasn't registered?"

"No, it hasn't."

"So if I visited you later, I might see some genuine angst?"

"Maybe. Or maybe I'm simply frozen with astonishment and you'll never pry a reaction out of me."

He pulled out a pair of dark sunglasses and put them on, and I understood that it was a calculated maneuver intended to intimidate me. My gaunt, haunted self was reflected in the lenses.

"Not so much as a whimper of dismay?" he taunted.

"Is there some book that tells how I should behave at a moment like this? If there is, why don't you loan it to me so I can give you the responses you expect?"

"How long were the two of you married?"

"We're practically newlyweds."

"Congratulations." His tone was too snide for my liking. "Then there's nothing further I need to know, is there?"

His smug grin warned that he wasn't about to forget me, that he would be pondering and discussing, reviewing and debating.

In the meantime, I was so out of there!

"Good-bye, Sheriff."

"Good-bye, Mrs. Blair. I'm sorry for your troubles."

"So am I."

I got into the cruiser, and the deputy followed my directions to the beach house. Very soon, we arrived, and I murmured my thanks and hurried out of the car without waiting for him to assist me. I waved, then skirted the side of the house, pretending I was headed for the rear door. I didn't want him to loiter and observe me, then report to his boss that I wasn't sufficiently upset.

I spied on him from behind some bushes. He sat there for a few minutes, the engine idling, then he left. After the sound of the motor faded in the distance, I sneaked around and tried every window and door, but they were all shut and locked. On the front stoop, I peeked under the mat and the flowerpots, and I was stunned to find a key.

In light of how anal Jordan had been, it was out of character for him to have been so foolish, but I wasn't going to quibble over the discovery. I let myself in and dawdled in the quiet. I was weary and needed a nap, but there were too many lurking ghosts and I couldn't bear to hang out with them.

I made myself a sandwich, and as I nibbled on it without fearing that Jordan would materialize to take it from me, I decided it was the most delicious thing I'd ever eaten. I finished slowly, adjusting to the sensation of solid food hitting my shrunken stomach, then I went through every room, hunting for cash, for jewelry or other costly items I could carry away and pawn.

Amazingly, in the back of a closet I stumbled on one of my old outfits: black jeans, T-shirt, jacket, and boots. I stripped off the clothes Jordan had bought for me and put on my own. I was enormously comforted by the change, even though the jeans were much too large and I had to scrounge for a length of rope to use as a belt so I could tighten the waist.

I walked out and locked up, stuck the key under the flowerpot, and trudged down the hill to the highway. I had several hundred dollars in my pocket, as well as a necklace and some earrings that probably contained real gems. I had no idea if Jordan had kept a record of his valuables, if the gems would later be cataloged and missed, but at the moment I didn't care.

I'd been his fucking wife, and I had no doubt I'd be cut out of any inheritance due to the prenuptial agreement he'd forged. While I didn't want much, I wanted enough to start over. I *deserved* enough to start over. I thought of it as combat pay. If anybody complained about my having the jewelry, I'd merely contend that he'd given it to me for my birthday. Who'd been around to say he hadn't?

I managed to catch a ride with the first trucker who passed by, and he took me all the way into the city. I went straight to our building and checked in at the lobby. I'd been afraid that the security guards might stop me, that there might have been a hold slapped on Jordan's property while his death was investigated, but no one said a word.

I signed the roster and climbed in the elevator.

I suppose I could have stayed in the apartment. I'd been legally married to Jordan, so I had the right to be there. I could have contacted lawyers and had them fight for a share of what should have been mine, but in my tormented state I didn't want anything except to be away. I had an absurd and panicked feeling that if I remained, the doors would magically close and I'd be trapped again. I had to escape while I could.

Everything in the place reminded me of Jordan, when I simply wanted to forget. I was exhausted, but as with the beach house, there were too many ghosts. I wouldn't lay my head on a pillow and shut my eyes. I was terrified by how they'd haunt me. I might fall asleep and wake up only to learn that Jordan wasn't really dead and I was still his prisoner.

I searched thoroughly, emptying my secret caches of twenties that I'd hidden in every nook and cranny. In Jordan's office I scored big-time, locating several thousand dollars in the desk, as well as a bunch more jewelry which I stole without hesitation or remorse.

Though I looked and looked, I didn't find Steve's phone or CDs, and I couldn't guess what Jordan had done with them. But I *did* find the videos he'd made of me and Adrian, as well as those of himself in disgusting situations with many other women. They were hard evidence of why I'd ended up hating him, of why I'd ended up killing him. I didn't want anyone to ever watch them, didn't want his other victims humiliated if the cops ever came and rummaged around.

I stuffed them in a duffel bag and set it in the front foyer, then I stood at the picture windows that faced to the east. I'd hoped for a last glimpse of Mount Hood, to see the evening sky shading it in magnificent hues of pink and purple, but it was raining, the valley gray and dreary with clouds.

I paused to remember Steve, what a great guy he'd been,

how much his friendship had meant to me. I mourned for how I'd discounted its value, how I'd tossed it away without a second's consideration. I wondered where he was buried, how I could discreetly obtain the information, if I dared visit his grave or send a card to his mother or Marie.

Steve was murdered because I'd been greedy and stupid and had run off with Jordan. I forced myself to recollect the first time Jordan had brought me to the penthouse. I'd assumed I was deliriously in love, that I was happier than I had any right to be, that I was making all the right choices, all the right moves.

It scared me to realize how wrong I'd been. Would I ever again trust my judgment?

I'd arrived in his life with only the clothes on my back, and after all I'd been through I was leaving in much the same condition. There was a moral to the story, but I had no clue what it was.

I returned to his office and pulled out a folder with Brittney's name on it. She and I were about the same age, the same height, and I took her birth certificate and Social Security card. I'm not sure why.

Jordan had tried to alter me so that I became her, and in many ways he'd succeeded. I didn't know who I was, but I wasn't Meg White anymore. If there was some scrap of her remaining deep inside, it would be quite a while before I could lure her to the surface. I was at a crossroads, and I was too overwhelmed to figure out what was best. I might want to just let her rest in peace.

I wasn't positive how it was accomplished, but I knew I could use Brittney's personal papers to build a new identity. In case I ultimately decided to disappear—if I someday *needed* to disappear—I ought to have them.

I left the apartment with tons of money, jewelry, and Brittney's file crammed in my coat, the bag of porn videos slung over my shoulder. I took the elevator downstairs and strolled out to the sidewalk. It was a cold autumn night, a depressing drizzle falling, but the drenched pedestrians were accustomed to it and didn't seem to notice. They were ambling along, chatting and laughing. There was still heavy traffic, cars and bicycles whizzing by on the wet street.

Down the block I saw a dumpster, and I went to it and threw in the duffel of videos. I said a prayer for Brittney and the other women Jordan had tormented. A spurt of gladness shot through me as I recognized that my action guaranteed he'd never hurt anyone ever again.

Then I closed the lid and glanced in both directions, wondering where to go next.